Books by Tracie Peterson

*with Kimberley Woodhouse **with Karen Witemeyer, Regina Jennings, and Jen Turano

For a complete list of Tracie's books, visit traciepeterson.com.

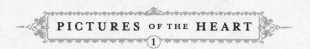

PICTURES OF THE HEART
1

Remember Me

TRACIE PETERSON

BETHANYHOUSE
a division of Baker Publishing Group
Minneapolis, Minnesota

Published by Bethany House Publishers
Minneapolis, Minnesota
www.bethanyhouse.com

Bethany House Publishers is a division of
Baker Publishing Group, Grand Rapids, Michigan

Printed in the United States of America

Library of Congress Cataloging-in-Publication Data
Names: Peterson, Tracie, author.
Title: Remember me / Tracie Peterson.
Description: Minneapolis, Minnesota : Bethany House Publishers, a division of
    Baker Publishing Group, [2023] | Series: Pictures of the heart ; 1
Identifiers: LCCN 2022037874 | ISBN 9780764237386 (trade paperback) | ISBN
    9780764237393 (cloth) | ISBN 9780764237409 (large print) | ISBN 9781493440580
    (ebook)
Subjects: LCGFT: Romance fiction. | Novels.
Classification: LCC PS3566.E7717 R46 2023 | DDC 813/.54—dc23/eng/20220808
LC record available at https://lccn.loc.gov/2022037874

Scripture quotations are from the King James Version of the Bible.

This is a work of historical reconstruction; the appearances of certain historical figures are therefore inevitable. All other characters, however, are products of the author's imagination, and any resemblance to actual persons, living or dead, is coincidental.

Cover design by LOOK Design Studio
Cover model by Alexey Kazantsev / Trevillion Images

Baker Publishing Group publications use paper produced from sustainable forestry practices and post-consumer waste whenever possible.

23 24 25 26 27 28 29   7 6 5 4 3 2 1

Prologue

DAWSON CITY, YUKON
JUNE 1902

Adeline Byrant, or rather Moerman, since she'd been forced to marry Sam Moerman last year, tried her best to sleep. It was the wee hours of the night—her birthday, or it had been the day before. There had been a big party for her, and Sam had presented her with a gold-nugget necklace worth a fortune. She had felt the entire atmosphere of the party turn dangerous and threatening when Sam put that piece around her neck.

"You're the most beautiful woman in Dawson City, Addie. You deserve to be covered in jewels," Sam had whispered in her ear.

Addie had felt the weight of the necklace. It was like a chain that bound her to a life she despised. She wanted to say as much, but Sam had been mostly good to her, and she didn't want to cause a scene.

She touched the place on her neck where the gold piece had lain. It was safely put away for the time being, but she knew Sam would expect her to wear it. She heard someone say it was worth one hundred thousand dollars, but she couldn't believe that. How could any one thing be worth that much money? Addie rolled over and tried again to get comfortable.

Thankfully, Sam had still not come to bed. Probably working downstairs at the Moerman Gold Palace, which included a gambling hall, saloon, and brothel. Unfortunately, Addie's suite of rooms was on the second floor, with many of the brothel rooms just down the hall, and the noise seemed to never die down.

She punched the pillow and flipped onto her left side. She had lived in the Yukon since her father and brothers dragged her north in 1898 during the gold rush. She'd been just fifteen years old and had no say over the matter. Just as she'd had no say in marrying Moerman. She supposed it could be much worse. When her brothers sold her to Moerman after the death of their father, they had tortured her, telling her she would have to work as a lady of ill-repute. Barely eighteen, Addie had tried desperately to find a way out of Dawson City, but she had no money, and even her best friend, Millie Stanford, couldn't help.

But thankfully Sam was more impressed with her cooking skills and had bought her mainly to keep her baking and serving up meals for the gambling hall. Addie hadn't minded that, except she wasn't paid . . . at least not regularly. From time to time, Sam took pity on her lack of decent shoes or clothes and gave her money to buy herself what she needed. He was better to her than her brothers were. It wasn't long, however, before he took advantage of her situation and forced her to be his mistress as well as his cook. Addie reluctantly gave in, knowing there was no one who could stop it from happening, and maybe as Sam's woman, she wouldn't have to endure being passed around to the customers. At least that had turned out as she'd hoped. In time, Sam married her, although to this day Addie wasn't exactly sure why. Maybe he was afraid of losing her to another man. Maybe he honestly cared about her reputation. It seemed unlikely, still . . . who could say?

As Mrs. Moerman, she had protection from the men who showed up begging to have her as their partner for the hour. Sam made it very clear that his wife was not for rent and that one of the other girls would have to do. But now, even a year later, Addie was still propositioned by strangers.

She gave a sigh and rolled onto her back, staring at the ceiling. Despite the hour, dim light filtered in from behind black curtains. Midnight sun was what they called it, but Addie had never quite gotten used to a sun that never really set in the summer.

She thought of when she'd first arrived in Dawson City and met the charming seventeen-year-old Isaac Hanson. They used to take long walks around Dawson. They would inevitably lose track of time, and Addie would get in trouble for showing up at home near midnight. It had been love at first sight, and in truth, Isaac was the only man Addie would ever love. When he left the Yukon for college, Isaac promised her he would find her again no matter where she went. He gave her a small tintype picture of himself, and on the back, he scratched out the words *Remember Me*.

Addie knew she would always remember him, even after being forced to marry Sam. Poor Sam. He knew she didn't love him and never would.

Addie pulled the cover over her head and closed her eyes. She fell asleep almost immediately. Thoughts of Isaac put them together in her dream. They were walking along the river, talking about their future. Isaac had just said something when Addie felt her body being shaken awake. She opened her eyes and blinked hard. A lamp on the table had been lit, and Millie Stanford was beside her bed.

"Addie, wake up. Something happened."

"Millie, what in the world are you doing here?" Addie rubbed her eyes. "What time is it?"

"Nearly five. Look, Sam's been shot. There was a fight." She paused as if perplexed.

Addie sat up. "What is it? Just tell me."

"Sam's dead."

Addie was fully awake now. She threw back the covers. "Let me get dressed."

She slipped into a navy blue skirt and gray blouse. Millie helped her do up the buttons in the back.

"Who did it—Hiram? Shep?" She named her brothers as prime suspects due to their well-known hatred of Moerman. They had once worked for him and been good friends, but after selling Addie to Sam, they thought they were due much more than Sam was willing to give. It made them enemies.

"No, it was a stranger in from the outer regions. I don't know anything else. Jack was . . . visiting me, and we both heard the shots, so he dressed in his uniform and went downstairs to see what had happened. Then he came and got me so that I could break the news to you."

"Thank you. I appreciate that it was you and not someone else." Millie had been the only person to make her life bearable when Addie was forced to change her living arrangements. Millie worked at the saloon and brothel, and Jack, one of the local policemen, was quite fond of her. He often commented about buying out her contract, and Addie had assured Millie that when the time was right, she would see to it that Sam did the right thing. Now he was dead.

Addie ran the brush through her long brown hair and tied it back with a ribbon. "I suppose I'm ready." She headed for the door with Millie right behind her.

By the time Addie reached the gambling hall's large open room, quite the crowd had gathered. She spied her brothers standing off to one side, and Jack and another policeman were standing near a blackjack table with the stranger.

Sam's body lay in a pool of blood on the floor near the door. No one had even bothered to cover him. Addie steeled herself and went to Jack.

"Addie," he said, nodding. "Sure sorry about this."

"Thanks for sending Millie. What happened?"

"This guy said he was being cheated. Pulled a gun and threatened Sam, who happened to be dealing. Sam told him to put the gun away and leave. But he didn't, so Sam started for the door and was nearly there, as you can see, when the man told him he wasn't going to be cheated and shot him in the back."

"He cheated me. I know how to play blackjack, and he cheated me. Dealt off the bottom for himself."

Sam's right-hand man, Bud, came to Addie. "Sure sorry about this, Mrs. Moerman. What do you need me to do?"

"Get Sam to the undertaker and have Joe clean up the mess." She spoke with the calm of someone who had done this before, when in truth she had never had to deal with anyone's death. Sam always managed the fights and killings. Dawson City was a dangerous town—especially when the Moerman Gold Palace was involved.

It was nearly eight in the morning before everything had been tended to. People were coming and going throughout the morning, but Addie remained to oversee the entire matter. Unfortunately, Addie's brothers, Hiram and Shep, stuck to the place like glue. They kept their distance, seeming to understand that she was in no mood to deal with them, but nevertheless they stayed around.

"Everybody needs to go home. I need sleep," she announced. But it wasn't to be. Mr. Lundstrom walked through the doors. He was a middle-aged man who handled legal matters for Sam.

"Mrs. Moerman, I'm mighty sorry to hear about what happened."

"Well, it's the nature of the business, isn't it?" She fixed him with a stern look. "Sam always said he'd probably die dealing cards."

"Yes, well, I know it's all just happened, but we will need to discuss Sam's arrangements."

Addie was more than a little aware of her brothers moving closer. It reminded her of wolves sneaking in for the kill. She ignored them. "The only thing I need to know right this minute is if he had arrangements for his funeral."

The man considered the question for a moment. "Yes, I believe he did. If I recall, he has had a plot at the cemetery for some time. Thankfully, it's June and the ground isn't frozen."

"Yes, that is good. Whatever arrangements he wanted, Mr. Lundstrom, would you please see to them and then let me know when the funeral will be?"

"Of course." The man gave her a sympathetic nod. "You have my deepest condolences, Mrs. Moerman. If it's of any comfort, Sam left everything to you."

It wasn't a comfort at all. The only thing Addie wanted was to be free of Sam and Dawson City. Now this man was telling her she was the owner of a gambling hall and brothel.

"Mr. Lundstrom, would you find me a buyer for the Gold Palace?" This brought Hiram to her side. Shep followed. Addie continued to ignore them. "I want to sell out."

Mr. Lundstrom looked confused for a moment, then seemed to understand. "Yes, I suppose it would be difficult for a widow to run such a place."

"She's got me and Shep to help her. She don't need to be selling. Besides, she's our responsibility now. We're her brothers." Hiram put his hand on Addie.

She gave him a sharp elbow in the gut. "You are nothing to me, Hiram. I am the widow of the man you sold me to. Nothing more."

Hiram growled and took hold of her. His hand tightened around her upper arm in a most painful grip. "You got no say in this. You're our property."

"I'm afraid you're wrong," Mr. Lundstrom interjected. "Mrs. Moerman is no one's property. She is her own authority and her husband set her up to be well served. She'll have plenty of money to see to her needs."

Addie jerked away from her big brother. "You had your chance. You sold me once, but you'll never do it again." She gave Mr. Lundstrom a nod. "I'll be waiting to hear from you regarding the funeral."

She turned and swept past her brothers. She had nearly reached the stairs when Hiram's voice boomed out. "This ain't over, Addie. You owe us."

"That's right, Addie," Shep chimed in. "You got more than enough, and we got nothing."

Addie fought against making a scene and calling them both out on their lack of concern for her welfare. They sold her into slavery as sure as Joseph in the Bible was sold by his brothers. She just kept walking up the steps with Millie close behind.

The minute she reached her room, Addie hurried inside and motioned for Millie to follow. "Close the door and lock it," Addie said, moving to open the drapes. "I can hardly believe those two. They think I'll come back to them as if I have no ability to see to myself."

"They're very dangerous, Addie. They won't stop until they have their way."

Addie turned and met Millie's worried expression. "That's why you're going to help me get out of Dawson City without them knowing."

"How will we do that?"

"I'm not entirely sure, but I think we can figure out a plan." Addie went to the small writing desk and drew out a key. "I've saved up gold and jewelry—gifts from Sam. With that, plus what I'll inherit from him, I have more than enough to get out of here."

Addie went to the armoire in the corner and unlocked the bottom drawer. She drew out a heavy lockbox and placed it on the bed. She took another key, which she'd hung on the back of the armoire, and unlocked the box.

Millie moved closer to see the contents. "Oh goodness!"

Inside was a variety of jewelry and gold nuggets. She had several bags of gold dust, but perhaps most impressive was the gold-nugget necklace she'd taken off just a few hours ago.

"That necklace is really something." Millie lifted it from the box. "Heavy too."

"Yes." Addie studied the piece as Millie turned it one way and then another. A heavy gold chain had been used for the base of the necklace, and from that hung the gold nuggets in various sizes, starting small near the clasp and gradually increasing in size until the center, where a large teardrop-shaped nugget marked the middle of the necklace. It was a ghastly thing as far as Addie was concerned.

Millie carefully put the necklace back in the box. "Oh, Addie, surely we can get you out of Dawson with all of this."

"I know Bud and Joe will help me. Even if Mr. Lundstrom doesn't manage to sell the Gold Palace, it won't matter. Dawson City is losing people every day. Surely I can just slip away with those folks and start anew somewhere else."

She paused and took hold of Millie's hand. "I'm setting you free, cancelling your contract. Tomorrow, I'll go through Sam's papers and set everyone free. If they want to renew a contract with the new owner that will be up to them, but I will see that they have their freedom and some cash to leave this place."

"Oh, Addie, that will cost a lot."

"All of this gold cost someone a lot in either work or their very life. I want to do whatever good I can." She put a bag of gold dust into Millie's hands. "Tell Jack this is for the two of you. But I'm going to need your help first. I can't trust anyone else."

Three days later, Addie had a plan. Hiram and Shep had tried to force her to meet with them more than once. The armed guards for the Gold Palace refused them entry as Addie had ordered, which only served to make them all the madder. Hiram stood in the street yelling up at her window for nearly fifteen minutes, making it clear that he wasn't about to drop the matter.

It gave Addie a certainty that she needed to get out of town as soon as possible. The funeral for Sam had been short and simple the day before. Afterward, Mr. Lundstrom had quietly bought the Gold Palace from her. She'd practically given it away, knowing that she had more than enough gold to see her through the rest of her life if she was careful. Her one provision was that each of the girls who had worked for Sam be given some money and set free. If they chose to stay in that lifestyle, Lundstrom would deal with them honestly. He agreed. That gave Addie great comfort.

She and Millie had hit upon a plan. Because she was still quite small, they figured she could pass as a boy. A down on his luck boy who had gone to the Yukon hoping to find a fortune and instead found hunger and homelessness like so many.

It was almost comical to resort to such a thing. Her father had brought her into the Yukon the same way. He didn't want anyone knowing she was a girl as they traveled because he knew there could be conflict should someone take a fancy to her. Men were often ruthless when it came to women. Her father knew that full well because he and her brothers often acted that way. And Addie had been happy to pretend to be a boy. She very much liked the idea of being ignored. Hopefully, it would work again.

Millie arranged to find some ragged boy's clothes and an old knapsack. Addie arranged for Mr. Lundstrom to get her passage on a boat that would take her south. Eventually she'd catch the train and then a ship to head to Seattle. That big city was surely large enough to hide anyone who wanted to be hidden.

The trick would be getting away from the Gold Palace. Hiram, Shep, or someone working for them watched the place at all times. Addie had heard they were promising their friends a piece of her fortune if they would help keep Addie under observation.

Bud and Joe, however, figured out how to help her with that as well. They rounded up a bunch of boys to come into the Gold Palace, making a commotion. Bud would usher them out, and Addie would slip into their ranks. They set it all up for when the Palace was at its busiest. With so many people coming and going, Addie ought to be able to just leave without being noticed.

Now, waiting for the appointed time, Addie made one last decision. "Millie, help me cut my hair. I snuck into Dawson with my hair cut off, I might as well go out that way. At least this way if my hat falls off it won't give anything away."

"Are you sure?" Millie asked.

"Yes. Quite. We'll have to be quick. Don't worry what it looks like, just cut it."

Millie took up the scissors and nodded as Addie started to undo her braid. "No, just leave it. I'll cut it at the top of the braid."

"Smart thinking."

Millie began snipping away at the thickness. Finally, she held the braid up in front of Addie. "There you go."

Addie looked in the mirror. They had already smudged her up with dirt and soot. She didn't even recognize herself. "Cut some more. Trim it up a little shorter."

Millie did her best. When the clock chimed the hour, Addie was ready. She grabbed the heavy knapsack. She had packed it with a change of clothes and another pair of boots. Each of the boots was stuffed with gold and jewelry, and on top was a pair of wool socks to keep everything contained.

She secured her cap in place. "How do I look?"

Millie studied her a moment. "I honestly wouldn't recognize you."

"Good." Addie's voice sounded confident, but inside she was fighting back her fears.

She sent Millie downstairs first to let Bud know she was ready. Meanwhile, Addie snuck down the back stairs and waited in position for the boys to show up. It wasn't long until a half dozen or so urchins wandered into the Gold Palace. They started begging for food almost immediately, causing a disruption to those who were dining. Addie slipped into their numbers and found herself welcomed without words. The boys crowded around her, as Bud and Joe had no doubt instructed. Across the room, Addie spied Hiram drinking at the bar. She prayed he wouldn't recognize her or even care about the rowdy boys.

He didn't. He glanced up only once that she saw and then went back to his beer. She had no idea where Shep might be, but so long as neither recognized her, she'd be safe. At least she prayed she would be. She wasn't all that sure God heard her prayers, since she'd never been in a church, but Isaac had once told her that He would.

"You boys get out of here. You're not old enough to be of use to me." Bud grabbed her by the collar and put his arm around another boy to push them through the door. Once outside, he gave Addie's shoulder a squeeze. "Go on and

16

stop causing me trouble. You boys know better. Why don't you go beg down by the docks?"

The boys moved en masse with Addie in the middle of them. They shouted crude insults back at Bud and continued their way to the river. The steamer waiting there blew its whistle to let everyone know it would soon be leaving. Again, the boys made a scene, racing up the gangplank and past the man taking tickets. Addie slipped away from them and was helped by one of the captain's men. It was all over in a matter of minutes. She was with the boys one second, and in another, she was being pushed into a small cabin by one of the captain's men. How in the world Bud had managed it all, she didn't know, but she was ever so glad she'd left him a nice bonus with Mr. Lundstrom.

"You'll be safe now, boy. Stay here. Someone will bring you something to eat in the morning."

Addie nodded and said nothing in reply. She'd been practicing a lower voice but wasn't at all convinced that she could pull off speaking as a boy. Once the steamer was underway, she breathed a sigh of relief and sat down on the bed.

The room was stuffy, but she didn't mind. The last few days had been unbearably hot, so at least she wouldn't have to worry about freezing to death on her trek south. She leaned back and closed her eyes, her pack still secure on her back. It was all she had to her name, except for some ready cash Millie had insisted she hide in the socks she was wearing and the binding they'd used for her breasts.

She thought of her brothers back in Dawson City without enough money to leave. They would be livid when they learned she was gone. Millie was going to cover for her for a few days, telling them Addie was sick, and the doctor agreed to help by insisting she needed to be quarantined. That would buy her precious time so that just in case they were able to come up with enough for their passage south, Addie would have a good head start.

Now, if she could just reach Seattle.

1

O h, what a busy day," Pearl Fisher said, coming into the kitchen. "How's supper coming along?"

Addie Bryant stirred the thick beef stew. It was one of Pearl's favorites. "The stew is ready. I just pulled it from the oven. If you want to call Otis, I'll have it and everything else on the table momentarily."

"Wonderful. I swear I have such an appetite these days. I believe it's all due to the extra work with the expo. I've never worked nearly so hard." The older woman left Addie to finish up and went in search of her husband.

Placing the stew in a serving bowl, Addie smiled at the creation. She had always been a decent cook. People in the Yukon used to come calling just in hopes of getting a sample of whatever she was serving for supper. That was saying something, too, because they had to endure her father and brothers in order to eat at the Bryant table.

She hurried to gather up the vegetable side dishes and biscuits. Once Otis knew supper was on the table, he'd waste little time getting there. The Fishers were good people, and Addie thought Pearl was right. The soon-to-be-open expo was making them all work harder and eat more.

The Alaska-Yukon-Pacific Exposition was opening in Seattle on the first of June, and Addie's employer, Otis Fisher, had the brilliant idea of creating what he called "Camera Girls" to promote photography and in particular the sale of Kodak's new Brownie camera.

Otis had hoped to be the expo's official photographer, but that went to his rival Frank Nowell. To counter his disappointment, Otis had come up with the idea of training pretty young ladies to take pictures with the new cameras, and then folks could stop by his little store at the expo and buy the postcard-sized photo that had been taken. And with any luck, they'd buy a new camera as well.

Addie thought the entire thing was brilliant. She knew the pretty and personable young ladies would attract attention. Otis and Pearl had even invented a uniform for them to wear. Black skirt, high-necked white blouse with long sleeves, and a straw boater hat trimmed in black ribbon, which they provided for each girl, as well as a name tag that Pearl had fashioned. The uniforms were smart looking and distinguished them as Camera Girls to the roaming expo crowd.

Pearl returned to the kitchen to help with the coffee. Addie handed her a tea towel so that she wouldn't burn herself.

"Otis is so worried that people aren't going to buy the photographs or cameras," Pearl tsked as she followed Addie to the table.

"I think folks are really going to be excited about this, and Otis is selling the photos quite inexpensively." Addie grabbed the sugar and cream from the sideboard.

"So long as he has the camera sales he anticipates, we should do fine," Pearl replied.

"I believe the sales will go well. The girls are quite excited about the commission they'll earn for each camera they sell."

They went to the table, where Otis waited to take his place. Addie surveyed the scene, making sure nothing was missing, then took her seat as Otis helped Pearl into her chair. Once seated he offered grace, then immediately dug into the stew to serve it up.

Addie passed her bowl to be filled, as was the routine on something like stews or soups. They never stood on formality here.

Once the stew was served, Addie passed the biscuits and butter. After that the creamed peas and a platter of asparagus made their way around the table, and they were finally ready to eat.

Otis sampled the stew and smiled. "Good, good. Our Addie is quite the cook and takes the load off you, Pearl. We are blessed."

He was a pleasant employer and even better landlord. Addie had found them on her first day in Seattle, seven years ago. She had spied a notice declaring there was a small room for rent on the third floor downtown. Fisher Photography occupied the first floor of the building, while its owners were on the second floor. The small room on the third floor suited Addie just fine. She was living with other people, and there would be no need for her name to be listed at the address.

Knowing she was newly arrived, Otis asked if she was interested in a job. He had presumed her a boy in need of work, and for a time, Addie let them both believe that. It got her established and solidified her friendship before she confessed the truth.

The Christian couple had been loving and kind, very nearly becoming the parents Addie had always longed for. Eventually she confided in them, explaining that she wasn't a boy at all, but rather a young woman trying to make it on her own after her father's death. She told them of how her brothers sold her in marriage to a man she didn't love. Pearl was horrified at the thought. Addie was careful not to reveal the truth of the matter in full. When she'd seen Pearl's upset over the idea of being sold in marriage, Addie could hardly admit to the situation being so much worse. Fortunately, the Fishers had told her they would do whatever they could to help her. In turn, Addie admitted to having some gold in the bank. She had offered to help them on several occasions, but always Otis told her no—that he would find a way to provide for Pearl and himself.

"Well, the shop is ready for opening day," Otis admitted. "I stocked the last few crates of supplies and made sure the darkroom was ready."

"Do the expo coordinators have everything ready for tomorrow's opening day?" Pearl asked.

"I think so. They were going to lay the last bits of sod tonight after the University of Washington graduated its classes and ended the school year," Otis replied.

"It's all so very exciting." And Addie meant that too. There had been very little that she'd taken such pleasure in as she had the expo's birth and development. She had watched the area come to life as the men built grand and glorious buildings, fountains, and gardens on property belonging to the University of Washington. Of course, there was a bargain to be made. Those in charge of the exposition agreed to build several permanent buildings amidst the temporary ones, so that the college could use them after the expo. Locally, it was seen as a great boon for the school and the city.

The plan was for millions of people to attend and learn about the various cultures represented in Alaska, the Yukon, and the Pacific. The focus of the exhibits on Alaska was meant to encourage a push for it to become a permanent territory or even a state. It was hoped that there would be renewed interest in people wanting to settle there if visitors knew about the place and its peoples. The emphasis on the Yukon exhibits would also be tied to the rapid development of the local area. Seattle exploded with people in 1898, when the gold rush was on. There were to be several displays devoted to the requirements for each citizen heading into the Canadian wilderness. Lastly, the Pacific exhibits would focus on anything and everything in the islands of the Pacific Ocean. Representatives for Hawaii would share its culture and history, as would those for the Philippines, Japan, and other locales.

Despite whatever might happen in the next few months, Addie, and many others, thought the expo had already changed Seattle for the better. There had been new streetcar lines added, the sewers and electric services had been extended, and new neighborhoods were springing up faster than anyone had expected. Added to this was the betterment of the university. Even if the expo should fail overall, Seattle had benefitted.

"Do you think the girls will do well, Addie?" Otis asked, sounding a little more anxious than she'd heard him before.

"Of course. I've had them over there every day to learn

the locations of everything they could. They know the position of the shop and where it stands in contrast to various buildings and amusements. I think most of them could find it blindfolded."

"And they understand all about the camera. Are you sure we don't need to call them together tonight?"

Pearl responded before Addie and patted her husband's arm. "It will be good, Otis. You'll see. The girls will do well. It might be rocky at first, but I believe by the end of this grand event, they will be quite comfortable and have sold every camera you have available."

"I hope you're right. We've invested so much."

"Otis, I believe it will be a complete success."

He still looked worried. "But you know the last expo did not do well. The one in Jamestown was a huge failure. Millions of dollars were lost."

"That's true," Addie admitted, "but I don't believe it's going to happen to us. The newspaper said they were poorly managed and had overly ambitious goals that they knew they could never accomplish. The planners here have been very wise and the people equally supportive. Just look at all the money they were able to raise from regular citizens alone."

"She's right, Otis. It's going to be just fine."

Addie smiled. "Besides I've already told you that if all else fails, I'll buy your entire inventory and sell it elsewhere. You two are the only ones who know that I have plenty of money in the bank to do exactly that."

"No, no. I want to earn the money myself," Otis said, shaking his finger at her. "I will build my new shop with my own blood and sweat. This is a matter of pride. My father always told me anything worth having was worth giving your all. Sometimes chances have to be taken, and this is that time for me."

"Then do not give it further concern, husband." Pearl smiled so sweetly at the man. Theirs was a true love match, and Addie couldn't help but be a little envious.

Pearl began again. "We prayed about this and felt it was the right thing to do—the thing God called us to do. Satan wants us to doubt. We cannot spend all of our time in worry."

He drew a deep breath and refocused on the food. "You are right. I will stop my fretting."

Hiram Bryant was tired of being bossed around, but as a part of an early release agreement with the Canadian government, he and Shep had signed on for the hard work in order to get out of prison.

They had been sentenced to ten years for an armed robbery that had resulted in a man being severely wounded. After serving seven of it, they were offered a deal. If they would participate in helping with the heavy lifting aspect of moving artifacts to Seattle for the Alaska-Yukon-Pacific Exposition, they would receive an early release. The news was well received by Hiram and Shep, who had more than wearied of life in prison.

"You fellas have done a good job," the overseer announced. "I have paperwork here that declares you've served your time and met all of the requirements for early release from prison." He handed out the envelopes to a dozen men and smiled. "The Alaska-Yukon-Pacific Exposition is going to be better for all of your work on the Yukon exhibit. You'll find a small amount of pay included in your release papers. You're welcome to spend the night in our tent, but tomorrow it's coming down."

Not a single man there cared one whit as to whether the exposition would be better, nor did they have any interest in staying in the prison tent. Hiram took his papers and elbowed Shep.

"Let's go into town. I'm sure we can manage to find something else. At least a decent meal, and maybe some female companionship." He took up the sack of their worldly possessions and threw it over his shoulder.

Shep nodded and followed his brother away from the Yukon exhibit. As they neared the front gate area, a man called to them.

"Hey, you two. Wanna earn some money?"

Hiram stopped, and Shep ran into him. His growl was enough to cause Shep to jump nearly three feet to the right.

"What did you have in mind?" Hiram asked, turning around.

"I'm helping with landscaping. We're laying the last of the sod tonight. I could use a couple more fellas to help with carrying the sod from the wagons to the areas where it will be planted. It pays well."

Hiram considered it only a moment. "I suppose we could."

"We'll probably work quite late," the man added, "so if you want, you can stay in the dorm we have for the groundskeepers. I know for a fact there are a few empty cots—private too. They arranged rooms for the men who would be working throughout the fair."

"Sounds good." Hiram nodded. "Where can I put our gear?" He nodded to the sack.

"I can take it to the place where you'll stay. After we're done laying sod, I'll escort you there as well. I promise you it'll be safe."

"It better be." Hiram looked to Shep and then to the man. "Let's go."

It wasn't that he wanted more meaningless work to do, but the promise of good pay and a place to stay was too much to pass up. He was determined to get a drink as well, but this exposition was dry. Whoever thought that was a good idea was obviously blind to the profits that could be made by whiskey and beer. People would get thirsty, and the advertised lemonade and iced tea didn't satisfy like a cold beer. The exposition planners were fools.

They worked until midnight, and when the last of the sod was laid and the last adjustments made, the man who'd hired them reappeared.

"I'll walk you over to the dorm."

Hiram and Shep were covered in dirt and sweat, but it didn't matter. They'd never worried overmuch about cleanliness. It took money to stay clean.

As if reading Hiram's thoughts, the man pointed. "At the far end of the building are showers. There's plenty of hot water. Soap is provided as well as towels."

Suddenly settling for dirt and sweat didn't seem nearly so appealing. "Thanks," Hiram said.

"I never really introduced myself. The name is Riley Martin. You fellas worked hard. Want a job helping to keep up the grounds? Pick up trash and so forth. You'd carry a canvas bag around and use a pickup stick to get the trash. It doesn't pay as well as what you just made, but I can keep you in the dorm for no charge."

It wasn't at all what Hiram wanted, but he was starting to think it might be to their benefit. "Any time off? We haven't had even a day since they brought us down here."

The man smiled. "I can give you opening day—tomorrow—but you'll need to be available at the crack of dawn on Wednesday. We'll need to have the entire campus cleared of trash before the expo opens that day. The other trash collectors will do what they can through opening day, but we're anticipating around seventy thousand people or more, so it'll be difficult to keep up. Your regular days off will be Thursdays and Sunday until noon. The expo doesn't open until one in the afternoon on Sundays."

He opened the door to the groundskeepers' dormitory and led the way to a small room with two cots. "This will be yours for as long as you're employed by the exposition. Oh, and you get a free lunch each day—part of your pay. Otherwise, you can get food from the expo at a discounted price. Just show them your work pass." He handed one to each man. "This will get you in and out of the expo for free, and like I said, discounts on food and drink and a free lunch."

Hiram looked over the small room. The cots were made up with a pillow, sheet, and blanket. There wasn't even a window in the room or another piece of furniture. It wasn't all that different from prison. "Sounds good." Hiram and Shep received their pay and waited until the man was gone to speak.

"Why'd you do that?" Shep asked. "I thought we were going into town. I wanted to get a beer."

"I know, and we'll have tomorrow off to do just that." Hiram noted that their sack of goods was placed at the foot of one of the cots.

"I thought we were gonna make some money for ourselves. Make money our own way," Shep said, sounding quite disgruntled.

Hiram pushed him aside. "Look, I had an idea. If we work here and live nearby, we can pick the pockets of all who come to the expo. It should be an easy way to make a living—at least until this fair closes down. As employees of the expo, no one is going to expect us to be picking pockets."

Shep actually smiled. "I hadn't thought of that."

"We've got a place to stay, showers, and free meals. There's been many a time we've gone hungry in the past, so at least there's that. We've got some good money in our pocket and the day off tomorrow to figure out what all we want to do."

"You suppose Addie might come to the expo?"

Hiram frowned. "That's hard to say. We don't know exactly where she ended up." They had overheard Millie telling one of the store owners that Addie had moved to Seattle. That had been enough to set Hiram's mind on future plans. He figured to beat it out of Millie, but instead he and Shep had gotten caught robbing a man who just happened to be a judge. There had been no mercy for them—only prison.

But now they were in Seattle, and if she hadn't moved away, Addie was here as well. Hopefully, it wouldn't be all that hard to find her . . . and that gold-nugget necklace.

"I'm going to go take a shower. You'd do well to do the same. Maybe wash out your clothes, and we can dry them overnight."

"Seems like a lot of fuss to pick up trash."

"We're going into town tomorrow, stupid. And frankly I don't want to smell your stench all day."

Shep shrugged. "These clothes aren't all that good anyway. Just used clothes given to us by the prison. Couldn't even give us a change of clothes."

"That's all right. We'll steal what we need tomorrow." Hiram smiled. "Remember how to do that?"

His younger brother laughed. "I reckon I do."

"I thought as much," Hiram said, heading for the door. "Now, come on. I'm worn out and want to get to sleep. We've got a lot to accomplish tomorrow. Including figuring how to sneak some whiskey back with us."

2

At precisely noon, President William Taft was contacted by the expo's president, John Chilberg. He announced that the fair was ready to begin. With that, Taft wired back a telegram to officially open the Alaska-Yukon-Pacific Exposition of 1909.

At Fisher Photography, Addie considered each of the Camera Girls, making sure their black skirts and white blouses were spotless. Each girl was ready for her new job, with a camera around her neck and satchel over her shoulder.

"Everyone should have cards for the shop to hand out, as well as sample photographs to show interested camera buyers. Make certain you stress the purchase of the camera. Frank Nowell is the official photographer for the expo, and he has a great many photographers positioned around the exhibits. When Mr. Fisher arranged for this shop, he stressed the sale of the Brownie camera as his goal so that no one would think he was trying to interfere with Mr. Nowell's work. We need to make sure the cameras sell."

Each of the girls nodded. Addie continued her inspections.

"Make certain that your hats are secured." She waited while each of the young ladies adjusted her hat.

"Mary tore my ribbon!" Esther protested. Mary stood looking confused, while Esther continued to whine. "She tore it away from the rim. It's a mess."

Addie looked to Mary, who continued to say nothing. The other girls looked away and pretended to be busy with their uniforms. It wasn't the first time Esther had blamed Mary for her woes, and the others simply didn't want to be involved.

Poor Mary was such a shy girl that Addie almost didn't hire her on. How in the world would she be able to sell anything? But it seemed that with the camera and pictures as the purpose for her interactions, Mary did perfectly well. She focused on the object for sale and talked about it quite freely. In all truth, she was better than the others at interesting a buyer in the benefits of being a Brownie owner.

"Let me see the hat," Addie said, reaching out to Esther. She handed over the straw boater and pointed at the dragging ribbon. "This will be easy enough to fix." Addie took the hat in the back room, where they had some paste. She slathered a coating of paste on one side of the ribbon and secured it back in place around the brim. She made a couple of quick stitches to be sure it wouldn't move while drying, and everything was as it should be.

She came back to the front room just as Otis returned.

"The exposition is open!" he announced. "We must get to our jobs, but first we will pray."

Addie handed the hat to Esther, then bowed her head. She was glad that Otis and Pearl were strong Christians who believed in the power of prayer. Addie had to admit the faith of others had helped her many a time. In the Yukon, she had believed because Isaac assured her that God loved her and the Bible was true. When she came to Seattle, it was Pearl and Otis who convinced her of that. But it was difficult to find her own faith in God. Even when her heart cried out for it.

Otis finished the prayer of blessing on the business and each employee. "I want you to do your very best, girls, and above all be considerate and kind to everyone. You are above no one, but neither are you beneath them."

"My mother says we're all better than those natives," Esther sneered.

"I haven't the time to argue with you, Miss Esther." Otis went to the door and opened it. "Now go and do your jobs. Remember, when you complete a roll, bring it straightaway to the shop for development. Leave the camera, and we'll have another already loaded, so there will be little time to wait. Stress to the people that they can see their photos the same day so long as they get here before five. Remind them that we will only hold them for one week before destroying them."

The girls hurried through the door. Already there were people milling along the walkways and heading for the Pay Streak, where the concession stands would ease their hunger and vaudeville shows would entertain. Addie had read about some of the various acts and shows that were being offered. Everything from simple souvenir shops to food vendors and shows to the more elaborate reenactment of the Battle of Gettysburg. Though why they would have it at an expo about Alaska, the Yukon, and the Pacific was beyond Addie's understanding. She had never even heard of the battle until Otis mentioned it. Only then did she learn that it had taken place in the state of Pennsylvania back east. Even Otis was unsure why it was included.

Addie followed the girls into the growing crowds. Folks had been allowed to come through the gates earlier that day, but none of the buildings were open to the public until the president's telegram officially began the exposition. Now the crowds were growing larger by the minute. It reminded Addie of when ice blocked a waterway and how at first there was just a trickle of fluid, then as the ice broke apart and melted, a gush would flood through, making it necessary to move to higher ground. Only with people, there was no higher ground.

Supplied with everything the other Camera Girls carried, Addie began to look for folks who might appreciate a photograph. Otis had particularly encouraged family photos, as well as those of couples.

"Would you care to have a photograph of your family?" Addie asked, approaching a group of people who were already resting on the steps near the Cascade Fountain.

The woman looked up and smiled. Beside her were three children ranging in age from what Addie figured were three or four years to about eight. A man approached carrying a baby. He glanced at Addie a moment and then to the woman.

"I got directions," he told the woman.

"This young lady offered to take our picture."

Addie turned on her charm. "I work for Fisher Photography, positioned at the edge of the Pay Streak and Bonanza, by Klondike Circle. After I take your photograph for free, you have only to pick up the picture later today for a very small fee."

"We haven't had a family photograph with the baby," the woman said, sounding hopeful.

The man still seemed unconvinced, so Addie tried to further entice him. "I can position you in front of the falls over here with the Court of Honor building in the back. It will make a wonderful souvenir for your family. Also, if you like what you see, you might want to consider purchasing one of these new Kodak Brownie cameras. They are the latest in technology and start at the low price of ten dollars. They're also very easy to operate."

Now she had the man's interest. "A ten-dollar camera from Kodak?"

Addie laughed and gave him an enthusiastic nod. She reached into her satchel and pulled out postcard-sized photographs. "And just look at the quality of the pictures."

The man handed the baby to the woman and took hold of the pictures. "These are amazing. Not blurred at all. I might want to check into this camera."

"Of course. You should do that when you pick up your photograph." Addie smiled and lifted the camera that hung round her neck. "Shall we?"

The man nodded. "Come, children, we're going to have our picture taken."

Addie helped them get in position and took the photograph without any difficulty. Even the baby seemed content to pose.

"Stop by the shop later today—no later than five—and it'll be ready. The photographs will be destroyed after one week. And here's a card to remind you." She handed him the business card Otis had created for the fair. "You'll see my name at the top, and the time I took the photo. It's also nice enough to be a souvenir."

She turned the card over to reveal the circled logo where

three women were positioned as representatives of the expo. Dressed in red, white, and blue, they each stood for something related to the fair. The woman in red was the essence of the Pacific. Her right hand was extended in welcome, and in her left hand she held a train representing commerce by land. The woman in blue stood for the Orient, and she extended a ship to represent commerce by the sea. The woman standing in the middle wore white and represented Alaska. In her hands were gold nuggets to remind people of the vast mineral wealth the north had to offer.

"That's very lovely," the woman said. "I shall put it in our scrapbook of adventures." The two older children clapped their hands and danced around.

Addie smiled and continued on her way. The expo was an entirely different place with thousands of people strolling the streets. It took her no time at all to take another nine pictures and complete her roll. She hurried back to Otis's shop just as Mary was doing the same.

Pearl was running the counter while Otis was already at work in the darkroom. "We've brought more film to be developed." They left the cameras and picked up others that were loaded and ready to go.

Addie gave Pearl a smile but didn't stop to talk. She wanted to do her part to make the Fishers successful. It was times like this that Addie wished she had a whole lot of friends and family that she could gift with one of the new cameras. She had plenty of resources in the bank, but no one to bless with them. She'd tried on numerous occasions to help Otis and Pearl with their dream of a bigger shop and home, but they'd hear nothing of it. The best Addie could do was to show up with the occasional roast or steaks, maybe a gift for one or the other. But they were proud people, and in the seven years she'd been with them, Addie had been quite limited on what they would allow her to do.

The day passed quickly with Addie taking pictures and exchanging cameras. At three o'clock, over three thousand people gathered to witness the dirigible launch. Unfortunately, the pilot couldn't get the engine to fire, but he promised in the days to come he would, and the dirigible would fly. Addie had hoped to take a picture of the thing moving through the air. It maneuvered so slowly that she figured she could get a decent shot without too much of a blur. But it would have to wait.

After returning her eighth camera, Addie decided to seek out something to eat. She hit the Pay Streak and enjoyed a German sausage on a skewer before continuing to walk around. It wasn't long before she came up to an exhibit on Eskimos. The designer had fashioned plaster icebergs and snow mounds, and outside there were a dozen native people dressed in fur parkas and sealskin pants. Today wasn't all that warm, but Addie couldn't help but wonder how they would bear up come summer. Thankfully, Seattle weather was usually cooler than other places Addie had read about in the paper.

As she stood there a moment, the past came washing over her. There were men dressed in similar fashion when her family had climbed the Chilkoot Trail. The Ice Staircase some had called it. Others named it the Golden Stairs. But the name didn't matter. By either choice, the people had to take pack after pack up the mountain in order to transport a ton of goods per person.

She shivered even though it wasn't cold. The reminders of her family left her momentarily fearful. She glanced around, looking as always for her brothers. The entire matter upset her so much she decided to go for a walk by the lake.

It wasn't all that more peaceful down by the shore. The noise from the expo was quite prevalent. There were rides, music playing to attract crowds to various exhibits, and the constant hum of voices. Addie continued to walk along the lake, where cottages dotted the waterfront. Since she'd first come to this area during the building of the expo, Addie had fallen in love with the lake cottages. She vowed to Pearl that one day she would buy one of these places, but it seemed none were ever for sale.

"Not there, Caledonia," Addie heard a woman state. She glanced up a slight rise in the landscape and spied two older ladies struggling with a sign at the end of their walkway.

"Can I help you, ladies?" she asked.

"That would be so kind," one of the women announced.

"We'd like to get this sign in the ground," the other woman added.

Addie looked at the sign. They had hand painted in black the words, *FOR SALE*. She looked at the cottage and then to the women. "Are you really selling this lovely home?"

"We are. We thought to sell it before the expo began, and now that it's started, we are even more determined to move."

The shorter of the two drew out a handkerchief and put it to her forehead. "We cannot take the noise. First, there was all the ballyhoo about creating the exposition."

"Sister, there is no need to speak so crudely," the other woman chided.

"Well, I simply cannot take any more. After that came the construction and all the noise of supplies being moved in and out and buildings being erected and more people coming to promote what was happening. We haven't had a peaceful moment since."

"But the expo only lasts until October," Addie reminded her.

"It doesn't matter. The university has promised to push for more enrollment. Not to mention the plans for boat races and other challenges on the lake. There will simply be people tramping all about."

"Perhaps I could buy your cottage." Addie smiled. "I have quite a savings and have been wanting to buy a little place near the water."

The smaller woman perked up. "Could you buy it right away?"

"I could. If it suits me."

The woman dropped her hold on the sign. "Let's not worry about this right now. Come in and see the place." She motioned to the walkway. "I'm Patagonia Montgomery, and this is my sister, Caledonia. Now come on."

"Sister, you shouldn't be so bossy," Caledonia remarked. Nevertheless, she gave Addie a nudge from behind.

"It's all right," Addie said, allowing the small woman to pull her toward the house. "I would love to see it."

Inside, Addie was all the more certain this was the place for her. There was a sweet little living area with a nice fireplace to heat the house. The kitchen was very small, but certainly big enough for Addie. In the back were two small bedrooms with a bed and dresser in each.

"We'd like to sell the furnishings as well. You could just buy it all, save our personal bric-a-brac," Patagonia announced. "They've already hooked us up to sewer. Did it last year, and we have running water and electricity. Through that door, we added on an indoor bathroom." She pointed to the door at the back of the house—between the bedrooms. "It used to be a mud porch, but it was thoroughly made over. We hired it professionally done."

Caledonia nodded. "We thought it would be a nice convenience."

"I love it," Addie said. "It's charming and exactly what I need. Why don't we sit down and discuss the price?"

"We have a good friend who can draw up the papers and bring them to you tomorrow, if you let us know where you live." This came from Patagonia, who suddenly seemed just as eager as her sister to vacate the property. As if fearing this might drive Addie away, she added, "We've a sister who lives in Spokane. She's recently widowed and has begged us to come and stay with her. She has a very large house."

"That sounds like a wonderful thing. All the sisters together again." Addie couldn't begin to explain to them how she had always longed for a sister. She reached into her bag and pulled out one of the cards advertising the Fishers' shop. "Here is where I'm working. You can have the papers sent there, and if the price and terms are agreeable, I will happily purchase your house."

"Oh, that would be wonderful," the one said, looking to the other. "And we needn't worry about that sign."

Addie nodded. "By the way, my name is Adeline Bryant, but most folks call me Addie. I wonder if you ladies would like to have a picture taken of you in front of your sweet little house as a memory keeper?"

"Are you a photographer?" Patagonia asked.

Addie held up the camera. "That's what I'm doing at the expo. We are called Camera Girls, and we're going around the fair to encourage the purchase of these Brownie cameras. We take people's photos and then explain how easy it is to use the camera and show them what marvelous pictures it takes. I'm certainly not trying to sell a camera to you, but I think it would be nice to have a picture that you can keep to remember this place by. It won't cost you a cent. It's my treat."

"I think it would be grand," Caledonia declared. "Let's do it, sister."

Patagonia gave a giggle and nodded. "I say yes. What marvelous fun."

Addie looked at the developed photo of the two old ladies. She went to pay Pearl for the picture, still smiling.

"What's that?" Pearl asked.

Addie handed her the ten cents Otis was charging and smiled. "I took this picture of two sisters who just sold me their house."

"What?" Pearl looked more than a little surprised. "Why did you not seek counsel before agreeing to buy it? Otis will be terribly hurt."

"I'll explain it to him. I don't want him to be offended. Still, it was one of those things I felt compelled to do, and you know how it is when I feel a thing is right to do."

"I know, but it happens so rarely. I suppose that provides all the more surprise. Where is the house located?"

"It's just beyond the expo down on Lake Washington. It's a little cottage, and it's perfect for me. I fell in love with it at first glance. I'd gladly keep the old ladies too, but they want to move to Spokane to be with their sister."

"Goodness, how did you accomplish all of this in an afternoon?"

"Well, it's not finalized. They're having a lawyer bring over papers tomorrow. They'll come here to the shop so Otis can have a look at them before I sign them."

"I'm glad you're at least doing that much."

"It really is a wonderful home. And it's been fully modernized with sewer, electricity, and running water. It even has an indoor bathroom. And they are selling me most of the furniture and items that aren't of sentimental value—like dishes and pots and pans. I'll be fully set up and ready to go without having to do much at all."

"Well, I have to admit it does sound like a good deal."

"Don't worry about me, Pearl. I think it will be perfect. You and Otis can come with me tomorrow night after we close the shop and see the house if you like. Otis can tell me if he thinks there are any problems. Remember," she said, leaning close to Pearl, "I can afford to fix things up. It's not like I'm spending all my money buying the place."

Pearl considered this a moment, then took the photograph from Addie. "They look reliable."

"I think they are, and I want to believe God put us all together for just this reason." Addie's brow raised. "You're always telling me that this is how God works, just when we least expect it. Now, pray about it if you must do something, and I will try to as well."

Pearl handed back the photo. "I will pray. Otis, too, when I tell him all about this." She smiled at Addie. "I hate the idea of losing you. I love having you live with us."

"I've enjoyed my time with you too. You and Otis are as dear as anyone could ever be to me. I don't intend for that

42

to come to an end. And besides, we'll both be here at the fair working, and you can come and see me at the house anytime you like."

Nodding, Pearl reached out and hugged Addie. "Perhaps that will make it so that I miss you less, but I doubt it."

3

Isaac Hanson took another headcount of his eighth-grade students, then handed out the tickets as they stood in line. It was Children's Day at the exposition. He knew most of the class had been looking forward to this day all year. The expo was all anyone could talk about. There were rides and entertainments as well as the educational things that Isaac intended to show them.

"Everyone listen, please." His group went silent, but everyone around them continued to talk. The students leaned in to better hear. "We will spend the first half of the day focused on learning. At noon we will have lunch near the bandstand, and after that, you will have two hours to do whatever you please. But you must stay with your assigned buddy, and you must meet back right here by the gates at three o'clock. Does everyone understand?"

The class of students nodded, although by now they were all bored with waiting. Isaac smiled. "Very well, let us go."

The class was well behaved. After all, the principal had arranged for these summer forays, and they came with a warning: if anyone acted out of line, they would suffer a suspension when the new school year started. Given this class was about to pass into high school, they were on their best behavior.

They went first to the Natural Amphitheatre on the opposite side of the expo grounds, where seventeen hundred children from various schools sang patriotic songs while accompanied by the official expo band. After a time, the band duties were given over to the Japanese naval band and the children sang the Japanese national anthem in English. At the end of speeches given by school officials, the children who had been dressed in red, white, and blue formed a human flag and the American national anthem was sung.

After this, Isaac led the children to some of the exhibits. He had come the day before to get a feel of what would be most beneficial and studied up on what he might say to each of the groups he would escort in the weeks to come.

Just before noon they ended at Ezra Meeker's house. "Who can tell me about Mr. Meeker's contribution to our great state?"

No one seemed to want to be bothered, but finally one young man raised his hand.

"Yes, Thomas?" Isaac smiled. "What can you tell us?"

"Mr. Meeker is worried about the Oregon Trail disappearing. He wants to preserve it for future generations by retracing it and leaving markers."

"Why does he feel so strongly about this?" Isaac asked the group. No one volunteered the information, so Isaac continued. "Ezra Meeker was an Oregon Trail immigrant who came to Washington determined to make his fortune, which he did and then lost it. He has been very supportive of Washington State, promoting it wherever and whenever he could. He even went to Alaska to search for gold, so he definitely deserves to be represented here at the expo."

The children already had their minds on lunch, as well as the many attractions there on the South Pay Streak area of the expo.

"Does everyone have their lunch money?" Isaac asked.

They all seemed to be set, and Isaac decided that even though it was ten till twelve, he'd let them go early. "All right, everyone listen and listen well. You can get your food and come and sit as a group by the bandstand if you like. If you prefer to eat at one of the restaurants, that's all right too.

"You know where the main gate is—the place where we entered the expo. And if you don't know how to get back to it, ask any expo official and they'll be able to point it out. Meet me there at exactly three o'clock. We'll be catching our trolley right after that, and if you get left behind, you will suffer suspension."

The students all appeared to comprehend the gravity of the situation and agreed to the arrangement. Isaac released them, and they disappeared so fast he wondered if they'd ever really been there. Even the girls were quick to get away, and almost always one or two lingered behind to ask him silly questions because they fancied themselves in love with him.

He wondered if he got the university teaching position if things would be any better. Girls could certainly be a silly bunch. He wondered why they couldn't all be as stable and considerate as Addie Bryant had been.

Thinking of Addie always brought him both pleasure and pain. He had been in love with her since he was seventeen. They had promised each other they'd marry after he got his doctorate, but things hadn't worked out the way Isaac had hoped.

He had only been in the Yukon because his father wanted to take up a large stock of store goods and set up a shop for a year. He felt they could cash in on the hard work of the miners and provide what they needed. Then after a year, they would return to the States richer and better able to send Isaac to Harvard, where he intended to study history and teaching. He wanted to one day teach at a university level. Teaching children was all right, but he wanted, even at the age of seventeen, to converse with students who could be taught to become real thinkers. The kind of students who would plumb the depths of human thoughts and deeds. It was something he had loved while learning at Harvard. He found it to be even better than he'd dreamed it would be.

However, it had been harder to leave the Yukon than he'd anticipated. He met fifteen-year-old Addie shortly after his arrival and lost his heart to her. At first, he thought it was just because her father and brothers were so cruel to her. He had tried to intercede for her on occasion and always ended up being threatened with death. Addie made him promise he'd stay out of it. They were killers, she told him, and they would think nothing of eliminating him. But Isaac couldn't just let it be. He loved her and wanted to protect her.

"We'll marry and be together always," he had promised, and she'd agreed to wait for him.

But her family had other plans.

"Do you know where the Fairy Gorge is, Mr. Hanson?" one of his students asked with a large roast beef sandwich in hand.

Although he had earned his doctorate and was entitled to be called Dr. Hanson, Isaac never used the title with his young students. He pointed to the left. "I've been told it has quite the twists and turns and can actually induce vomiting. You might not want to eat first or else wait a good hour before going on the ride."

The boy shrugged and took off in the direction of what Isaac had heard was fast becoming the fair's most sought-after form of entertainment. Isaac gave a chuckle. He'd done similar outrageous deeds when he was young.

Walking along the avenue, Isaac noted the various entertainments. There were other rides besides the Fairy Gorge. There were plenty of places to buy food, of course. Isaac noted that at the far end he could see a horse trained by Prince Albert and then walk a little ways to see a scenic arrangement of the streets of Japan. Farther down, old-timers who had returned from the Yukon would teach you how to pan for gold.

Isaac couldn't help thinking of Addie again. He'd promised to come back to her after his college studies. Undergraduate and graduate classes had only taken him seven years, less than most, but still a long time to be away from the woman he loved. He'd gone back for her after graduating from Harvard, but she was gone. Her brothers too. The brothers had gone to prison in late 1902 after having nearly killed a man while robbing his store, but no one seemed to know where she had gone, and Isaac felt most hopeless. Eventually, he remembered Addie's friendship with a woman named Millie Stanford. Millie was hesitant to tell him much, but finally confessed that Addie had gone to Seattle.

She told him other things as well. Things that broke his

heart. Addie had gone through so much. Isaac was originally from Seattle, and his sister, Elizabeth, still lived here. So he had come to stay with her and her husband, Stuart, while he looked for Addie. They had two adorable little girls, Mina and Lena, who filled Isaac's days with laughter. Elizabeth had insisted he live with them until he was able to secure a position, but even after he went to work teaching at a local school, Isaac remained. They were the only family he had, now that their father had passed on.

He told Elizabeth all about Addie and his desire to find her. At one point, Stuart suggested that he hire a Pinkerton to search for her, and Isaac did just that, but to no avail. The man told him it was akin to looking for a needle in a haystack. But Isaac didn't care how difficult the task was, he had to find her.

As a last resort, he had put an ad in the papers seeking Addie, but no one had responded. It seemed so hopeless, and he eased his pain by telling stories about Addie to Mina and Lena. They called her Princess Addie, and Isaac was the handsome knight who would save her from the evil dragon. He had asked them how he could do this, and Mina had answered, *"Your love will save her, Uncle Isaac. Just like God's love saved us from sin."*

Isaac remembered how impressed he'd been with the then eight-year-old Mina. He had even commented on how her assessment was quite astute for one so young. Mina countered by telling him God had given her an old heart, and Isaac believed it. Now at age ten, Mina had quite a depth of understanding.

At three o'clock, Isaac met his students at the gate, just as instructed. They were all talking nonstop about what they

had experienced. Most of the boys were starving because
they'd used their lunch money for other things, but that was
of no matter now. They would soon be home and could seek
food there.

Isaac was glad when they were all finally released from his
charge. He made his way home, walking up the hilly street.
He reached his sister's house with the wrought-iron fencing
and massive gate. Stuart was from a moneyed family and had
invested wisely. Although he taught English at the University
of Washington and made very little, he was quite well off
with investments. He had once joked that he had enough
family money that he could afford to teach as a lifelong position. Even colleges couldn't afford to pay all that well.

But Isaac didn't care. He knew Addie wouldn't either.
They were both quite practical, and money wasn't their rai-
son d'être. Addie hadn't been brought up to fear God as
he had, but even then, she hadn't sought riches and wealth
as her goal in life. She saw how the madness affected the
people around her. She pitied them and even wept when she
saw them break from the strain. Addie was a girl who felt
everything deeply.

Isaac had shared his faith with her, and Addie had seen
the value of it but wasn't sure she understood or could fully
embrace it, given the cruelty of her own family. How could
she trust a heavenly Father who seemed to ignore her situation? Isaac reminded her that God had sent Isaac into Addie's
life, and that he had pledged to always be there for her—just
as God had. Gradually, Addie had softened to the idea of
salvation through Jesus. Isaac had led her in a prayer and
encouraged her to join him at church services on Sundays,
but her family would hear nothing of it.

He wondered how she felt about God after all these years . . . ten to be exact.

"Uncle Isaac!" Two little girls came bursting out the large double front doors.

Isaac scooped them both up at the same time and hugged them close. "Wait a minute," he said, putting them down again. "Did you grow while I was gone?"

Six-year-old Lena giggled and gave an enthusiastic nod. "I did. Mama had to buy me new shoes." She held up one foot.

"Oh, those are handsome shoes, Miss Lena. I think you chose very well."

"I didn't choose. Mama did." She pranced around the porch and gave a twirl. "They're very good for dancing."

"Indeed, they are," Isaac agreed. "I don't think I've ever seen anyone twirl quite as well." She lifted her chin in pride. Isaac might have laughed, but the child was dead serious. "And what did you get, Miss Mina?"

"A new hat and gloves."

"We both got new gloves," Lena had to interject.

Mina frowned at her. "Yes, we both needed new gloves for church."

"What kind of hat did you get?"

"It's a straw hat to keep the sun off of my face so that I won't freckle. Mama hates freckles."

Isaac put his arm around Mina's shoulders. "Well, I like freckles."

"Did Princess Addie have any freckles?" she asked.

Lena danced over to join them. "Did she?"

Isaac thought back to Addie's creamy complexion. Though slightly tanned by the sun and her outdoor work, she didn't sport any freckles.

"No, Princess Addie didn't have any freckles, but that doesn't make them any less valuable to me." He leaned down and kissed Mina's forehead. "So if you should get any freckles, I will cherish them."

"Mine too?" Lena asked.

"Of course." He kissed the top of her head. "Now what say we go in and see if the cook has arranged tea for us?"

By the imposed will of the University of Washington, the expo was a dry affair. Liquor of any type was not to be allowed on the premises. Most world fairs and expositions knew the value of making alcohol available, but that was of no concern to the university. They felt it was an abomination and, as an example to their students and citizens, had refused. But that didn't stop Hiram and Shep Bryant. After all, they hadn't agreed to the conditions, and after all those years in prison, they weren't about to continue to abstain.

The day after they got their exposition jobs, Hiram had managed to slip the liquor past the gate guard, telling them that his backpack was full of clothes and other needs for his employment. They hadn't even cared. Despite it being a special turnstile for employees, the place was overrun with people, and the guards and others manning the stiles didn't have time to worry too much about what people were bringing in.

Shep had carried what looked like a strongbox, while Hiram managed the backpack. The box was empty and easy enough to show if one of the guards did want to make a fuss. But no one did, and once they reached their room, Hiram removed the liquor from his pack and put it in the box. Afterward, he had Shep secure a padlock on the box, and then Hiram took the key.

They had divided up the clothes they'd stolen. Both were pretty much the same size. Hiram and Shep had visited several stores to acquire all that they needed. They stuffed some of the things under their shirts, while paying for other, less costly pieces. The stores were crowded, and no one ever seemed to notice.

After shopping their way, they went about seeking alcohol to take back to the exposition. Hiram and Shep had enjoyed plenty of the brew while in town, as well, but it made both of them feel a little happier knowing the stuff would be available to them whenever they wanted it.

Now, a few days into their new situation, Hiram stretched out on his cot and yawned. "I'm gonna take a nap."

Shep nodded. "Guess I will too."

Closing his eyes, Hiram thought of his miserable life. He might as well still be in prison. He was limited on what he could and couldn't do because of his job and the place where he lived. It wasn't what he wanted, but for the moment, it seemed about all he could arrange.

On the positive side, he and Shep had made two hundred dollars in picking pockets. They would be out walking around on their trash pickups and just bump into a person here or there. After all, the people attending were shoulder to shoulder in some areas. Hiram had always had a touch, even as a big man, for sneaking a man's wallet out. It was harder with women, but they seldom carried much with them and usually Hiram let them be. Women were always trouble.

They looked over their shoulders in fear of big men like Hiram and Shep. They were the first to move away if they felt at all that a man was taking liberties with their space. No doubt Addie was the same way. Hiram couldn't imagine her being very congenial to any man given the way she'd acted in Dawson City after Isaac left.

That boy had been nothing but trouble, and Hiram had to straighten him out more than once. But he had to give the boy credit. He never told Addie about Hiram's beatings. That gave Hiram a bit of admiration for the young man . . . but not much. He knew what the men of the Yukon were looking for in his little sister. And when it suited Hiram and made it worth his trouble, he was willing to give her over to them. For a price.

Sam Moerman had paid quite well for the privilege of having Addie for his own. Hiram never knew for sure what all he made her do at the Gold Palace, but after a while, Sam married her, surprising him and Shep. Why would a man bother to marry when he owned the woman?

Oh well. It was Sam's choice.

From now on, it would be Hiram's choice, and he didn't intend to waste any time taking advantage of the people and events going on around him.

4

Addie had never seen so many people in one place. There had certainly been plenty of souls in Skagway and Dyea, preparing to climb the Chilkoot Trail, but so many more roamed the grounds of the AYP, as folks working there had come to call it.

Keeping track of the Camera Girls was proving to be more and more difficult, but from the number of photographs being developed and people coming into the shop for said photographs, Addie figured the girls were doing their job. Still, she did her part to work the crowds and to promote the Brownie camera and family photographs.

Noticing Esther with a couple of young men, Addie joined them to see what was going on. "How are you doing with photography, Esther?" she asked upon reaching the trio. It was easy to see that Esther was promoting only herself to these two men.

"Another pretty girl," one of the men declared. "Aren't we the lucky ones today?"

"Sure are," the other young man replied. He stepped closer toward Addie, but she sidestepped his maneuvers.

"Esther, you should have a full camera by now. Have you taken these gentlemen's picture?"

"They didn't want a photograph taken."

The one who had moved toward Addie stepped closer again. "We're more interested in the beautiful women taking the photographs."

Addie nodded. "Nevertheless, taking photographs and selling cameras is what Esther is getting paid for. Come, Esther, there are plenty of folks who do want their photograph taken."

The blond-haired young woman looked none too happy at Addie's outstretched hand. She moved past them all in a huff, and Addie in turn bid the gentlemen good day. Catching up with Esther, she could see she was more than a little angry.

"I'm sorry you think it unfair of me to interfere, but you are getting paid to do a job. If you would like to turn in your things and resign the position, that can be arranged."

"I don't want to quit," Esther snapped. "I need this job."

"Then I suggest you *do* the job."

Esther stopped and turned to face Addie. "You don't know what it's like to struggle to pay bills."

"You know nothing about me, Esther, and right now, I don't have the time to enlighten you. Now, there's a family over there pausing to look at the map of the expo. Why don't you offer to take their picture and make them a memory keeper?"

Esther gave a huff and stomped over to the young family. Addie hoped her attitude changed before she actually said anything to them.

Addie continued to make the rounds, searching the growing crowds to find her girls. It was her birthday, but she refused to celebrate it, and Pearl and Otis knew better than to bring it up. After all, the last time she had celebrated her birthday, a man was killed. She tried not to think about it, however. It was just a birthday—her twenty-sixth. Nothing special at all.

A mass of people pressed in and passed her to reach their destinations. It was said that the fair was averaging thirty thousand people every day. It was amazing to watch. Almost more fascinating than the exhibits themselves, which Addie was taking in on her days off.

Finding herself outside the display on the gold rush, Addie listened as a man explained to the growing crowd that each visitor headed north to the Yukon had to take survival goods with them. She remembered that well enough. Remembered, too, that her father had argued with one of the officials, insisting that Addie was a child and certainly didn't eat like they did. Her father was adamant that they didn't need to take as much food for her as they were taking for themselves. The man finally grew tired of arguing with her father and pointed out that he and his older boys were larger than the average man, and they'd be glad to have Addie's extra poundage of food. But he finally gave in and let them go without Addie having as much food stocks as the others.

"Folks headed to the Yukon were anxious to get there 'fore the gold was gone," the lecturer told the crowd. "But you had to transport these goods, and it wasn't easy. Many of the people there hired Eskimos."

Without thinking, Addie piped up. "They weren't Eskimos. They were Tlingits."

The man stopped and looked down at her. "I'm sorry, miss, but were you there?"

Addie heard the condescension in his tone. "As a matter of fact, I was. I climbed the ice staircase with my father and brothers. How about you? Were you there?"

The man flushed and stammered. "Well, uh, no. Not exactly."

She smiled. "They were mostly Tlingit, with a few Haida and Athabaskans. Good people. Most of the prospectors would have died without them." The people around her turned toward her, ignoring the man onstage.

A woman nearest her asked about Addie's experience. "Did you haul packs of goods up and over that mountain with all the others?"

"No, I guarded our goods as they collected on the Canadian side. So I only made one trip up the mountain, but that was enough. I carried a pack with about thirty pounds of gear, and it was nearly too much."

"Did your father and brothers hire the natives to help?"

Addie remembered her brothers robbing and gambling to get enough money for a few packers and to pay the Canadian duty charges. "They did hire a couple of men," she told the woman. "However, my father and brothers were large men who were quite capable of carrying big packs—some probably weighing close to one hundred pounds."

The woman gasped, as did a few other people. Addie remembered them complaining with each trip they made, and she was always to have refreshments or a meal available to them when they reached the top.

"How did you, a little girl, guard your supplies?" a man asked, sounding doubtful.

"A little girl is well respected when holding a large gun. I had a pistol in my pocket and a rifle slung over my shoulder. Besides, most of the people were accommodating and used the honor system. There were also the Canadian police and government men. For the most part, people didn't want to get caught doing anything wrong because they wanted to get to the Yukon, where they were confident they could pick gold up off the ground without having to work for it."

"And did they?" a woman asked. "Did they pick up gold off the ground?"

Addie shook her head. "If anyone did, they were done with that by the time we got there. Searching for gold was grueling. If you panned in the rivers and creeks, you did so with hundreds of other people. Those who got rich were more often the businessmen and women running stores and saloons." She thought of Sam Moerman and added, "There was real money to be made in the gambling halls too." She didn't bother to speak about the brothel. That made even more money. "People would dig and pan and do whatever they could to find gold, then come into Dawson City to spend it, so being a store owner, you made all sorts of money and didn't have to work nearly as hard for it."

"Is it true that people lived in tents even when the temperature was forty below zero?" a man asked.

"It is. I experienced that myself." Addie shrugged. "But we had a tent stove, and besides me, there were three big, burly men." She remembered it all too well. Her father and brothers hadn't cared whether she froze to death or not. She had counted herself lucky to be allowed to sleep inside the tent. After she was sold to Sam, she had the luxury of sleeping in a bed. However, given the price she had to pay, she would have happily taken a tent any day.

The lecturer brought the crowd's attention back to the stage. "Folks, if you'll look up here, we have arranged a variety of goods just like the gold rushers would have had to pack. I have an Eskimo here to show you how it was done."

Addie turned her attention to the stage and hoped the others would too. She hadn't meant to interrupt the man's performance and was determined to listen to his lecture and then apologize for her interruption.

After the man had the native demonstrate how to load and carry a large pack of goods, he concluded his speech. "The gold rush was not for the weak or faint of heart. A lot of men and women lost their lives on the side of the mountain or on the rivers getting to Dawson City. We are proud to remember them and their brave feat."

The crowd clapped and dispersed while Addie made her way to the raised platform. The man saw her and came down to greet her.

"I am sorry for interrupting your lecture, mister."

The older man smiled. "I found myself enchanted, so no apology is needed. I was just as fascinated as the crowd to learn that you had actually gone north."

"It certainly wasn't my desire to have done so, but I was just fifteen, and my father made the decisions."

"I wonder . . . do you suppose you could come on Saturdays to speak to the children? We have a series of lectures going on all over the expo on Saturdays to further their education. There's one lecture given on islands of the Pacific, another on our fair state, and so forth. We tried to include a wide variety to give the children and others a better understanding of various locations. Might you consider speaking about your life in the Yukon? The difficulties getting there, how it was to live on the trip north, then how it was to actually live there?"

Addie had never thought about her experiences being of interest to anyone else. "I don't know."

He pressed on. "You saw how fascinated the people around you were just to talk to someone who had actually been there and experienced that life. They were mesmerized and had no end of questions. Had I not redirected the gathering, you would still be answering those questions."

"I suppose that's true enough. You say it would take place on Saturdays?"

"Yes, you would speak three times. Once at nine, once at ten, and then eleven. We stop the lectures after noon."

"I suppose I might be able to get permission to do that." Addie wasn't at all certain she wanted to remember all the details of her life up north, but she could see that the audience craved information. "I'll speak to my employer and let you know later today."

"I'm Jim Rigsby, by the way." He extended his hand. "And you are?"

"Addie. Addie Bryant."

"Are you certain that you want to do this?" Pearl asked Addie over supper that night. "I know there was a lot of pain for you up there."

"There was," Addie admitted, "and I must say that was my first thought. But I got to thinking that it might also be possible to lessen the hold of those days by sharing some of my experiences with others. I can focus on the positive and some of the fun I did have. And maybe talking about the difficulties folks had to endure will help me to remember I wasn't alone in my suffering."

"I suppose we can spare you for those three hours on Saturday," Otis said, cutting into the pork chop his wife had prepared.

"Well then, I guess I'll give it a try." Addie smiled. It actually felt like the right thing to do.

Pearl looked momentarily worried but then smiled. "I would imagine the children will be fascinated to learn about it from the perspective of someone who was a child when they experienced the Yukon."

"I wasn't a child for long." Addie's smile faded. "You grew up fast in Dawson City. Too fast."

"Thank you for coming this evening," Isaac said to the auditorium full of parents and schoolchildren. "As you know, the area school districts have set up an arrangement with the AYP Exposition to have lectures for the children on Saturday mornings. We have also arranged special transportation and tickets. For the simple price of one dollar, your student can attend each Saturday lecture all summer. They will have transportation to and from the school and admission into the fair. If you choose to attend with them, you will have to purchase your own tickets, as this is a special pass for the children only."

A woman raised her hand. "Yes, you have a question?" Isaac asked.

"What about lunch? Will they need to provide their own?"

"The lectures are in the morning from nine to noon. After that, the student is free to stick around or head home. Lunch will be the responsibility of the parents, so if you want them to stay at the fair, you'll have to give them money to buy food or send them with a packed lunch."

He paused and looked out over the crowd. "I want to highly recommend this opportunity. We can teach from a textbook all day long, but seeing things in person is a marvel that doesn't come around often. I'll continue to take questions now if you have any."

A woman in front raised a hand. "I heard that there are naked natives dancing and eating dogs."

Isaac tried not to smile. There had been quite an uproar over the Igorot tribespeople from the Philippines.

"You are speaking of the Igorot. These are native peoples from the mountains in the Philippines. They have a village at the expo where they dress in their native way, which, in our way of thinking, is quite scandalous. However, this is their natural manner of dress and is allowed at the expo to teach others about these people and their daily living.

"It is also true they occasionally eat dog, but so do many cultures. Cats too." He smiled. "And while that is hardly appetizing to most Americans, I would venture a guess that there have been Americans who have done likewise in times of desperation. However, I want to encourage you to not be offended by the difference of cultures represented at the expo. The important point of all of these exhibits is not to titillate but to educate."

There were other questions regarding the transportation and ages allowed for the children to participate. By seven o'clock, everyone seemed satisfied, and the signup sheets were filled out and monies paid. Isaac was pleased, as were his fellow teachers, at the response. Whether the parents actually saw the value of the education being offered or were simply glad to rid themselves of their children for the whole of Saturday morning, who could say?

"Are you ready for this?" one of the other teachers asked him.

"I am. I think it will be a great deal of fun."

"I'm just glad you suggested we each focus on one exhibit and take multiple groups of children, rather than try to familiarize ourselves with all of the lectures that will be given."

"I still plan to somehow experience each of the lectures, but given my background with the Yukon, it seemed natural for me to take the children to those lectures so I could also handle their additional questions. Since they only leave about fifteen minutes at the end of each talk for questions, I'm sure the children will still have plenty to ask afterward."

"I'm relieved to only have to study up on Washington state history," the man said, laughing. He slapped Isaac on the back. "Guess I'll see you in the morning."

"Transportation leaves at eight thirty sharp," Isaac reminded him.

The man nodded and pulled on his hat. "I'll be there."

Isaac walked home the few blocks, thinking about all he had to do. He was still waiting to hear back from the University of Washington as to whether he would be hired to teach history. He'd thought his interview went very well. The questions they asked him about his personal experience had impressed them. Isaac's father had been quite good at investing their Yukon money, and it had allowed Isaac to travel during his college years. He had gone to study the history of England, Ireland, and Scotland one summer, and France and Spain another. He even spent time with a group of young men traveling to various American Civil War battlefields.

To Isaac, it had been important to grab on to as much learning in his college years as possible. Besides, it kept him from thinking too much about Addie. Well, at least it did in theory. Addie was never far from his thoughts.

At home, Isaac made his way to the kitchen. He was starving and had missed dinner that evening in order to attend to his duties at the school. A plate of food awaited him in the warming box on the stove. He smiled at his sister's thoughtfulness. She had been so very attentive to him since he'd come to live with them.

"Uncle Isaac! You're home," Mina said, coming from the back stairs. "I told Lena I heard you come in."

"It's me, and I'm very hungry, so I'm not going to play with you until after I eat." He grabbed some silverware and his plate and headed for the kitchen table. "But you can come and sit with me if you want to."

Mina danced across the kitchen soon to be followed by Lena. "Uncle Isaac, would you take us to the exposition? Mama said she can't because she's busy getting ready for her trip to California."

"Your mother won't be leaving for a few weeks, and she'll only be gone another couple. She's going to be with a friend who's getting married, but she should be back in plenty of time. The expo runs until October." He could see the disappointment in the girls' eyes so he continued. "However, if your mother and father say yes, then I will happily take you to the expo."

"Yay!" The two little girls clapped and danced around in their nightgowns and robes.

Isaac couldn't help loving them. They were so sweet and innocent. They epitomized everything that was good and precious. They made him long to have his own children.

"When can we go?" Mina asked, finally settling down.

"Well, like I said, I'll have to speak to your folks. I can't take you on Saturdays because I have students to oversee. But maybe during the week or even Sunday after church. The fair doesn't even open until one o'clock in the afternoon on Sunday."

"I'm so excited to go," Lena said. "Nanny said it was magical."

Isaac laughed. "Well, I don't know if that's what I'd call it, but it sure is full of people and sights to behold."

"Nanny said there are rides too. A Ferris wheel that goes way up in the air." Lena raised her arms high.

"There is that." Isaac began eating his supper while the girls chattered on about what they wanted to see at the fair.

"I heard a ruckus and knew the girls must be involved," Elizabeth said, coming into the kitchen. "Why are you girls out of the nursery?"

"We wanted to see Uncle Isaac." Mina hugged her mother's skirts. "He has something to ask you."

"Well, first I'd better see the two of you march up those stairs and back to your beds." Elizabeth pointed to the back staircase. The girls frowned but nodded and did as they were told. They were good children.

"Good night, Uncle Isaac. Don't forget to ask," Mina said at the base of the steps. When her mother pointed her index finger at her, Mina quickly headed for the nursery.

Once they were gone, Elizabeth sat down at the kitchen table opposite her brother. "What is it you want to ask me?"

Isaac laughed. "The girls want me to ask if I may take them to the exposition. I know you and Stuart are enormously busy, so I would be happy to escort them there."

"Goodness, I don't know. I'm worried with the confusion that might be stirred up in such crowds. The girls have never been a part of anything like that. What if they stray?"

"You know I'm fully capable of keeping track of the girls. I'll just threaten to take them back home, and I'm sure they'll be good as gold."

"I'm sure. For you they do almost anything." She smiled. "It's been good for them to have you here."

"Good for me as well. Having family around has been good for the soul." Isaac started to get up.

"What do you need? I'll get it."

"A glass of milk to wash this down."

Elizabeth went to the cupboard for a glass. "I know you still hope to find Addie, but if that doesn't work out, I know some lovely ladies who might suit you."

Isaac tried to keep his cheery disposition. "Now, Lizzy, you know my heart isn't able to just cast aside the love of my life. I'm completely pledged to her."

Elizabeth opened the icebox and grabbed a bottle of milk. She brought it to the table with the glass. She poured Isaac's milk without saying another word, then took the bottle back to the icebox and closed the door. For a moment, Isaac thought maybe she would leave the subject well enough alone, but that wasn't to be.

"What if she's . . . married to someone else? Or dead?"

"I've loved Addie with my whole heart all these years. I

believe God put us together, and I will find her again. I'm going to hire another Pinkerton man. I should have done it already."

"I hate to see you disappointed." Elizabeth looked genuinely worried.

Isaac shook his head. "Lizzy, I long ago agreed to give my life to God. Whatever happens, I will find contentment in Him. I trust that He has my future, and that if Addie and I are meant to be together, as I've always believed, God will bring it about."

"Your faith has always bolstered my own," Elizabeth admitted. "I wish I could believe as completely as you do."

"You can. It's not about anything I've done. Not really." Isaac shrugged. "I prayed for faith to trust Him. Then I prayed for more. It's all His doing."

"Well, it serves you well."

"No, I believe it serves God well. My faith in Him encourages others, as it has you. People see and hear and then begin to think, 'Well, maybe God can do . . .' whatever it is they're praying about. I just want my life to be an example of faith and hope. God truly can do anything and everything."

"Then why isn't Addie with you?"

Her words pinched a bit, but Isaac nodded. "In God's time, she will be. I know that. That's why I'm not worried. I know I will find her again. God will bring her to me."

5

With the transfer of the house deed complete, Addie was excited to move into the little lakeside cottage. The ladies had left most of the furniture, as well as the dishes and pans, so there wasn't a whole lot that Addie needed to arrange for. Pearl, however, had other thoughts. Without letting Addie know, Pearl had spoken to the women of the church, and they decided to help on moving day with food and new bedding, dish and bath towels, and other little things. There was even a brand-new braided rug made by the pastor's wife. Addie was deeply touched.

Mary and Bertha had the day off from their duties as Camera Girls and came to help Addie set things into order. Bertha was a mild-mannered young woman, pretty in a classic way with blond hair and blue eyes. Her personality was especially joyful most of the time, and Addie enjoyed her enthusiasm for her job.

"This is the perfect cottage," Bertha declared. "I could live here quite happily, and I'm sure that you will find it homey and peaceful."

"I hope so," Addie replied.

Mary was especially enthralled with the house. "It's so quaint. Just like a little haven."

"That's exactly what I thought the minute I saw it," Addie admitted. "I knew it was for me."

Most of the ladies had gone home, but a few remained speaking to Pearl. Addie looked around the room and smiled. It already felt like home. The curtains hanging from the living room windows had been freshly washed and pressed, and the same was true of the ones hanging elsewhere. The Montgomery sisters had been most insistent that the house be cleaned from top to bottom before Addie could take it over. She hoped their new life in Spokane would be a good one, because she was certain this place would be a blessing to her.

"How old are you, Addie? If you don't mind my asking." Mary looked almost embarrassed at having posed the question.

"I'm twenty-six. Why?" Addie adjusted a landscape picture that the sisters had left her.

"I'm just nineteen and was thinking about how you have this house and a great job. I wonder if I can do as well by the time I reach your age."

Addie laughed and gave a shrug. "How well or poorly a person does in life is conditional upon a great many factors. Circumstances around us often knock us down, but I've learned we have to keep trying."

"Mama says that God controls our fate," Bertha chimed in. She looked at Addie. "Do you believe that?"

Addie was always uncomfortable talking about God. Isaac had taught her that God was love. That He cared about her every need, but if that was true, why had He allowed so many bad things to happen to her? If God controlled her fate, why hadn't He kept her safe from the horrible things she'd endured?

"To be completely honest, Bertha, I don't know. I want to believe that God is good and watches over us in tender love."

"I do too," Bertha replied. "But sometimes it is hard to understand why things happen as they do. Like when my little sister died last year."

"My mother died when I was fourteen," Mary stated. "I was really mad at God."

"When Beulah died, I didn't even want to pray," Bertha admitted.

Addie motioned them to sit and took her own seat in one of the overstuffed chairs left to her by the sisters. Once the girls were settled in, Addie spoke. "I think losing a loved one is always difficult. My mother died giving me life. I never knew her, and yet the pain of that loss is very real to me. I've often asked God why He took her from me. However, having grown up in great cruelty delivered by my father and brothers, I came to be glad my mother didn't have to go through that. I can only imagine how she probably suffered before I was born. I think it is possible that someone's death can prevent them from further suffering."

"But Beulah was only ten years old," Bertha protested. "She was a good girl, and our family loved her very much."

Addie nodded. "I believe every word you say. Again, I don't have any answers, just possibilities."

"When Mama died," Mary began, "I asked my father how God could be so mean as to take a mother away from her children. I have two brothers who are younger than me.

They needed their mother. I need . . . needed . . . her too."
Mary's voice broke, and she paused to regain her composure.
"Papa told me that we don't always get to know why God
does what He does, but we must keep putting our faith in
Him. For me, that has been so hard."

"For me as well," Addie admitted. "I had a friend who
would always tell me much the same. I really do try to have
faith, but mine is very weak, and it's easily trampled by life."

The conversation depleted her of the joy the day had originally given. She wanted nothing more than to forget about
why God allowed things to happen and focus instead on
anything else.

"Mary, you live with several other girls, don't you?" she
asked.

Mary perked up and nodded. "We have an apartment
with three bedrooms, and we all share together—two girls
in each room. It's the only way we can afford the rent. I was
desperate for a job. I'd just lost my other position. The owners sold their shop and moved to California."

"I remember when I read your application," Addie said,
smiling. "Your former employer gave you a great letter of
reference."

"They did. They were wonderful people. I enjoyed working for them. And the girls I live with are good too. We are all
kind of shy. None of us go out at night, nor have boyfriends."

"Why did you leave your father and brothers?" Bertha
asked.

Mary's expression saddened. "Papa died last year, and my
brothers went to live with our uncle and aunt, while I went
to work. I see them once in a while, but not nearly enough,
so the girls at the house have become my family."

"It's really wonderful that you have a place like that to live and to be a family for one another." Addie turned to Bertha. "And you live with your family, don't you, Bertha?"

"Yes." She was fidgeting with her hair, as the bun seemed to have come loose. "We live not far from here, so when there were jobs to be had with the fair, I decided to find one. Taking pictures was of such interest to me. I had always loved watching photographers work, and now to be able to take pictures myself suits me very well."

"And you have quite an eye for it." Addie looked from Bertha to Mary. "You both do. You have an artistic eye. I think you're the best of all our girls when it comes to posing your subjects and arranging them in good lighting. You've paid attention to what Mr. Fisher taught you, and the photographs are quite amazing."

"I just hope that after the fair is done, I can find work with photography," Bertha declared. "I'm in no hurry to marry. Owning my own little shop would be perfect."

"I wouldn't want the responsibility of ownership," Mary said, shaking her head. "When I think of all that I would have to do, it terrifies me."

"Yes, there is an awful lot of business that goes on behind closed doors," Addie admitted. "A lot of paperwork and keeping track of inventory and customers. I'm more inclined to be like Mary and avoid the extra responsibility."

"I like being in charge," Bertha interjected. "I like the challenge of doing several things at one time. That's why I like photography. You have to pay attention to the lighting and the camera's abilities. You have to keep an eye on what you're photographing, be it land or people. There's just a lot happening at one time."

"Well, as I said, you two are the best of our Camera Girls, and I think you are both quite gifted. You have true artist's eyes."

Mary blushed and Bertha smiled. They were very different girls, but such good company, and Addie couldn't help but laugh. "I think there's some lemonade and cake left if you'd like some before you head off."

"No, I need to get home," Bertha said, looking at her pocket watch. "I didn't realize it was getting so late."

"I should go too," Mary said, getting to her feet. "I want to get home before dark."

Later, after the girls had gone home, Addie curled up in the chair near her bed. She was dressed in her nightgown and robe and sat looking at the tintype Isaac had given her so long ago.

"Remember me," she read from the back. How could she not remember him? He had been her whole world back then. And even now, he was the first person she thought of when she awakened and the last person on her mind when she went to sleep at night.

"But I'm no longer worthy of his love." She bit her lower lip and tucked the tintype under the doily on the little table beside her chair.

Sam had made her his mistress, and while he had married her, Addie was forever tainted. She had pledged herself to Isaac. But thanks to her brothers and their desire for money, she had broken that pledge. Or rather it had been broken for her. She had no say in the matter.

She had to admit that Sam had been kind to her. He wouldn't let anyone else handle her and never considered making her a part of the brothel. Addie had been grateful for that.

Cooking had also been her saving grace. Addie was a great cook. She learned quite by accident, watching this person and that one, and then experimenting with whatever was at hand. She'd found a cookbook in the rubbish after one of the families left Dawson City for the States. Addie had hidden the book away, and whenever possible, she snuck it out and read it from cover to cover. She'd learned how to measure ingredients and substitute one thing for another. She remembered the first time she made cinnamon rolls. Her father and brothers had brought home friends to play cards, and Addie served up the rolls with coffee. The men devoured them and begged for more. She explained that the baking process took all day, since the dough had to rise a couple of times. They were disappointed, but not mean and ugly like usual. From then on out, she tried to always make cinnamon rolls whenever she had extra time. It was the one thing that usually saved her from a beating.

After a while, she made extra and took them to Isaac and his father's store. Isaac's father insisted on giving her store credit, and Addie was sometimes able to get herself little things she needed. Then other places heard about her rolls, and they wanted to buy some as well. She told her father about the requests. He took care of the details, and after that, Addie was allowed to spend most of her time baking. When Isaac and his father left the Yukon, Addie was glad for the task. It hurt so much to lose Isaac, and keeping busy was the only thing that helped. It still was.

She yawned and stretched. It was time to go to bed. She had to be up early tomorrow. She'd go to work first at the camera shop helping Otis with whatever he needed and then run over to the Yukon exhibit and teach her classes. How ironic it was to take on this task. She'd spent the last seven years trying to forget the Yukon.

Addie crawled into bed and turned out the light. She snuggled down under the covers, but thoughts of her conversation with Mary and Bertha returned. There was always that one question that came to haunt her: If God controlled her fate, why hadn't He kept her safe from the horrible things she had endured?

"Where are you, God?" she murmured in the dark. "Where were you when my father beat me? Where were you when my brothers sold me to Sam?"

She thought of Joseph with his coat of many colors in the Bible. Millie had told her the story when Addie learned that her brothers had sold her.

"Joseph's brothers sold him, too." Millie had done her best to comfort Addie, who was on the verge of hysterics, convinced she was going to have to work in the brothel.

"His brothers were jealous of him," Millie explained. "And they just weren't very nice fellas. They sold him, then took his coat home and told their father Joseph was dead."

"I wish I were dead," Addie had declared.

"Addie Bryant, you take that back. You have no idea of what the future holds for you, but God has it. He does, and He will protect you and see you through. Even if bad things happen, God will keep you in His care."

But why not just keep the bad things from happening? Addie could never get a good response to that question. She'd asked the pastor here in Seattle once and got the answer that the world had fallen from grace and that sin abounded.

"But isn't God able to overcome anything?" she had asked in return.

"He is able, Addie, but not always willing to interfere in the situations we've created."

It had never made sense to Addie. She hadn't created anything. She hadn't asked to be sold or made a mistress. She had a dream to be Isaac's wife and to live with him far away from the Yukon.

"They want me to trust you, God," she said, staring into the darkness, "but they don't tell me why I should. They just tell me to have faith—to believe that you love me."

A sob broke from her throat. "But I don't feel loved."

"Why are you in such a hurry, Uncle Isaac?" Lena asked. The girls watched him rush around the dining room, grabbing breakfast from the sideboard, then racing to the coffee pot to pour himself a cup.

"I'm running late. I need to get to the school, or I won't be able to take the students to the expo."

How he'd managed to oversleep was beyond him. He remembered his brother-in-law's valet waking him, but then he must have fallen back to sleep.

Isaac folded some eggs into a piece of toast. He gulped down the hot coffee, ignoring the heat, and hurried for the door, sandwich in hand.

"I love you girls. See you later."

He dashed down the steps, and despite the fact that it went against social acceptance, Isaac ran the full four blocks to school.

As he ran, he tried to eat, but finally gave up on it and tossed the makeshift sandwich to one of the local dogs who was matching him step for step. When Isaac finally reached the school, his students were assembled, thanks to one of the other teachers, and waiting to be led to their trolley.

"Sorry I'm late," Isaac told the class. "Bad timing on my part, but we're going to have a wonderful time today."

The class was a group of seventh graders that Isaac didn't really know. He recognized a couple of the boys whom he'd helped with some tutoring, but otherwise the children were strangers. It wasn't going to be easy knowing whether or not they belonged to his group.

"Does everyone have their pass?" he asked.

The children held up their tickets, and Isaac took a count. There were only fifteen in his group. That should be manageable.

"You know, Mr. Hanson, every time I'm late for something it always seems to be the best day ever," one of the girls told him and smiled. "Maybe today will be a really wonderful day."

Isaac smiled. "I'm sure you're right. It's going to be a very good day."

Hiram looked at the new route Riley Martin wanted them to cover. "Sorry to move you fellas after you were probably just getting used to the area you had to cover. We had a couple of folks quit on us already. I really need you to cover this area at the boat dock and park along Lake Washington."

"Over by the model farm, eh?" Hiram studied the map. "I'm not gonna pick up manure."

"No, I'm not asking you to do that," Riley replied. "Just trash as you've been doing. Folks tend to picnic in the park and fail to use the trash receptacles. You'll have plenty of work just in that small area."

Hiram nodded. "Come on, Shep."

They started on their way, but Hiram wasn't happy about it. While working on the main thoroughfare, they were able to pick quite a few pockets and occasionally even find a dropped purse. Which, of course, they always turned in to lost and found—once they'd gotten what they wanted from the contents.

There was no way of knowing how easy or difficult it might be to pick the pockets of folks coming in from the boat dock or who had come all that way to picnic. If it failed to net them some good catches, Hiram was going to complain . . . or quit. The job wasn't exactly to his liking anyway. He wasn't even sure why he'd said yes, but it did put him at the fair every day, and he didn't have to pay for a ticket. It also gave them a small salary and lunch, as well as a roof over their heads. For the time being, he told himself to be patient. He told Shep the same thing.

As if on some unspoken cue, Shep began to complain. "I don't know that I want to keep workin' here, Hiram. I don't like picking up trash."

"I don't recall askin' you what you like or don't like."

"Just seems we'd make more money in town. I don't like havin' to get up at five every morning and get out there to work before folks come and make a mess all over again. It's the same thing day after day."

"We've had this job less than two weeks, so stop your whinin'. It's givin' us a place to live and a wage. It could be a lot worse, as you well know. So just mind yourself. We'll leave when I'm good and ready to leave and not until." He fixed Shep with a look that he'd been told was fierce enough to melt a man's resolve.

Shep quieted immediately and didn't offer another word.

6

Isaac quieted his class of children as a young woman took to the stage. A man followed closely behind and raised his hands to further signal the crowd to quiet.

"Ladies and gentlemen, boys and girls, today we have a special speaker to share with you about her adventures to the Yukon during the big gold rush north. I won't further delay, but introduce to you, Miss Adeline Byrant."

Just hearing her name gave Isaac the sensation of a clamp being placed around his chest. He could scarcely breathe. He had seen the woman step onto the edge of the stage but had paid no attention. Now his gaze went to her, starting at her shoes and rising ever so slowly to her face.

Addie. It was truly Addie.

The woman smiling down upon them was more mature —even more beautiful if possible—but nevertheless she was the same girl he'd fallen in love with all those years ago.

"I'm so glad to be with you here today," she began. "As Mr. Rigsby mentioned, I came here to share stories of my time in the Yukon. I went north with my father and brothers, and we lived there for four years during the height of the gold rush."

Isaac was mesmerized as he watched her. She was dressed quite simply in a black skirt and white blouse. On her head, she had a straw hat trimmed sedately with nothing more than a black ribbon. Her dark brown hair was plaited in a single braid, hanging over her shoulder.

"It wasn't easy to get from Seattle to Dawson City, nor was it without expense. A person wanting to go north to the gold rush needed to have a lot of money. I know that sounds funny because most were headed north to make their fortune, but there were costs associated with the trip that most never consider."

She walked to the side of the stage where supplies had been gathered. "You were required by the Canadian government to bring all of this with you to Dawson City. It's a year's worth of supplies.

"Just a few of the requisite goods included one hundred fifty pounds of bacon, four hundred pounds of flour, and one hundred twenty-five pounds of beans. You also had to have all sorts of building materials because once you climbed the Chilkoot Trail—that ice staircase so many speak of—you had to build a boat. But I'm getting ahead of myself." She gave the audience a sweet smile.

Isaac kept his straw hat low so as not to distract her. He knew once she saw him, Addie would be hard-pressed to finish her presentation.

"You registered with the authorities and let them know how many were in your particular party. You proved you had the required goods, even though the Mounties would recheck your supplies once you reached the top. It was very difficult. Probably harder than anything I ever did. I was only fifteen years old at the time. Thankfully, I was allowed to sit with our stock of goods once I made the first climb up the mountain."

It was as if Isaac had gone back in time. He remembered every detail of that climb. How everything suddenly got much steeper after you were about a third of the way up. How those last fifty feet seemed impossible to navigate. Then there was the madness at the top. Once a person reached the top, they were inclined to stop and park their gear, making it even more difficult for those coming behind.

Addie continued with her speech, even giving commentary as native men came onto the stage and demonstrated the packs they had made and carried for hundreds of climbs up and down the Chilkoot. Finally, Addie concluded and asked for questions. A dozen hands went up.

"If you had to buy all these things, hire people to help you, and make a boat, how could anyone afford to go?" a young man asked.

"It wasn't without its sacrifice, to be sure," Addie replied. "My father and brothers were gamblers and played cards for the money needed."

Isaac knew they'd also stolen a fair amount of money and goods to get north, but Addie was probably not going to tell the crowd that. She always bore the shame of her family in silence.

"Sometimes you could earn the money you needed once you got to Skagway. There were some jobs available, and if you were willing to pack goods for other people, you could make a fair amount of money. But in all seriousness, you needed to have plenty of money to spend just to get to

Dawson City. You needed strength and health too. It was a brutal trip, and folks died on the route. Some were killed in avalanches, some froze to death, some were lost in the river rapids. Money wasn't the only price you paid."

Addie took another question. This one from a young lady. "How did you climb wearing a dress?" She giggled, and several other girls beside her laughed as well.

"I didn't wear a dress or skirt. I posed as a boy for the trip. No one knew that I was a girl. I was small for my age, and it wasn't all that hard to do. My father decided with all the dangers at hand, it would be better for me to pretend to be a boy. So I cut my hair and dressed in trousers and a heavy coat. There were women who wore dresses, but most had trousers underneath them for modesty's sake."

Several other questions were asked, and Addie handled them all very well. Finally, she announced she could take one more, then she needed to let everyone go so the next groups could come in.

"Did you love your adventure to the Yukon?" a teenage girl asked in a rather dreamy voice.

Isaac couldn't help but look up at this. He knew Addie had suffered unspeakably from her life in the Yukon.

"There were parts of the adventure that were wonderful," Addie said, smiling. "I made good friends and learned so much. But there were also very bad things that happened. I saw men killed, and I saw them die from the cold or injury. I saw women and children sorely used and die from lack of food and exposure."

The crowd went silent even though the other sounds of the expo continued.

"Everything I endured made me tougher."

"Would you do it again?" the girl asked. This time her tone had changed to one of concern.

Addie considered the question for a moment. "There is nothing in the Yukon that could ever compel me to return. As for going back in time to do it again . . . well, we know that's impossible to do, so an answer to that question would be a moot point." She smiled. "Now don't forget there's a class photo to be taken, so meet to the left of the stage in your groups, and we'll take your photos."

The students clapped. Isaac's pupils gathered close. "Did you see people die too, Mr. Hanson?" one of the boys asked.

Isaac had told his group on the trip over to the expo how he had gone to the Yukon with his father to set up a store.

"Sadly, I did. It's a hard and unforgiving land." He nodded toward the side of the stage. "Now let's go get our photograph taken so we can move on to the next lecture."

Isaac knew this was where he would announce himself to Addie. He hated that it would have to be such a public matter, but he had hardly been able to keep from rushing up onto the stage as it was.

A young woman dressed identically to Addie came to Isaac. "Is this your class?" she asked.

"It is. We're here for our photograph."

"I'm Mary," the girl said. "If you and your class will gather over here and arrange yourselves in three rows. Taller students in back and the teacher at the side of the group."

"Could I have Miss Bryant take our picture?" Isaac could see the smile fade from the young woman's face. "It's just that I know her personally."

Mary's brow raised slightly. "I'll ask her if she has time."

"Don't tell her about me. It will give away the surprise." Mary nodded and took off in the direction of where Addie was speaking to a couple of men.

There was a tug on Isaac's suitcoat. "Do you really know her?"

Isaac looked down at the girl. "I did. I do. I haven't seen her in a very long time, however."

Isaac saw Mary interrupt whatever Addie was saying. Isaac turned to address the students. "Come along, we're supposed to form up. Three rows. You tall boys in the back." This allowed him to keep his back to the ladies.

Soon enough, Mary returned. "I've brought Miss Bryant," she announced.

"I understand you think you know me?" Addie's comment was more question than statement.

Isaac turned and couldn't help grinning. "Remember me?"

He watched her blue eyes widen as she barely whispered his name. "Isaac."

It was completely against propriety, but Isaac couldn't stop himself. He went to her and pulled her into his arms. He pressed his lips against her ear. "My love. I thought I'd never find you again."

At first, Addie did nothing, but as he continued to hold her, she relaxed and put her arms around him. When he finally let her go, he found tears in her eyes.

"I can hardly believe it's you," he said. "I've searched all over. I went to the Yukon to find you, but you were gone, and Millie told me she thought you were here in Seattle, so I took out ads and hired a Pinkerton. No one could find you."

"I'm sorry. I suppose . . . well, that is to say . . . I didn't want to be found."

"But why? You knew I'd come back for you." She looked away, and Isaac couldn't be sure, but she seemed embarrassed. "Addie, didn't you want me to find you?"

Addie pulled a handkerchief from the cuff of her blouse. Her hands were shaking. She dabbed her eyes. "I have to get back to work. It's good to see you, Isaac." She started to leave.

"Wait. Addie, please."

She turned back. "Yes?"

"I'd like you to take our school picture." Isaac wanted to say so much more, but for now, this was the only thing that came to mind that might keep her from leaving.

Addie seemed momentarily perplexed but then nodded. "Are they lined up?"

Isaac looked at his group of children. "They are. Just let me slip in beside them."

Addie thought she might faint dead away when she realized who the mysterious man was.

"We're ready," Isaac told her.

Doing her best to be strong, Addie focused the camera on the class and took the picture. She held up her hand. "Let me get one more, just in case."

But this time she centered the picture on Isaac. She might never have another chance to do this. This would be her photograph to put along with the tintype. She would have it to keep her memories alive long after this moment passed.

"There. All finished."

While Isaac spoke to his students, Addie gave in to her panic and disappeared into the throng of children and teachers. She ducked into the exhibit building and into a storage room. She hid behind one of the unused display cases while she fought to regain her breath.

How could he be here? Why now?

"Oh, Isaac."

She lowered her gaze to the floor and let the tears come. She had always prayed she would see him again, but at the same time, she feared it. Nothing could ever come of it. She had been a man's mistress. She had lived in a brothel. Her reputation had been destroyed. Had Sam not married her, the few decent folks left in Dawson City would have completely ignored her.

Planting her hand over her mouth, Addie did her best to stifle her sobs. The pain of the moment was just too great. She still loved Isaac. She would always love Isaac, but she could never be with him now.

"Addie!" She heard him call her name frantically from just outside the door.

He would know she'd be obligated to speak to the next group of students. She was nearly out of time before Jim Rigsby would be calling her to the stage.

I can't face him. Not yet. Not now.

She pulled herself together and wiped her face. Her handkerchief was soaking wet. She left it on the back of a nearby chair and smoothed her black skirt before heading for the storage room door. She had no idea of what to say or do to ease the desperation she'd heard in Isaac's voice.

God, how is this showing me love?

Isaac found one of the teachers from his school and got him to put their classes together for the next hour. He promised to catch up at the eleven o'clock lecture, then waited by the stage for Addie to return. When he caught sight of her, Isaac could see she'd been crying. But why? Was she so overwhelmed with joy that she couldn't bear it? Or was she grieved at seeing him again?

The man who had introduced her was now trying to rally the crowd and get them into their places so that he could introduce Addie once again. Isaac had no time to waste. He slipped around the partition that was meant to keep him out and came up the steps to where Addie was. Without warning he pulled her back down the stairs with him.

"Please don't run away again. I must talk to you. We must."

Addie looked up at him. "I-I can't, Isaac. I have to work. I have two more lectures to give and then my job as a Camera Girl. I can't stop and talk to you."

"I've looked for you everywhere. I'm so happy to see you."

"Isaac. There are things . . . I . . ." She shook her head. "I can't. We can't."

"You're obviously shaken by the surprise of seeing me here. Just as I am you. It's been so long, and I just want to hear about you—to know what you've been doing. Can we please just meet and talk?"

"I don't know."

"The expo won't open until one tomorrow. Could we meet at the park down by the lake? Please, Addie. We have so much to discuss."

She finally nodded. "All right, let's meet there at eleven. I'll wait by the boat dock."

Isaac smiled as Jim Rigsby called Addie's name. "I'll be there." And with that she was gone.

Later that night, Isaac questioned whether the encounter had even happened. It certainly wasn't the reunion he'd dreamed about.

He slipped upstairs into the nursery to tell the girls goodnight. That was when he often told them stories of his life in the Yukon and Princess Addie. Tonight, he could tell them that he'd found her, and they would get to meet her in the morning. He had already gotten permission from Stuart to take them to the park after Sunday school.

"Are my two favorite girls still awake?" he asked.

"Of course. We were waiting for you," Mina said, sitting up in bed.

Lena popped up from the bed on his right. "We thought you weren't coming."

"I had something wonderful happen today." He sat on the edge of Mina's bed, and Lena joined them.

"What happened?" Lena asked as she crawled onto Isaac's lap.

"I know what happened," Mina said. Her eyes sparkled.

"You do?" Isaac asked. He wanted to laugh at the way her excitement came alive as she bounced up and down on the bed.

"You found Princess Addie!"

"Princess Addie?" Lena asked.

"Yes, indeed, I did. I found Princess Addie, and tomorrow after Sunday school, you are going to meet her too."

Mina clapped her hands and dove at Isaac with her arms wide to hug him close. The trio embraced in a tight knot until poor Lena gave protest.

"You're squishing me, Mina."

"This is so wonderful," Mina said, backing off. "How can I ever sleep, knowing we'll see Princess Addie tomorrow?"

Isaac chuckled. "I don't know how I'm going to sleep." He kissed both girls and carried Lena back to her bed. "But I'm going to because I want to be well rested before I see her again."

Mina was still sitting up in bed as Isaac headed to the door. "Oh, Uncle Isaac, this is really the best day ever."

He paused at the door. "It is, Mina. It really is."

7

When a knock sounded on her cottage door, Addie feared that Isaac had somehow found out where she lived. She thought about ignoring it, but when the knocking continued, Addie knew she would just have to face the situation.

"Just a minute," she called, struggling to do up the back buttons of her blouse in her hurry. Finding the last couple in the middle almost impossible, she gave up.

She opened the door and found Mary with a worried expression. "Addie, are you all right?"

"Yes." Addie nodded and stepped back. "Please come in." Immediately, she went back to fighting the buttons.

Mary turned Addie so she could help. "I can get these," she said, brushing Addie's hand aside. "I was afraid you'd already be gone to church."

"I have an appointment at eleven and so decided to stay home." Addie closed the door and turned to face Mary. "Have you had breakfast? I could fix something."

"No, I've eaten, but please go ahead for yourself."

"I couldn't eat a bite," Addie replied. She drew a deep breath and steeled herself. "What can I do for you, Mary?"

"You seemed worried after you met with that man yesterday. Is there something I can do? I feel responsible since I brought you to him."

"Don't. Isaac is a very good man, and it's quite all right that we met again. I had always hoped we might. We knew each other well in the Yukon. We were just children, but we spent a lot of time together." Addie motioned to a chair. "Why don't you sit?"

"I don't want to cause you delay with your appointment."

"It will be fine. We're just meeting a short way from here at the park by the boat dock."

Mary nodded and took a ladderback chair. "I really didn't mean to put myself in the middle of your affairs. You just looked so upset yesterday, and last evening, you headed out before I could talk to you. I usually keep to myself, but you've treated me like a real friend, and I want to be one to you."

Addie let down her guard and took a seat opposite Mary on the sofa. "You are a dear friend, Mary. You and Pearl have both been worried for me. It's wonderful to have friends who care."

"And I do care. I was worried that maybe that man had caused you some sort of trouble in the Yukon, and now that he was here, he would cause you trouble again."

A smile touched Addie's lips. "No, he would never cause me trouble, so don't let that concern you. However, I'd just as soon you don't speak of it to anyone else."

"Of course not."

"Thank you, Mary. I appreciate your friendship."

Addie noted the time. "I guess I'd better get ready for my appointment."

Mary popped up. "I'm glad you're all right. I'll see you at work."

Opening the door, Addie thanked her. "I'm sure glad you came by. I never would have gotten those buttons done up."

"Happy to help." Mary took off down the pathway. As she left, Addie noticed the lawn needed to be cut. One more worry.

Addie locked the door behind Mary. It was kind of the girl to care. It touched Addie deeply. She had wanted to explain to Mary the circumstances but knew it was best to leave it lie. As soon as she met with Isaac and told him that nothing could ever come of their relationship, Mary would have nothing more to worry about.

But just the thought of putting Isaac out of her life again left Addie feeling a sense of hopelessness and sorrow. This sorrow cut even deeper than losing him the first time because he clearly wanted to renew their relationship and move toward the future they had pledged to each other.

Considering the path her life had taken, Addie knew it would be unfair to enter into a marriage with Isaac. He deserved a woman above reproach. Thinking of her past brought thoughts of her brothers. She despised them for what they had done to her. Their father may have beaten her and expected her to do the work of a dozen people, but he was clear about keeping her from being manhandled. But Hiram and Shep had no such convictions, and when money was to be made for absolutely no effort on their part . . . Addie's innocence was of no concern to them.

She tasted blood and realized she'd been biting her lip.

Her brothers were in prison, and she hoped they died there. The fear of seeing them as she had Isaac, however, crept over her. It had been several years. They might not be in prison anymore. It was possible they were free. That turned her stomach even more than the thought of having to tell Isaac why they couldn't be together.

Pushing those thoughts aside, Addie did up the buttons on her boots and drew a deep breath. Everything would be all right. She would simply tell Isaac that too many years had passed by. She'd be firm with him and explain that she was happily settled on her own.

It was a lie, of course, but what else could she do?

At a little before eleven, Addie left her house and walked to the park. The trash collectors had already cleaned the area, and it looked quite beautiful. The landscapers were managing some of the flower gardens, and Addie admired the work they had done. It was said that there were over fifty-thousand plants just in this one area of the exposition. Maybe she should plant more flowers around her little cottage. The Montgomery sisters had some lovely flowers arranged, but there was room for so many more.

Addie took a seat on a bench near the path and stared out across the water. A part of her knew she would never have the strength to say good-bye again to Isaac, while another part told her she had to find that strength. No man wanted to marry the mistress of another man, even if he did marry her in the end. All it would take would be running across one person they had known in Dawson City, and Isaac would be completely shamed.

She knew she should just tell him the truth and be done with it, but Addie couldn't even do that. Isaac would hear it but not really receive it. He would tell her it didn't matter, though Addie knew it did. He wanted to be a great professor at a university one day. He'd told her that on more than one occasion. Those types of men needed impeccable reputations and the admiration of all who crossed their paths. With her at his side, he could never have that. If it was learned that his wife once lived in a brothel as mistress to the owner . . . well, it wouldn't matter that it wasn't her fault nor his.

"Addie."

She looked up and found Isaac and two little girls. Her heart skipped a beat. "Hello, Isaac."

"Girls, this is Addie."

"Princess Addie," the taller of the two declared.

"Princess Addie," the smaller one said as if in awe.

Addie looked to Isaac for an explanation. He smiled and put his arm around the girls. "This is Mina," he said, nodding to the older one. "And this is Lena."

He had children. Addie relaxed a bit. If he had children, then there was no doubt a wife. She let her breath go. Almost immediately, however, the thought of Isaac speaking about their future came to mind.

"I'm pleased to meet you, Mina and Lena."

The girls actually curtsied. "Princess Addie, you're more beautiful than I ever dreamed," Mina said, smiling.

"Why do you call me Princess Addie?" she asked.

"I told them stories about our days in the Yukon and of our adventures," Isaac explained.

"And of how much he loved you and still does," Lena added in her little girl voice.

Addie put her hand to her heart. "And what does your mother think of your father telling you stories like that?"

Mina giggled and that made Lena laugh as well, although she looked as if she wasn't quite sure what they were laughing about.

Mina jumped in. "Uncle Isaac isn't our father—he's our uncle. Our mama is his sister."

Addie recalled that Isaac did have a sister. She was married and living in . . . Seattle. The thoughts chased around in her head. Isaac had told his nieces stories about her . . . so many times that they called her Princess Addie. They knew that he loved her.

"Mama knows he tells us stories. You are the princess and Uncle Isaac is the knight who has searched for years upon years to find you and rescue you from the horrible dragons who took you away. Now that he has, you can both live happily ever after," Mina said.

Addie thought she might be sick. Her stomach roiled at the child's descriptions of them being like characters in a fairy tale. This certainly wasn't a fairy tale. In a story like that, the hero always arrived before anything bad could happen to his lady love. She looked up and met Isaac's steady gaze. This time the knight was too late, and the princess had been hurt.

"I thought you might enjoy meeting my nieces," Isaac said after a few moments of silence. "They feel like they already know you. When I came to live with them, they wanted to know all about me, and I couldn't very well tell them all without including you."

Addie looked at the girls. "I'm glad I could entertain you both, but I'm really no princess."

"We know, but in our fairy tale you are," Mina answered, and Lena nodded enthusiastically.

"Girls, remember I told you that I would need to speak to Princess Addie for a few minutes by myself?" He pulled out a small ball. "I want you to go up there away from the water and play catch for a little while. Stay where I can keep an eye on you."

Mina took the ball and then grabbed Lena's hand. "Come on. We promised, and then afterward we can go to lunch with Princess Addie." They hurried to a place where they could play and immediately began to toss the ball.

"Why did you promise them lunch with me?"

"I didn't think you'd mind. I remember how much you love children."

"I do love children, but this situation is already awkward enough." Addie looked back to the water, knowing that if she looked at Isaac, she might not be able to say the things she needed to say.

Isaac sat down beside her on the bench. His nearness immediately sent her back in time to memories of them in Dawson City. Addie had snuck away so many times to meet Isaac at the little cemetery. It was on a hillside just outside of the town proper. They would sit side by side amongst the wooden crosses. It was peaceful there, and it would be most unusual if anyone came there to look for them.

"Addie, what's wrong?"

She shook off the memory. "Everything. At least for the two of us."

"But why? I've searched for you so long. I thought you were a mirage yesterday when I saw you on that stage. I thought I was just so desperate to see you that I conjured you up in my mind and gave life to you."

Addie didn't trust herself to speak. She focused instead

on her breathing, reminding herself that hurting him now would be better than marrying him and letting him find out the truth later. Again, she reasoned with herself to just tell him the truth, but she refused. She knew Isaac too well. He would tell her their love was stronger than any ugliness of the past. He would assure her so convincingly that Addie would believe it too—until the past caught up with them.

"You aren't listening to me. What's wrong, Addie?" Isaac touched her chin to turn her face to his.

Addie stiffened. "It's too late, Isaac. You have your life, and I have mine. The promises we made were those of children in an uncertain life. There's no future for us. I'm sorry."

He was completely crestfallen. "That can't be, Addie. Yes, we were just children, but our love was real enough. My love is still real."

"I can't talk about this anymore."

She got to her feet, which caused Mina and Lena to come running. "Is it time for lunch?"

Addie felt horrible for hurting them. "I'm sorry. I have to go to my job, and I cannot take time out for lunch. I'm sure your uncle will still take you for something good."

"But you must come with us. We want to hear you tell us stories about when you first met Uncle Isaac." Mina's tone was pleading, and Lena just stood by nodding over and over.

Addie felt guilty for disappointing them. It wasn't their fault, after all.

Not far from the boat dock a vendor was setting up his stand. The sign read that he could offer them ice cream cones. That wouldn't be a good lunch. Addie glanced around but found nothing else available to them at the moment.

"I'm really sorry, girls. Perhaps another time." But Addie knew there'd never be another time. There couldn't be.

Isaac felt gut-punched as Addie hurried away from the lake. He had been so sure that only the shock of his showing up unannounced had kept her from wanting to be with him the day before. But the scene he'd just endured made it clear that it wasn't shock that was keeping her from him. Addie didn't *want* to be with him anymore. He frowned.

"It's okay, Uncle Isaac. You said that you and Princess Addie were destined to be together forever. Maybe after she's done with work, you can propose, and then she can quit working because you'll take care of her."

Isaac looked down at Mina. He'd like to believe her words, but there was a sinking feeling inside that suggested it might be otherwise.

Oh, Addie, what did I do wrong? Why are you running away from me?

"I'm hungry, Uncle Isaac," Lena said, tugging on his coat. "Can we go eat and then find Princess Addie again?"

He glanced in the direction she'd gone. Would she ever meet with him again? He could easily force his attention on her. She worked at the expo and his students would be expecting to hear her presentation. She would be in a position where she couldn't refuse his presence. But that wasn't what he wanted from her. He wanted her to rejoice that they were reunited. He wanted her happiness. And above all, he wanted her love.

Hiram recognized Isaac Hanson right off. The woman and children were a mystery, but not for long. With the little girls calling out for their "Uncle Isaac," their relationship was clear. The woman was shadowed, and her hat made it difficult to see her face. Still, there was something about her that made Hiram continue to watch her.

Making a pretense of cleaning at the far edge of the park, Hiram waited until she stood to leave. And that was when he realized he'd been watching his sister all along.

"Well, I'll be." He elbowed Shep. "It's Addie."

Shep looked up to see what Hiram was talking about. "Where?"

"Right there, stupid. The woman in black and white with the straw hat."

"That pretty one?"

"She's the only lady around." Hiram grew irritated with Shep's lack of understanding. "That's Addie. I'm telling you it is."

"Sure grew up pretty. Who'd have thunk that?" Shep asked.

"Of course she's pretty. She's got enough money to buy whatever she needs to make herself look beautiful." Hiram clenched his teeth a moment, then relaxed. "And now she's gonna have to share that money with us."

8

Hiram and Shep followed Addie at a distance. She didn't go to the expo, even though Hiram recognized the outfit she was wearing. She was apparently working at the fair as one of the Camera Girls he'd seen around taking pictures. It surprised him that she would be working a job. If his sources had been right, Addie left the Yukon with over a hundred thousand in gold. That was enough to take care of her needs for the rest of her life. Surely she hadn't already gone through it all.

He supposed it was possible she had squandered it or lost some, but that wasn't like Addie. She was meticulous with her money. He had once found out she had been saving a few cents here and there when they'd lived in the Yukon. He had demanded she give it to him for tobacco, telling her she had no need for it. Only immoral women had their own money. She had handed it over to him without a word. Just like he planned for her to hand over her fortune now.

"Where do you think she's going?" Shep asked as they wound their way through the pines, trying to keep out of sight.

"Who can say, but she'll have to stop sometime."

"Why don't we just grab her now?"

"Because I want to see where she's going. Now shut up." Hiram wearied of Shep's questions. With him it was always questions. He never seemed to have sense enough to figure out the answers on his own, and frankly, Hiram wished he'd drop off the face of the earth.

Hiram pulled Shep behind a tree and used a group of blackberry bushes to take cover when Addie stopped to talk to a woman. He waited while the two exchanged words and then began walking together.

He gave Shep a push to go but found him eating berries. "Stop it," he muttered, "those aren't ripe yet."

"I like 'em tart."

"You'll get a bellyache and won't be able to work, and I'll end up having twice the trash to pick up."

They progressed a little farther, then Addie led the woman to a small house on the edge of the lake. Apparently, this was where she lived because she was the one who unlocked the front door. The two women disappeared inside, leaving Hiram to wonder what his next move should be.

It was convenient to think Addie had a house near the expo. It would allow him and Shep to quit their jobs and stay with her instead of that wretched dormitory. Their room was far too much like a prison cell to suit him.

"Let's get back to work. We'll figure this out by and by." Hiram pushed Shep back in the direction from which they'd come.

"Aren't we gonna make her give us her gold?"

"Of course we are, just not right this minute. Timing is everything, Shep. We can hardly go make ourselves present with that other woman in there. We'll wait. You'll see. It'll be all right. Maybe we can grab her tonight."

"I'm sorry that I feel unwell," Addie told Pearl. "It was kind of you to see me home, but really I'm all right."

"No, you aren't. I've known you for years, Addie. You aren't all right. Something is wrong, and I want to understand so that maybe I can help you."

Addie sighed. "Would you like some tea? I think tea might settle my stomach."

"Then you let me make it while you get into bed. Turn around and I'll unbutton that blouse."

She did as Pearl commanded, then headed back to her bedroom. Addie felt dizzy, almost weak. She wondered if she was coming down with something but knew it was most likely her encounter with Isaac and his nieces that had her feeling this way.

With the clothes discarded and her nightgown and robe on, Addie went back to the kitchen. "Thank you for your help." She started to sit at the table, but Pearl would have none of it.

"Go get in bed. I'll bring your tea and maybe a couple of crackers. Do you have any?"

Addie shook her head. "I don't think so. I haven't had to go shopping since you and the ladies set me up with food."

"Well, that's all right. I'll go back to the shop and tell Otis what's going on while you rest. Then I'll come back with some soup and crackers for you."

"Pearl, I don't want to cause problems for Otis. Your shop

is doing so well. I saw the numbers on the sales of the cameras. He'll soon have to send away for more."

"He already has, but never you mind. We can have Bertha help in the shop today. She seems to have a real knack for that kind of thing."

"She's good at taking pictures too. She told me she'd like to have a little shop of her own someday."

"I think that might work very well for her." Pearl motioned Addie back to her room and followed to tuck her in.

Addie climbed obediently into bed and allowed Pearl to draw her covers up. Outside a light rain had started to fall, and Addie could hear the drops against the window. For reasons beyond her understanding, the sound made her sad, and tears formed in her eyes. *What's wrong with me?*

"Oh, Addie, I'm so sorry you don't feel well," Pearl said. "I wish you would unburden your heart and tell me what's wrong."

Addie wiped at the tears with the edge of her sleeve. "I don't know why I'm crying. Something about the weather just made me feel blue."

The tea kettle started to whistle. "You stay put, and I'll bring you a cup of tea."

Pearl left the room, and Addie propped another pillow behind her and sat staring out the window. She'd pulled back the curtains when she'd first awakened that morning. Her mind had been on her meeting with Isaac. Who could have ever guessed that he'd been so fixated on her that he'd told his nieces stories about their time in the Yukon?

"Do you want milk or sugar?" Pearl called from the other room.

"Nothing, thanks."

Addie thought of those precious little girls and how delighted they'd been to meet her. She would have loved getting to know them . . . befriending each one. She could imagine the fun she and Isaac could have spoiling them. Then maybe one day with children of their own, they could have outings with the girls. They could help with the children. It would be like one big family.

"No," she whispered, shaking her head.

"Here you are." Pearl brought her a cup and saucer. "There's a clear place on your nightstand to put the cup once you're finished. I will head back to the shop and return as quickly as possible. I know the restaurant near the Ferris wheel has chicken soup. They use it to ease the upset stomachs of folks who've ridden the rides one too many times." She smiled. "Don't fret. I'll have you feeling better before long."

Addie wished that might be true. She sipped the hot tea and thought of the situation with the due diligence of someone figuring out a puzzle. Isaac was the type of person who would pursue the truth at all costs. She would eventually have to tell him the truth, but the truth wouldn't matter to him. He would never let her go.

Perhaps if she left Seattle before seeing Isaac again, then he would understand that she meant business. It would hurt him, but then maybe that pain would keep him from following her.

Of course, there was the house to consider. Perhaps Otis could rent it out for her. Maybe someday Addie could return to it and live a quiet life there by Lake Washington. She sighed. Ever since Isaac left the Yukon, she had longed to see him again. He was the same as she remembered. The boyish charm was still there, the twinkle in his eyes and his playful spirit. It was just like him to make their time together sound like a fairy tale.

A heaviness settled over her heart. She would always love him. Always.

Pearl was back within an hour and true to her word she'd brought chicken soup and crackers. Addie had found sleep impossible, but the tea had helped to settle her stomach.

"I think you'll find the soup will go even beyond what the tea has done," Pearl announced, bringing a tray to Addie in bed. "It's a very tasty soup. I sampled it to make sure I didn't need to do something to help it along."

"Thank you, Pearl. You've always been so kind to me."

Pearl settled the tray on Addie's lap and drew up a chair. "I'm going to take advantage of that comment and tell you that you owe me an explanation."

"I do." Addie knew she could trust Pearl. But still, there was that tiny seed of doubt. Pearl was well respected in the church. If Addie told her the truth of her past, Pearl might feel obligated to separate herself from their friendship. She might feel compelled to have Otis fire her.

"What has happened to cause problems for you?"

Addie swallowed the lump in her throat with a spoonful of soup. "I saw a friend from the Yukon. The boy I told you about."

"The one you had hoped to marry one day?" Pearl asked, sounding excited.

"Yes, Isaac Hanson. He came to one of my presentations on the gold rush. He's a teacher, just as he always wanted to be, and he was there with his students." Addie reached beneath her pillow. "I took the photograph of his class and then this one." She handed the postcard to Pearl.

"My, he is a handsome fellow." She looked up to meet Addie's gaze. "So why isn't this a good thing?"

Addie looked away and shook her head. "The past holds too many issues to allow us to be together now. I can't tell him about it. I really can't tell you . . . everything. It's too horrible, and I'm afraid it would change everything between us."

"Nonsense, Addie Bryant. I would think you'd know me better. You've been like a daughter to me these last seven years. There is nothing that would keep me from caring about you."

"I know you feel that way now, but in time, the truth might make you feel differently."

"I should be insulted by what you're saying, but instead, I'll tell you this." She fixed Addie with a stern expression. "There will always be things we hope will never be found out about our past. Some are small and insignificant, but others can be quite profound, and people of lesser character will use them against you. I am not one of them. No matter how horrible you believe your sins, I will love you as I always have."

Addie's eyes filled with tears. "But your reputation in the church is so important to me."

"You let me worry about my reputation, Addie. That is my concern, and mine alone. The Lord already knows what's happened, so why not share it with me and let me help you bear your burden?"

A sense of relief washed over Addie at the mere thought of someone helping her to bear this burden. Millie had helped in Dawson City, but over the years, they'd lost track of each other. Addie didn't even know if Millie was still alive.

"I'll tell you, but if you feel you must walk away from our friendship, I'll understand."

Pearl said nothing. She shook her head ever so slightly and gave Addie a tolerant smile. It made Addie smile as well. Pearl would never desert her. Pearl's love wasn't given lightly.

"Isaac was only in Dawson City for a year. He wanted to attend Harvard, and the cost was far more than his father could come up with. They got it in their mind to go north with the gold rush. Someone had told them that the real money to be made was in the services they could offer to the miners. And it proved true. They opened a general store and sold all of their goods within the year, then headed back down."

Addie set the tray aside on the bed. "Isaac promised to come back for me, although we both knew it would take years for him to attain the education he needed. He was only eighteen. It was so hard to see him go, but we were both confident that we were meant to be together."

"Did he write to you and you to him?"

"The cost made it almost impossible for me to send him letters. I know he sent several to me, but my father always threw them directly into the fire making sure I knew he didn't approve."

"How awful. So what happened that you no longer feel you can be together?"

Addie frowned. "When I was eighteen my father died. He and my brothers had made a living gambling and stealing. You know those cinnamon rolls I make?" Pearl smiled and nodded. "Well, my father realized there was money to be made in my making and selling them, so he put me to work doing that. It made good, steady money for them, and I didn't mind. It was easy and kept them out of my business. None of them wanted to spend time in a kitchen.

"When my father died, my brothers were restless. I think they originally planned to leave Dawson City. I suppose they considered me a burden and decided to dispense with me." Addie's discomfort grew, and she stopped to reconsider what she would say. She didn't have to tell Pearl everything.

"They decided to . . . to . . . sell me to a man who owned a gambling house and . . . brothel." She hurried to continue. "He married me, and that was the end of my dream with Isaac."

"Are you still married?"

"No, someone accused him of cheating them and shot him dead."

"I see." Pearl seemed to consider all of this a moment, and Addie hoped she wouldn't ask anything else.

"My brothers were there, and as soon as I appeared, they told me I belonged to them again. I knew that I could never be under their control again, so my friend helped me escape."

"And you came here and found us."

"Yes, Isaac would have said it was by God's guidance that we came together, you and I." She smiled. "I suppose I can accept that. However, in accepting that, I have to also accept that He had a hand in the other things that happened. That is harder to deal with."

"Addie, we've talked about this before. God doesn't always like what happens down here."

"But He lets it happen. If He's all powerful and really loves us as you claim, why doesn't He stop it? Why did He allow my brothers to sell me?"

"I'll admit, I don't have the answer to that, except to say that God does care, and He does love you. Man is terrible at times. His sins are great, and he will answer for what he has done. Your brothers will answer for what they've done to you. So too the man who bought you. Even though he made you his wife, you were not a willing participant. Your marriage was not based on love."

"But it ruined me just the same. I can't give myself to Isaac knowing that will always stand between us."

"If the boy loves you, it won't matter to him."

"I know . . . and that makes it all the worse."

"Why do you say that?" Pearl looked at her in disbelief. "The Bible says love covers a multitude of sins, and the only sins in this situation are the ones that were committed against you. I believe the Bible is speaking of God's love for us, but it can easily translate to Isaac's love for you."

Addie shook her head. "Nothing can cover this, nor wipe it away and give me a clean slate. I need to find a way to make it clear to Isaac that we cannot have a future together, and it breaks my heart."

9

Isaac sat at the desk in his sister and brother-in-law's library and wrote out his letter of resignation to the school district where he currently worked. That morning a message had come from the University of Washington telling him he had been chosen as the new instructor for the history department. Everything was falling into place, and his dreams were coming true.

Even finding Addie again fit into that plan. He had been so excited when he'd first seen her, and even though she was keeping him at arm's length, Isaac knew they were meant to be together. And if that took time, he could be patient.

He paused in his letter and put the pen aside. But why was she acting the way she was? He could see in her eyes that she had longed to speak—to say something more. She had acted as though their being together didn't matter, but he knew otherwise.

"You look awfully deep in thought. Should I leave?" his sister asked from the doorway.

"No, stay. Please, I need to talk to someone, and you would be perfect."

Elizabeth smiled and came to where he was sitting. "Well, why don't we go and sit on the sofa together? The fire looks inviting on this damp, cold day."

"That's why I made it," Isaac said, smiling. "Summer isn't supposed to be quite this chilly."

"That's the way it is in the Pacific Northwest. You can never tell what you will get. We've had very hot days in June and very cold days. It just doesn't seem to follow any logic. You'll get used to it."

"And of course, there is always the rain."

"In all its various forms from mist to deluge," Elizabeth replied and chuckled. "Still, I love it here. The flowers are beyond beautiful. They take on their own special quality, as do the garden vegetables and fruits. The dampness of our climate is a blessing."

Isaac got up from the desk and followed her to the sofa. "I've been writing my letter of resignation for the school district."

"I'm so happy for you to teach at the university. I know you've wanted this for a very long time."

"I have. I love the minds of young adults. They aren't afraid to think in a different way—to explore possibilities that might never have otherwise been considered."

"I can't imagine such thinking being all that useful in history, but I'm glad you're happy."

"Well, of course it can be useful in history," Isaac countered. "It is important to consider why things happened the way they did. People are always trying to avoid digging deeper when it comes to the reasonings behind choices in the past. It makes them uncomfortable to find out perhaps someone they admired had a wrong mindset for the deeds they performed."

Elizabeth took a seat on the edge of the sofa and straightened her lavender skirt. "I still fail to see why you would care. It won't change things at all."

"But it does have the power to alter the way we look at history, and sometimes that affects the present. And in truly bad situations, it can sometimes help us not to make those mistakes again."

She smiled. "I'm glad you enjoy it, and I'm very happy you'll be sticking around the area."

"Me too."

"And what about Addie, now that you've found her again?"

Isaac sat and stretched out his legs in front of him. "That's a problem. I have wanted to talk to you about it, but then I'd think surely I can figure it all out myself."

"What's wrong?"

"Addie doesn't want to be with me. At least that's what she's said, but her eyes tell me another story. She was never very good at lying."

"Why are you so sure she's lying? Maybe the years have changed her feelings for you."

Isaac shook his head. "She's been through a lot, that much is true. Her family treated her like a slave. If I could have taken her with us when we left Dawson, I would have. She deserved so much better."

He folded his arms. "She's so strong. I never admired a woman more, unless it was you or Mother. You are a strong woman like Addie, and I've always held great respect for you. You don't let the problems of life defeat you."

Elizabeth laughed. "If I did, I would be long gone by now. Problems abound from every side of life. Even for those who

117

have a decent situation in life. The poor are hardly the only ones who face difficulties."

"Addie faced difficulties for so many reasons. Her father and brothers held no respect for women. They were unkind and vicious. She was humiliated and defeated by them no matter the situation. They were terrible people."

"Aren't the brothers still living?"

"Yes, I suppose I should have said that they *are* terrible people. I don't know if her brothers are still in prison or not. When I spoke to them, they still had a few years on their sentences. I suppose it's possible they could have died or gotten into a worse situation in prison, causing time to be added to their sentence. I only hope they never catch up to Addie. She snuck out of Dawson to escape them. Did I tell you that story?"

"I think so. You said you had talked to her friend and learned that she left town to escape them."

Isaac gave a sad smile. "Her friend Millie. She told me how she helped Addie escape dressed as a boy. She had come to Dawson City in the same fashion, and they both thought it fitting that she leave that way."

"Still, it was no doubt difficult for her." Elizabeth fixed him with a sympathetic expression. "But you know that she's safe now."

"Yes, she's working at the expo. She takes photographs and sells Brownie cameras. She's quite good. I've seen some of her photographs."

"Where is she living?"

"I heard one of the girls say she lives nearby, but I don't know where. I plan to visit her at the shop, and perhaps she'll tell me."

"Do you think it's wise to pester her? She needs to get used to the idea that you're back in her life. These things can be quite hard on a woman."

"I've taken that into consideration, along with all that happened to her after I left. I won't rush her into marrying me, but I want her to know that I don't care about anything that's happened . . . at least not in the sense that it would keep me from loving her. I've never stopped."

Elizabeth leaned toward him and took hold of Isaac's hand. "But you must listen to me. You may not care about those things that happened to her, but Isaac, if they were bad enough, they have the power to change who she is. She's no doubt different from the young girl you left in Dawson."

"She is changed. I know that. I know that the things that happened took a toll on her." He tried not to think of the things her brothers and Millie had said to him about Addie's plight. It hurt him so much to know her brothers sold her to Moerman and the brothel. He wouldn't ever admit that part to Elizabeth, as he didn't want her to think less of Addie. He didn't think his sister would be that petty, but he feared it was the type of thing that had the potential to wreak havoc.

Still, Elizabeth made a good point. The horrible things that Addie had endured could have changed her profoundly. He knew she still loved him, but he wasn't at all sure she cared about herself. Maybe she didn't believe herself worthy of love. That made him angry.

"You're frowning. What's the matter?"

Isaac shook his head. "I just don't like the idea of Addie going through so much that she might no longer feel deserving of love. She told me she never had the slightest bit of love until I came into her life. Her mother had died in childbirth, and her father and brothers were incapable of it. No one has ever been there for Addie except me. When I think of her as a little girl like Mina and Lena and how she had no one to comfort her when she was afraid or to encourage her when she was challenged . . . it makes me angry."

"It does me as well, Isaac." She squeezed his hand. "All I can tell you is to pray for her and give her time. If God still means for the two of you to be together, He will make it happen."

"I feel completely positive that He intends it, Lizzy. I don't think my life would ever be complete without Addie."

Later that day, after delivering his letter of resignation, Isaac started back for home. His mind kept going over all the things that he and Addie had said to each other. He knew she was afraid. He could see that much. He wasn't sure why. Maybe she thought he wouldn't love her anymore. Maybe she thought the past would tear them apart.

But Isaac didn't care about the past. He remembered Millie telling him how terrible things had been in Dawson City. *"This place got all the worse after you'd gone. You must remember that Addie's had to witness a lot and endure more than most women."*

She'd told him a lot of other things too. Things that grieved him. He didn't like to remember any of it, especially the things her brothers had told him. Isaac sometimes wished he'd never gone to visit them at the prison. They were mean-spirited, angry men who held no love whatsoever for their sister. They spoke of her as if she were nothing more than dirt on their boots. When they talked of selling her, they had absolutely no feeling for her whatsoever.

"We knew we could get good money for her," Hiram had told him. "Moerman said she'd make it back for him almost overnight. The only regret I had was in not having asked for more money."

Isaac had wanted to punch him square in the nose, but Hiram probably wouldn't have felt it. The man was pure muscle and had had his nose broken so many times that once more from a man half his size wouldn't have mattered.

He let out a heavy sigh and climbed onto the trolley. He was nearly to the expo by the time he realized what he'd done. He was going to see Addie.

Pearl tapped Addie on the shoulder. "Are you sure you feel well enough to be here?"

"I'm fine, Pearl. Don't worry about me."

"We have a new girl coming today. She wants to hire on, and Otis thought her references were good. If you like her and think the same, would you mind training her?"

"Of course not. When will she get here?"

Pearl glanced at her watch pin. "Any time now. Her name is Eleanor. Eleanor Bennett. She lives here in Seattle and is twenty years old."

Just then, a young woman with strawberry blond curls walked into the shop. She looked around and then smiled at Addie and Pearl.

"Hello, I'm Eleanor Bennett, and I'm looking for Pearl Fisher."

"That would be me," the older woman replied. "I was just telling Miss Bryant here that we were expecting you to join us today."

Eleanor gave a broad smile. "I'm so excited. When I saw the girls walking around the expo taking pictures of people, I knew that was for me. I love photography. My father had his own shop back in Kansas, and I helped him all the time."

"That's what I read on your application."

Eleanor nodded. "I just can't get it out of my blood."

"By the way, this is Addie Bryant. She'll be training you." A customer came in, and Pearl nodded to Addie. "She's all yours."

"You can call me Addie, and I will call you Eleanor, if that's all right with you."

"Oh goodness, yes."

Addie liked the young woman's attitude, and she was quite pretty and dressed in a comely fashion.

"Our uniform is as you see me dressed. Black skirt, any style or type of white blouse so long as it's long sleeved and high-necked. We furnish the straw boater with its black ribbon, as well as a satchel to carry all of your supplies in, and then of course we have the Brownie cameras."

Eleanor moved forward to where Addie pointed. "I have been reading about these and just know they will be very popular. Imagine the common person being able to take their own photographs."

"Yes, the cameras are selling quite well, and this is the focus of Mr. Fisher's duties here at the expo. He wants to sell as many of these cameras as he can. That's why he created the Camera Girls. We go amongst the attendees of the fair and talk them into letting us take their photographs. Most people will come here that day or the next and purchase the postcard for ten cents. We will even mail them if need be."

"Are most of the people we approach willing to sit for a photo?"

"I have found them cooperative overall. I remind them, especially ones with little children, that this is a moment in time that will never come again. I also remind them that this is the perfect keepsake from the exposition. Most people like that idea because while there are other souvenirs to purchase, this one is personal."

"I love that idea."

"You will walk maybe twenty miles in a day as you walk from one end of the expo to the other. You'll need to be here by eight o'clock and stay until after we close the shop at five. Sometimes we have to remain behind for cleaning or inventory. If it's a particularly well-lit evening and the skies are clear, you might be asked to stay on and work."

"I don't have a problem with that." Eleanor glanced around the room. "I sure like the way you have some of the photographs in the window. That will really attract people's attention."

"Yes, I thought so too. I've seen quite a few stop to look at the pictures and then come into the shop. Mr. Fisher set up a little studio in the back where he takes photographs for folks who request it."

"How nice. And how is it we're to handle selling the Brownie?"

"Well, come over here, and I'll show you."

They skirted around Pearl and her customer and went in back, where Addie could show Eleanor the camera and its extra pieces.

Eleanor picked it up very fast. With all of her experience, Addie didn't have to worry about teaching her to be careful of lighting or to watch the placement of her photography subjects. In less than half an hour, they were out on South Pay Streak Avenue.

"This is the area where people are spending money." Addie pointed to some of the exhibits. "There are theatres and shows given round the clock and plenty of places to eat. A lot of folks like to buy something to eat and take it down by the lake or to the bandstand area. The gardens are another place where they go to stroll with their lunch. You can get some really great photographs in those places."

"Oh, I intend to. I love plants and flowers. I'm hoping to be a botanist one day."

"Then you'll have plenty to explore here."

"It is an amazing exposition," Eleanor said, looking all around. "It's hard to imagine ever having enough time to see it all."

"It's true. I've been trying to see a different exhibit every day during my lunch break. There's just so much to learn."

"I'll try to do that as well." She laughed. "I like the way you think, Addie."

10

Isaac purposefully waited until close to five to appear at the photography shop. A heavy rain was falling, and a lot of folks had taken cover in the various buildings, including Fisher Photography.

The people were wall to wall, and most were asking about their photographs. It dawned on Isaac that he might as well ask about the last class photos that had been taken on Saturday. When his turn came up, Addie was available to wait on him.

She gazed at him for a long moment. "How can I help you?"

"Class photo. I should have picked it up on Saturday, but I'm afraid my mind wasn't on business. I hope it wasn't destroyed." He gave Addie the detailed information of which class and what exhibition, and in a moment, she presented him with the photograph.

"Remind the students that copies can be made. Mr. Fisher is giving a nice discount on copies. We suggest you give a letter to each student with all of the information as to where they should come and how much the photo will cost. And, just so you know, Mr. Fisher isn't destroying any of the class pictures."

"Addie, would you have time to go with me to dinner tonight?" he asked, putting the photo card in his inside pocket.

"No." Her reply was quite curt. She frowned, and then apologized. "I'm sorry. I didn't mean to sound unfriendly or mean. It's just that I have a meeting to attend at church."

"Oh, where do you go to church?" he asked, hoping it didn't sound like he was prying.

"The Seventh Street Bible Church."

"That's a long ways from here," Isaac replied. "I'd hate to think of your traveling back and forth in the rain."

"Pearl and her husband live near there, so I'll find her at the meeting and then spend the night at their place. I lived with them until recently."

"Well, it's a relief that you won't have to travel back after dark."

"Yes." Addie kept her tone professional and distanced.

"I can at least accompany you there. I'd like to see where it is. I've been wanting to try a new church. My sister and brother-in-law attend a very large Episcopal church, and it's much too impersonal for me. The sermons are very formal, and frankly"—he lowered his voice and leaned closer to Addie—"they don't encourage personal prayer."

She nodded. "I'm sorry to hear that. I know how important that used to be to you."

"It still is. Prayer should be important to every Christian. Yet so few seem to realize the power to be had in prayer."

"Maybe they prayed, but things only seemed to get worse."

Isaac heard something in her voice that egged him on.

"Maybe they prayed but didn't understand God's provision and direction."

"That's very possible. Answers to prayer often look nothing like what I thought they should. I'm sure others must suffer the same problem."

"Can you help me with this?" a woman asked, pushing a business card at Addie. "This was when we had our photograph taken and the name of the girl who took it. There are some other notes on it—the photographer made those."

Addie took the card and nodded. "I'll be right back with your photograph."

Isaac decided to wait by the window. Slowly but surely the shop emptied out as Addie and the other Camera Girls helped the customers. He liked being able to just watch her work. She smiled so sweetly when working with people. At one point, she checked her watch and noted the few customers left.

"I'll be locking the door so that no one else can enter. When you conclude your business just let me know, and I'll let you out." She came near to where Isaac stood.

"Why don't you let me handle the door?" Isaac said. "I can act as a guard and keep new folks from entering, while helping the customers to exit."

Addie looked at him for a moment. "All right. That's kind of you and will help me a great deal." She handed him the key and returned to her place behind the counter.

After twenty minutes, the last customer headed out the door. Isaac brought the key back to Addie and smiled. "I can report that everything went well."

"Thank you, Isaac." She took the keys and put them in her pocket. "Girls, we'll be closing up in a few minutes, so tidy the counter and get your things. I can't stay late tonight."

The girls did as they were told for the most part. One pretty young woman began picking on a quieter Camera Girl, which served to delay things a bit.

"I know you didn't sell as many cameras as I did. I no doubt sold the most of anyone." The pretty girl gave a smug smile as she pulled on her galoshes. "I doubt Mary even sold a single camera. She's so mousy and ill-kempt. I wouldn't buy a camera from someone like her."

"That's enough, Esther. For your information, Bertha sold the most cameras," Addie declared. "Now stop making a fuss and picking on Mary. She sold her fair share."

"I don't know why anyone would buy a camera from her," Esther said, putting her nose in the air. "She hardly even says two words. She's not at all friendly."

"Yes, she is," Bertha countered. "She just sells things in a different way from you. Not everyone wants to deal with a flirt."

Esther raised her chin and gave a huff. "I find people like my way of doing things."

"Stop it now!" Addie put her hands on her hips. "I'm locking up in one minute."

The girls quickly gathered their things and cleared out. Isaac was rather amazed at Addie's authoritarian nature. She was quite different from the young girl he'd known in Dawson City.

Addie saw a look of surprise cross Isaac's face when she commanded the girls to stop. He didn't realize this was pretty much a daily thing with Esther bragging and putting others down. When she made sport of their appearance and it became personal like that, Addie really came down hard.

She hoped the interaction between her and the girls helped Isaac realize that she wasn't the same person he knew back in Dawson City. She and Pearl had discussed this earlier, and Pearl advised Addie to show Isaac how she had changed rather than just tell him. Addie hadn't been at all certain how she could do that, but this moment with the girls had provided an opportunity. She knew he wouldn't expect her to raise her voice and take charge in such a way.

"Are you ready to go?" He smiled in his old way and held the door open for her.

"Just about. Honestly though, you don't need to attend me. As you said, it's a long trip into town." She realized she had no idea where he lived. "I'm perfectly fine making the trip. I did this every day before I bought my cottage."

"You bought a cottage?"

"Yes, it's on the water not far from here. Two elderly sisters were completely unnerved by the exposition and decided to sell it fully furnished. I had been wanting to buy myself a place on the water, and so it seemed the perfect solution."

"I had no idea you could afford such a thing. Much less that you enjoyed such a view."

Addie frowned. "Yes, well, there's a lot you don't know about me. I've been working hard since leaving the Yukon." She left it at that.

She turned off the lights and locked the door. The rain had stopped, but she had an umbrella just in case. "If you're determined to accompany me, you should know that I need to go by my cottage and pick up a few things."

"You make it sound like that would be an imposition, but I'd enjoy seeing where you live."

Addie hadn't thought about how he would now know where to find her. But Isaac would never mean her any harm. She supposed it couldn't hurt for him to know.

They walked in silence across the expo grounds. People were starting to come out once again, and Addie knew there would be all sorts of activities planned for the evening. There would be a concert and probably fireworks. Someone had mentioned that a group of dancers was going to give a performance at seven.

"Do you ever stick around to enjoy the evening here at the fair?" Isaac asked.

"No, before I bought the cottage, it just took too much time to get home, and I hate to be out after dark. Now that I have the cottage, I just want to be there and enjoy my nice quiet evening. Well, it's not exactly quiet, but I like it."

"I like quiet evenings too. Of course, with two little girls running amok in the house, that doesn't happen too often."

She smiled. "They certainly seem to love you."

"They love you too. You would be amazed at the way they have shared my dreams of finding you. They were always asking me when I'd come home from school whether I had any news of you."

"You really shouldn't have done that to them. You built up expectations that can never be."

"Why can't they be, Addie?"

She cut a path across the grassy park area and tried to choose her words carefully. "Isaac, I know you don't understand, but things have changed. A lot happened to me in the Yukon—things that I don't want to talk about, but things that changed me. Some for the worse and some for the better. I just need you to understand that I'm not the same girl you fell in love with."

"You fell in love with me too, and I've changed. Does that mean you don't love me anymore?"

"Of course not," she answered without thinking.

"So you do still love me?"

She quickened her step. "That's not the point."

"I think it's a very important point. When two people love each other as we have and continue to do, nothing can come between them. Unless, of course, they allow it to."

Addie shook her head. Being with Isaac was dangerous. She couldn't control her feelings, much less her mouth.

"This is my cottage," she said, leading him up the walkway. "You should probably remain outside. I don't want the neighbors thinking I'm entertaining men at night."

"I would never do anything to harm your reputation."

Addie looked at him for a moment, then nodded. She unlocked her front door and hurried inside. She had planned to change her clothes, but with Isaac waiting, it probably wasn't a good idea. Instead, she gathered up the canvas bag she'd filled with scraps of material and old ragged clothes. She'd been gathering them from the girls and whoever else offered to donate. The pastor's wife would take them and make rag rugs to give away. Addie enjoyed the one she'd made for her and hoped to learn how to make them for herself.

When she appeared at the door with the bag, Isaac immediately took it from her, as she had known he would. She carefully locked the door and turned to face him. "I suppose I'm ready to go."

They walked back toward the expo and to where the

trolley would stop to pick them up. The transportation system had proven to be quite efficient, and for the most part, ran in an orderly fashion. It not only helped to get people to the expo, but afterward there would be new lines for students coming to the college and for those who were moving into the area to build houses. Addie had heard someone remark that over one hundred new houses were scheduled to be built in the area nearby. Some were already in the process. The AYP had brought all of that to the ever-growing city.

Once on the trolley, Addie tried to settle her nerves as she and Isaac sat side by side. Their shoulders touched, and Addie couldn't help but tremble.

"You're cold. I have to admit, I'm a little chilled myself," Isaac said. "I didn't think to bring a coat, but I could offer you my suit jacket."

"No, I'm fine. I should have grabbed a coat at the house, but my mind wasn't on it."

"What was it on, Addie?"

There weren't very many people on the trolley, so Addie couldn't use that as an excuse not to discuss her personal thoughts.

"My mind has been a jumble of thoughts lately."

"Does that include thoughts of us?"

Addie felt her chest tighten as if an iron band had wrapped itself around her. She couldn't lie to him. "I suppose so."

"Addie, we used to be able to tell each other everything. We never hid our feelings. Why are you afraid to be honest now?"

She didn't answer for a very long time. What should she say? What could she? As he had guessed, she did still love him. She had never been happier to be with someone in her life than she was with Isaac. But again, the past came to haunt her. She would never be that sweet, innocent girl Isaac loved.

"Why can't you leave it be?" She fought back tears. She wanted to be strong and bear up under this so that he wouldn't feel sorry for her. Nothing would be worse than to have his pity.

He lifted her chin. "Because I don't mean to live my life without you."

Isaac's words echoed in her head hours later when she was lying awake in her old bed at Pearl and Otis's house. She tossed and turned so much she wasn't at all certain she'd ever get to sleep.

A light knock sounded on her door, and Addie knew that she had probably awakened Pearl. "Come in."

Pearl opened the door. "Would you like some warm milk? I brought a glass just in case."

"I don't know that it will help, but it probably can't hurt." Addie turned on the lamp by her bedside and sat up against the iron headrail. "I'm sorry if I woke you up with all my moving about."

"You didn't. I haven't been able to sleep either after you told me about Isaac." She handed Addie the milk, then took a seat on the bed. "You can't go on like this."

"I know. I've told myself that over and over." She sipped the milk and found it soothing. "I suppose the only thing to do is just tell him all that happened, but Pearl, I know it won't matter to him."

"Then maybe it shouldn't matter to you. Nothing that

happened to you was your fault. So maybe you need to stop carrying the guilt and blame."

"I wish I could, but even you don't know everything." She put her focus on the milk. "I doubt you'd still want me in your life if you did."

"Addie, did you work in the brothel?"

Addie snapped her head up. "No!"

"Do you realize even if you had, you can be forgiven? Think of the woman caught in adultery in the Bible. They were all gathered around to stone her to death for her sin. Jesus told them that whoever was without sin could go first."

Addie nodded. "And they all dropped their rocks and walked away."

"And Jesus told the woman, 'Go and sin no more.' But first He told her that He didn't condemn her. He doesn't condemn you for whatever you think you've done wrong. Especially if you were forced to do it. You bear no guilt . . . no sin, Addie."

"I didn't work in the brothel, although I lived there." Addie put the milk on the side table. "But I was forced to be mistress to the man who owned the brothel."

"I thought you married him."

"I did. Eventually. I had no say in that either." Addie couldn't even look at Pearl.

Pearl took hold of her hands and held them tight. "Addie, what's done is done. What happened in the Yukon was not your fault. Not even the tiniest part. And do you know what?"

Addie forced herself to look up and meet Pearl's gaze. "What?"

"Even if you had chosen each and every thing that happened

to you—suggested you be that man's mistress or even asked to work in the brothel—if you sought God's forgiveness, you would have it." Pearl reached up and touched Addie's cheek.

"I know you hold God at a distance, fearful that He doesn't really care about you—hopeful that He does. Addie, He does care. He wasn't happy with what your brothers did, but like Joseph in the Bible, when his brothers sold him—God blessed him. And God has blessed you. You have a fortune in the bank. You have a good life and home of your own, and Addie, the man you have loved for so long is back in your life and still loves you. Tell him the truth. I don't think it will change a thing if he's the person you've related him to be."

11

Hiram and Shep had the day off, and it seemed the perfect opportunity to go visiting. There was only one place that Hiram had in mind, and that was Addie's cottage. He didn't know whether or not she was working today, but it didn't matter. If they showed up and she was at home—all the better. He was going to confront her sooner or later.

"Do you think she's keeping the gold in her house?" Shep asked.

"Who can say? If I had a treasure like that, I'd keep it close."

"What if she spent the money buying the house?"

Hiram hated it when Shep made sense. Most of the time he was as dumb as a stick, but even a broken clock was right twice a day, as their father used to say.

"I guess we'll cross that bridge when we get to it."

He continued up the walk to Addie's house. He had decided they would go as big and bold as could be. If she was there, so be it. If she was gone . . . that was fine. Hiram had no problem figuring a way into a house. In fact, he'd already decided that if the doors were locked, he'd break a window. He'd chosen a window that was more or less shadowed by a trellis of flowering plants. It wouldn't be readily visible if the police should walk by checking for loiterers.

The doors were locked tight. Both the front and side. Shep started to complain, but Hiram shut him up with a glance. All of their lives Shep had been a whiner. He'd complained every step of the way to the Yukon, and very nearly every step leaving it. Of course, they'd been prisoners being transported to a prison on the edge of Vancouver. No one cared if they were comfortable. Shep made it clear to the guards that he was miserable, but that only served to bring more torment his way. Hiram told him to shut up and lay low, so the guards would leave him alone, but his younger brother couldn't seem to understand the sense in doing so. Before they reached the prison, Shep had become a whipping boy for all of the guards.

"Stay here on the porch and knock."

"But nobody's in there."

"I know," Hiram declared, exasperation threatening to make him lose his temper. "But if you're knocking, no one is going to hear glass breaking. So when I break the window to get inside, no one will be the wiser. Understand?"

Shep nodded and stepped closer to the door. "I understand."

Hiram made his way around to where the trellis stood. He shimmied in between it and the house. The window was low, and Hiram checked to see if it was locked. It was. He picked up a rock and tapped the glass near the lock. He finally hit it hard enough that the glass cracked and broke. Hiram pushed pieces aside and unlatched the window.

He was in the house in a flash and made his way to the front door, where Shep waited. Opening the door, he practically dragged Shep in, then closed it again and locked it.

"Why are you locking the door, Hiram?" Shep looked confused.

"They have police patrolling the area, remember? They might come all the way up and try the door if they think there's a good reason. Now stop asking questions and look for that necklace and anything else of value."

They went in different directions, and Hiram ended up in Addie's bedroom. He spied a jewelry box almost immediately and went to investigate. He found a little cameo pin and a couple of necklaces, but none of it was anything special. He knew the difference between cheap paste stones and real ones. To his eye, the fake ones didn't hold a candle to the real. He didn't know why it was so clear to him, but the couple of times he'd been challenged, Hiram had been able to tell the difference. One of his old friends said it was a God-given gift, but Hiram doubted God had ever given him anything.

He was disappointed that there was no evidence of the gold-nugget necklace. He could still see that monstrous thing hanging around Addie's neck on the night of her birthday party. Those gold nuggets had been smoothed out a bit and shined to perfection. They encircled her neck, begging to be touched. Hiram intended to have that necklace. Of course, he wouldn't keep it, but he did intend to have it.

He searched through the rest of the room, and when he reached the night table, he saw something sticking out from the doily that sat under the lamp. He reached for it and found a tintype and a postcard. Both held the image of Isaac Hanson. Hiram tossed them aside.

The brothers continued to search through the house, but Addie had nothing of value. This started to really concern Hiram. She didn't even have a silver set for coffee or silverware for dining. The dishes were plain and serviceable, nothing fancy at all. Her clothes were nothing special.

"I've gone through everything out here, Hiram. I'm thinkin' she don't have money anymore. Besides, why would she work if she had money?"

"Maybe she likes being busy," Hiram said, glancing around the room. He hated to admit that Shep might be onto something, but it wasn't looking good.

"If she bought this house instead of rented it," Shep continued, "she probably spent all her money. Besides, it's been a long time since she left the Yukon. She had to have money to get down here and live all that time. She looks like she's doing real good, so she's probably spent it all."

"I can't imagine someone like Addie being able to spend a hundred thousand dollars. That necklace was said to be worth at least that."

"Maybe she didn't take it with her. I heard Sam had things locked up and hidden away in more than one place."

Hiram was getting more irritated by the minute. "All right, let's say she didn't get out of Dawson with the necklace. She still had the money for Moerman's place. I heard the lawyer paid her three thousand dollars. You only need a few hundred to live well for a whole year. In seven years, she'd need less than half of that to live. Especially since she's not buying herself all sorts of fancy dresses and jewelry. If she worked the whole time—and if I know Addie, she probably did—then she wouldn't have to draw on that money very often. So even if she only has a few hundred dollars, that's a few hundred more than we have."

Shep nodded but looked as if he were still trying to work out all the math.

There was a sound outside, and Hiram grabbed Shep and pulled him into the bathroom. Someone tried the front door handle. No doubt the patrol was checking up on things. Hopefully they wouldn't look in the window and see things thrown around. Shep had been none too careful with things, and stuff was strewn everywhere. Hiram had to admit he'd not done much better in the bedrooms.

They waited for a while, then Hiram peeked out the door. The bathroom was at the end of the hall that looked right toward the front door. It looked like whoever it was had gone.

"Let's get out of here but take it slow. We'll go out the front, but I'll check first to see if I can see anyone roaming about."

Thankfully, Shep didn't argue. He waited in the shadows for Hiram to give him the sign to come. He did, and they were on their way soon enough. Hiram didn't bother to re-lock the front door. If the patrol came by and found the place ransacked, so be it. Addie would no doubt call their attention to the place anyway.

He smiled to himself, wishing there had been something he could have left behind to let her know it was him. He'd visit her soon enough, he supposed, and it was nice knowing she'd be fretting over what had happened.

Addie had thought all day about what Pearl had said the night before. When lunchtime came, she made her way to the cottage and thought even more on how she might explain things to Isaac. She knew he'd tell her that what happened in Dawson City didn't matter, just like Pearl had said. She wondered if that was really true. But she couldn't get past what she knew of society. There were rules and expectations, and marrying a woman who had the kind of past Addie had was completely forbidden.

Isaac might not care, but his employers would. It would only take one person from the past showing up and remembering who she was to cause problems. Isaac just wouldn't see that, and she couldn't let him ruin his future when he'd worked so hard to get where he was.

Reaching her cottage, Addie felt the sense of something being out of place. She glanced around, but nothing seemed amiss. Even the lake was calm and clear. It was a beautiful day. But the closer she came to the front door, the more the hair on the back of her neck stood up.

She reached for her key and put it to the lock, but the door pushed open without need of unlocking. Addie froze in place, and the door swung back, revealing her ransacked house. Not thinking, she stepped inside and started to look around.

It was a shock to see it like this. Someone had come in and torn through everything. They had looked through her dishes and food, thrown things around as if it were nothing at all. Her books were scattered on the floor, and the chairs had been overturned as if the culprit had been looking for something specific.

She made her way to the bedrooms, starting with the guest

room first. There she found how the person entered the house. There was an open window and glass on the floor. With a trembling hand, she lowered the window and relocked it. Only after she'd done it did Addie realize it would do no good.

The room had been gone over in the same fashion as the rest of the house. She knew there was nothing of value for the robber to take. She owned nothing that could bring about much in a reselling situation. The only valuables she had were in a safety deposit box at the bank. She felt ill.

Making her way to her bedroom, Addie saw that the jewelry box had been emptied and thrown on the floor. She went to pick it up, but then heard footsteps on the porch. She grabbed the nearest thing she could reach for defense and hid behind the bedroom door.

Oh, God, she prayed in silence, *please help me.*

She heard the footsteps come ever closer and raised her hand to deliver a blow should the person or persons present themselves. The culprit stopped at the bedroom door.

"Addie?"

It was Isaac, and Addie let out a heavy breath, causing him to pull back the door. He looked at her for a moment, then followed her raised hand. His reaction was not what she had expected as he broke into laughter.

"Were you going to pummel me with your hairbrush or groom me?"

Addie looked at the object in her hand and realized her means of defense wouldn't have taken her far. "Oh, Isaac, I was so scared. I came home, and my front door was open, and the place was like this."

"You never should have stepped inside. The culprit might

still have been here. You should have gone immediately for the police. Come on now. We're going to go do that right now."

She could hardly think.

Isaac reached for her hand and took the hairbrush. "We won't need this."

Addie felt her knees grow weak and started to sink to the floor. Isaac took hold of her at the waist and half dragged, half carried her to a chair in the living room.

"Here, sit for a minute. Try to rest and gather your composure."

Glancing up, Addie shook her head. "What are you doing here?"

"I saw you head this way and thought maybe I could take you to lunch. We still have a lot to discuss."

She tried to comprehend his words, but nothing made sense in light of what had happened. "Who would do this? Who would break into my house and tear it apart?"

"I don't know." Isaac glanced around the room. "But they certainly did a thorough job."

"There . . . there wasn't any reason to think I had wealth in here."

"Well, you only just took the place. Maybe the older women who owned it before were known to have valuables. Who can say? It might have just been a random thing. The expo has brought out plenty of thieves and pickpockets. Crime has been reported up in the area."

"I just don't understand. To imagine there was a person in here who wanted to rob me . . ." She shook her head and looked around again. "It makes me feel very unsafe. What if they return?"

"Look, we need to get the police involved. I don't want to leave you alone, so you'll have to come with me."

"Addie?" a voice called from the front door.

"That's Mary." Addie got up and went to the open door. Mary was standing on the porch, looking rather confused.

"Come in, Mary. Someone tried to rob my house."

"They tried?" She looked around the room and then to Addie. "It looks like they did."

"I don't see anything in particular that's missing. There wasn't anything of real value. I had no silver or fancy jewelry. There weren't even any nice figurines or clocks."

"Oh, Addie, I'm so sorry." It was only then that Mary seemed to notice Isaac. "Who is this?"

"Mr. Hanson. Remember? He was the one who asked you to let me take his class's picture."

"Oh yes, the man you knew from the Yukon." She eyed him suspiciously even though Addie had explained about him.

"I'm going to go for the police. Can you stay with Addie?" he asked Mary.

"I can and will. I'll help you to get things back in place." Mary reached for one of the chairs.

"No!" Isaac's voice startled both women. "I'm sorry. I didn't mean to scare anyone. It's just that the police will want everything left as it was by the thief. Don't clean up yet."

He left Mary and Addie and hurried from the cottage. Addie could hardly think clearly as it was, but his demanding "No!" left her feeling completely shaken.

"Do you know anyone who would want to hurt you this way?" Mary asked.

"No." Addie shook her head. "Isaac said that crime was

up in the neighborhood because of the expo. It could have been almost anyone. It was probably just some random act to see what they could get. Isaac even said that maybe the old ladies who lived here before me might have been known to have wealth and valuables in the house."

Mary brought the chair close to Addie and sat down. "I'll remember where this was and can put it back when the police get here." She took hold of Addie's hand. "I'm so sorry that this happened to you. It's a terrible thing."

"I feel as if someone had caught me alone on the street and robbed me. It feels so personal."

Mary nodded. "I can imagine it does. To come into your home—to break in past your locks—it feels terrible."

It did indeed, and Addie wasn't sure she'd ever feel safe again.

Isaac hadn't wanted to say anything to Addie, but his first thought had been of her brothers and their style of dealing with things. If they had found out where she was, they wouldn't have cared at all about her and her things. They would have considered her property theirs.

He tried to remember when their sentence was up. He'd been there two years ago, and they still had some years to go. But there were all sorts of programs that prisoners could be involved in that would reduce their time spent behind bars. What if they'd been released early? On good behavior or because of some other deed that merited the forgiving of their sentence.

Still, it would require them finding Addie. No, it was probably some random thief. Maybe someone had watched her routine and knew when she'd be away. He could imagine them keeping an eye on her until she went to work, then sneaking in to see what valuables they could obtain.

The idea of Addie being vulnerable didn't sit well with him. What if she'd been there when they struck? Or what if she'd come home early to interrupt the attack? What might the person have done to her? He couldn't bear the thoughts that went through his mind. Maybe the culprit was interrupted and would return.

He spied a policeman and waved him over. Meeting him halfway, Isaac began to tell him what had happened.

"The house is a terrible mess, but she doesn't believe anything was taken," he told the officer.

They headed for the house, and Isaac fell silent. He couldn't shake the feeling he had.

"Tell me," he said, turning to the officer. "How can I find out if someone was let out of prison early?"

12

Two police officers went over every inch of her house, leaving Addie feeling even more violated. She knew they were looking for clues in order to help figure out who had done this to her, but Addie just wished everyone would go and leave her alone. Yet at the same time, she didn't want to be alone. What if the person who had done this came back?

"Well, the only real evidence we've picked up was the large boot print in the mud by the back window," the officer in charge announced as he and the other policeman rejoined them in the living room. "It was obviously that of a big man, but much more than this, I cannot say."

"Can more men be put on patrolling the area?" Isaac asked.

"We're doing what we can. The exposition has obviously attracted the type of characters who are going to be looking to make money by way of thieving. We've had a lot of trouble with pickpockets and even some after-hour break-ins." The officer looked at his notes and then to Addie. "Do you have somewhere else you can stay?"

"I suppose I do." She knew Pearl and Otis would take her in.

"If you don't, you can stay with my sister," Isaac announced. "I know she has more than enough room."

Addie met his eyes. She could see the love he held for her there. Why couldn't he understand that there was no future for them? Yet even as she posed the question, Addie felt her heart do a flip. She still loved him as much as ever, and nothing she said or did seemed to help her to extinguish those feelings.

"I'm quite comfortable staying with the Fishers," she commented.

"Well, if not that, perhaps you could have some other people stay here with you," the officer suggested. "I just wouldn't stay here alone for a time. Thankfully, the expo will only last through October, and then hopefully life will get back to normal around here."

Addie nodded. "Thank you for looking things over. I wish you had found more evidence of who did the job, but I do understand."

"Things like this often go unsolved," the policeman told her. "Especially under the circumstances where we have so many people visiting from all over the world. I doubt we'll be able to pinpoint the culprit, especially since you don't seem to have anything missing. Oftentimes, we can catch a thief when they go to sell an item. For very valuable items we make a list and distribute them to various secondhand and pawn shops."

"Yes, I see." Addie knew they weren't going to do anything more for her and decided to let the matter go.

"I'd get your window repaired as soon as possible," the

officer said, heading for the front door, where the other policeman waited.

"Thank you, I will."

Once the men were gone, Addie sat down on the closest chair. "This has been exhausting."

"I'll help you with the cleanup," Mary said, looking to Isaac. "I presume it's all right for us to tidy up now?"

"Yes." He knelt beside Addie. "I'm sorry they couldn't do more, but I promise I will keep checking into this and see what I can find."

"Don't bother, Isaac," Addie said. "There's nothing to be done. As the officer said, nothing was taken." She blew out a heavy breath and got back to her feet. "Mary, we can come back tomorrow evening if you have time and straighten it up then. I don't feel like facing it right now."

"I'll be happy to help you. Maybe Pearl will want to come too, or even Bertha."

Addie appreciated the girl's cheery attitude, but it did little to help. She went to her bedroom and surveyed the scene once again. This had been such a comfortable little home, but now it felt completely stripped of that feeling. She picked up her suitcase and began sorting through the mess to find the clothes she would need.

"Hopeless," she muttered. That was how it felt to face this. Hopeless.

Pearl was ever the mother hen. After hearing about Addie's cottage, she forbade her to return. Addie had been there today only long enough to straighten up before returning to the Fishers'.

"Just let some time pass, and we'll see what happens. Otis is arranging for the window to be fixed."

Addie sat nursing a cup of hot cocoa. "I just don't understand why someone should be so mean—so destructive. I've never done anything to hurt anyone, and yet they chose to hurt me."

Pearl brought her another blanket and tucked it around Addie as she curled her legs up under her and leaned a little closer to the fire. The evening had turned out rainy and chilly, and the dampness seemed to permeate clear to the bone.

"Try not to dwell on it. There are a lot of strangers in town, and I'm sure there are a great many evil people trying to make their own lives better while causing others to suffer. I'm just glad you had nothing of value that they wanted to take."

"I love that little cottage, and it makes me so sad that now that this has happened, my focus is all about someone breaking in. I don't know if I can ever see it as a happy place again."

"In time, it'll pass. You'll see."

"I hope you're right."

For several minutes, they sat in silence. Addie had little desire to do anything but stay exactly where she was. She knew that tomorrow she'd be expected to offer her talks about the Yukon, but she wasn't sure she could. Having the house broken into made her feel a weariness she'd never known before.

"I'm grateful to God for His protection of you. You could have been there when the thief came. You might have been hurt."

"I know. I should be grateful as well, but . . ." Addie shook her head and took a long sip of the cocoa. "Why did God allow it to happen, Pearl? All of my life someone has been telling me that putting my trust in God is the way to go. That He loves me and will take care of me. That He will keep me safe from evil. But then this happens, and I just can't help but question the matter.

"All of those years growing up—my father and brothers' cruelty, living with unsavory characters, and being left to fend for myself—how does that show God cares? These last few years with you and Otis have been good ones, but even then, I question them. You and Otis took care of me, not God."

"That's where you're wrong, Addie. God played a major role in us having anything to do with your life." Pearl took a seat and smiled. "We never intended to have a young woman take our room. When we advertised, we were certain we'd find a young man and hoped he would be someone who could work for Otis and learn the photography business. But instead, we got you. In fact, we didn't have a single other person apply for the room. It was quite clear that God wanted you to be with us."

"I want to believe I mattered so much to God that He arranged my being with you. I really do. I love the idea of belonging to the God of the universe—believing that I am special in His eyes and that He has made arrangements for me that include protection and eternal care. But when I look at the things that have happened in my life since asking Jesus to save me, I can't help but have my doubts."

"Getting us to doubt God is what Satan works hardest at. If we doubt, then we live in despair and sometimes even peril. We certainly never have comfort or peace of mind."

Addie sighed and stared into her cup. "I would so love to have peace of mind. The peace that passes understanding."

"'And the peace of God, which passeth all understanding, shall keep your hearts and minds through Christ Jesus,'" Pearl quoted from Philippians four. "Addie, it's yours to have. You have only to cast aside doubt and put your trust firmly in God. He is more powerful than the devil. The Bible makes it clear that Satan cannot win against God."

"Yes, but it also gives us examples that God allows Satan to test us. Look at Job or Simon Peter. Jesus even told Simon that Satan had asked to sift him as wheat. And apparently God allowed it to happen because Jesus told Peter that he had prayed for him. Wouldn't it have been better for God to just prevent it from happening?"

"But Jesus knew what would be best for Simon Peter in the long run. He knew what was necessary to strengthen his faith—to teach him the important lessons that he would need for life's journey. Especially a journey that would take Peter into many difficult and dangerous places."

Addie nodded. "But again, why not simply make it safe and easy for the Christian soul?"

"It would be lovely if we could just accept Jesus as our Savior and never have another worry or be tempted to sin." Pearl reached out and patted Addie's knee. "You're the closest thing I have to a daughter. If I were able to keep you from pain and suffering, I would do most anything. But we retain the ability to make choices for our lives. God doesn't force our obedience. I believe we go through the things we do to prove to us our need for Him—to show us how faithful He is even when bad times come. Life on earth is fraught with sorrows, Addie. You aren't the only one who has suffered."

"I never meant to imply that I was. I suppose I'm just weary. Seeing Isaac again and remembering the dreams we had for our future, then dealing with the destruction at my cottage . . . my heart aches. I want so much to believe God loves me and has brought all of this together to bless me, but I'm afraid."

"Fear doesn't come from God, Addie. God's perfect love casts out fear. The Bible tells us this in First John. Fear is something the devil uses to control us—to interfere in our relationship with God. Again, it's all about getting us to doubt our Father and His love."

Doubt and fear. Addie considered that a moment. Her entire life had been a story of doubt and fear. Those two things had been longtime companions. In fact, Addie couldn't remember a time when doubt and fear hadn't played a prominent role in her life.

Pearl got up. "I can see you need to think on this. Would you like more cocoa?"

Addie shook her head. "No, I'm fine. Thank you, Pearl. Thank you for everything."

The sound of the front door opening caused Pearl to smile. "That will be Otis. I'll go see to his supper."

For a long time, Addie thought of her life of doubt and fear. Those two simple words described every moment of her existence. How could there ever be peace in her heart when doubt and fear reigned supreme? How could there even be room for love?

Lord, I suppose all these years of listening to others encourage me to trust in You, I've never really understood. I truly do want the peace You promise—and the love. Help me to see what it is to trust You—to know You.

Fear for the future soured her stomach. When she'd left the Yukon, Addie had been determined to live a good life—a happy life. Instead, she'd lived a life of fear, always looking over her shoulder, always worrying about what might happen. Buying the cottage had been her way of moving forward into a new existence, and now that existence had been crushed.

"Oh, God, please help me. I don't know how to trust You."

Hiram and Shep sat in silence over supper. With a steady rain falling, it felt like a heavy, wet blanket had been draped over Hiram's shoulders. He'd been unable to find anything at Addie's that could help them, and even though they were doing quite well in their thieving amongst the expo attendees, Hiram was tired of working at the expo. He was ready to move on, maybe head to California. But they couldn't go—at least not until they had Addie's money.

"This is a good stew," Shep said, soaking another biscuit in his bowl. "Good and meaty."

"Cost enough, it ought to be meaty," Hiram muttered. He imagined Addie eating steak or something equally expensive. Her life at the cottage didn't suggest she lived in luxury, but given the way Moerman had treated her, he imagined she had it good. For sure she didn't go hungry or live in want.

Customers moved in and out of the tables around them, and still Hiram lingered over his meal. He'd long ago lost his appetite but had little desire to go back out in the rain, even to head back to the expo and the cot that awaited him.

"Would you fellas like some dessert?" the waitress asked.

Hiram looked up at her. If his mood had been different, he might have flirted with her or tried to get her to meet him later, but right now neither idea held any appeal.

"No dessert."

She smiled and put his bill on the table. "Just pay up front at the counter."

Shep finished the last spoonful of his stew and plopped the spoon in the bowl. "That will stick to my ribs awhile." He pulled off the napkin he'd tucked into the top of his shirt. "What do you want to do now?"

"I don't want to do anything," Hiram admitted.

"We can't sit here all night."

Hiram fixed his brother with a glaring look. "I know that. Just as you know we can't afford to do much of anything."

"Look, why don't we just go up to Addie at the fair and demand she give us her necklace? At least then we'll know if she has it."

"She's got friends. Too many of them, as far as I can tell. She's off staying with some of them since we wrecked her place. I thought maybe she'd come back, and we could pin her down there, but that's not the way of it. I'm not sure what to do about it."

"Addie's bound to be alone sooner or later. I think we should just walk right up to her and take her in hand. She's not expecting to see us at the expo, so it'll be a surprise, and you always say that surprise gives you the advantage."

Shep was right about that. Hiram imagined the surprise of presenting himself to Addie would cause her to be a bit reckless, maybe not think so clearly. She might even want to do whatever she could to avoid her friends meeting her brothers. Who could say?

"I suppose we really don't have much of a choice. We'll keep an eye out and do what we can. We need to get her alone. I don't think she'll come clean unless she feels threatened."

13

After church on Sunday, Addie was anxious to get back to Pearl and Otis's place before heading to work. Pearl had mentioned they were thinking of going out for lunch, and since church ended at eleven, Addie figured she could have an hour to herself before having to head out for the trolley.

"Addie, Pastor Jenkins and his wife have invited us for lunch at the parsonage. Mrs. Jenkins has everything warming in the oven, so we won't have to wait long."

"I hope you have a good time," Addie replied.

"No, silly. They intend for you to be there as well," Pearl countered. "I told Selma that I was sure you could make it."

Addie didn't want to show her disappointment and forced a smile. "But what about the photography shop?"

"We'll get there in plenty of time. As I mentioned, the lunch is ready and waiting. We're heading right over, and Selma has already gone ahead. The expo doesn't even open until one, so don't fret."

"Well, at least I wore my uniform." The black skirt and blouse were topped by a tailored red-and-black coat that

Addie had found at a secondhand store. Pearl had taken it in for her, and it fit Addie quite well. She added an older Marquis hat with a red feather trimming and felt quite smart.

They waited until the pastor had bid his congregation good day before heading off together to the little parsonage that sat next door to the church. Addie was just starting to relax and enjoy the conversation when Isaac appeared.

"Sorry I'm late." He gave Addie a boyish grin and tipped his hat at her and the other women. "Ladies."

"Glad you could join us," Pastor Jenkins said. "Otis, Pearl, in case you haven't met, this is Dr. Isaac Hanson. He has a PhD in history and is soon to teach at the University of Washington. He's new to the church but mentioned knowing Addie, so I thought it only right that he join us."

Pearl gave Addie a look of concern. There was nothing to be done but face the situation bravely. "Good day, Isaac," she murmured.

The pastor directed them toward the house. "Isaac tells me that you were both in the Yukon, Addie. I want to hear all about life in the far north."

Addie swallowed the lump in her throat and forced a smile. Isaac, however, seemed more than happy to accommodate.

"I'm sure we have stories enough to entertain you through a dozen lunches," he promised.

"That's good. Very good." Pastor Jenkins chuckled and held the door open for Pearl and Otis. "Come on inside. Lunch is already waiting to be served."

Addie followed Pearl and Otis with Isaac right behind her. She could feel his presence but refused to turn around. Oh, but this wasn't going to be easy.

The pastor directed them to the dining room off the main

living area. The wood-paneled walls gave the room a darker than necessary look, but the table was set with crystal glasses and silver that caught the light quite nicely and brightened the room. Alongside those were delicate china that bore a beautiful flower print and drew Pearl's attention.

"What beautiful dishes," Pearl commented.

"Those were given to my wife and I upon our marriage," the pastor explained. "A gift from her aunt and uncle."

"They're Haviland, if I'm not mistaken." Pearl looked to the pastor for an answer.

"They are. You've a good eye."

"Aren't they lovely, Addie?" Pearl asked.

She nodded, ignoring Isaac's nearness. "Yes, I was just noting how they catch the light."

"I'm going to see if I can help Selma," Pastor Jenkins said. "You folks be seated and make yourselves comfortable. I sit here at the head and Selma at my right, but you can feel free to have any of the other places." He headed off through the far side of the room.

"What a sweet little house," Pearl said as Otis helped to seat her at the table. "In all the time I've attended our church, I've never been inside."

Addie nodded. "Nor have I. It is quite roomy and stylish."

"Well, Mr. Hanson," Otis began, "I'm pleased to meet you. I think I've seen you in the shop at the expo." He assisted Addie into a chair opposite Pearl's.

"Yes, I'm a teacher and have been in there more than once to pick up class photographs." He wasted no time claiming the seat next to Addie. "And Addie and I have known each other since our time in the Yukon. I'm sure she must have told you as much."

"I believe something was mentioned." Otis looked at Isaac a moment, then moved back around the table to sit beside his wife. "How is it you came to be in Seattle, Mr. Hanson?"

"Please call me Isaac. I'm originally from Seattle. My sister and brother-in-law live here. They have two little girls of whom I'm very fond. Addie has met them."

"I have," she said, not knowing what else to do. "They are quite charming."

"They are. Such dear girls." Isaac's smile lit up the room. "Anyway, my sister invited me to live with the family. The house is quite large, and it's been wonderful getting to know everyone better."

"Here we are." Pastor Jenkins reentered the room carrying a large platter with baked salmon and rice. Mrs. Jenkins followed behind with a couple of bowls containing vegetables.

"I hope you don't mind our boardinghouse fashion," she said. "It's just easier to pass around the bowls and plates when you don't have servants to wait on you."

"It's hardly a problem for us," Pearl replied. "We live quite simply and have no servants."

"My sister has a houseful of staff, but I prefer it this way," Isaac said, taking one of the bowls from Mrs. Jenkins.

"We will return right away," she promised, setting the other bowl on the table. "There are just a few more things to bring out."

Pastor Jenkins positioned the salmon platter in front of his place setting, then followed his wife to the kitchen. When he rejoined them, he had a basket of dinner rolls in one hand and a sauceboat in the other.

Mrs. Jenkins brought a berry salad and took her seat while the bowl was still in her hands. "There, I believe we're all put together." She gave a light laugh as though amused with herself.

"Let us pray." The pastor bowed his head. "Father, we thank You for this food and for the friends who could come to share it with us. Bless all who enter this house in Your loving care. Amen."

"Amen," Isaac murmured.

Addie tried not to think of Isaac sitting beside her. She tried not to think of him being there at all. For the past few days, she'd done her best to put him out of her mind altogether but had done the job very poorly.

The food was passed from person to person. Addie found the salmon platter rather a challenge to balance, and so Isaac took it from her and waited while she served herself. She took a portion of the salmon and some of the rice concoction, then gave him a nod.

"This is a wonderful enticement that my wife makes," the pastor told Addie as he handed her the sauceboat. "The rice and salmon alone are quite delicious, but when you add this sauce, something quite magical happens."

Addie smiled. "It sounds intriguing." She poured some of the sauce as instructed, then passed it to Isaac.

With plenty of food on her plate, Addie sampled the sauce and rice. She couldn't keep the smile from her face. The lemony sauce seemed to draw out the herbs Mrs. Jenkins had used to season the salmon and rice.

"This is very good," she told her hostess. "Very nearly magical, just as Pastor Jenkins suggested."

"I'm so glad you like it, my dear. Marcus and I have it at

least once a week with fish of all kinds, but I'm particularly fond of it with the salmon."

"As am I," the pastor agreed.

They ate for several minutes without conversation, and Addie felt a little of her tension give way. After all, these were people she trusted, and while she feared what they might think of her if they knew the truth, Addie knew they wouldn't intentionally strike out at her.

She had just sampled the berry salad when the pastor posed a question. "So, Addie, tell us how it was that you ended up in the Yukon."

It was innocently asked, but not so easily received as Addie tried her best to remain calm.

"My father and brothers decided they wanted to go find their fortune. They didn't realize the work it took to get to the gold fields, however. I think they might have quit the trail but for the stories people told of the gold and how easy it was to be had."

"And was it easy to be had?"

She shook her head. "Not by the time we got there."

"And what of you, Isaac?"

Isaac paused with the fork halfway to his mouth. "My father and I saw it as a one-time opportunity to make a good amount of money. We had read up on the trip to the Yukon and knew of the difficulties, but with the help of a great many packers, we were able to take supplies to Dawson City and open a store there. We arranged for supplies to be brought in every week for nearly a year and made a good fortune in it. Of course, it was expensive to arrange for the goods and a large lot was lost in accidents or theft, but overall we made a good amount of money for my college education and left after just a year."

"And what of your family, Addie? Did you leave the next year?"

She took a sip from her water glass and tried to figure out what to say. Setting the glass aside she smiled. "No, it didn't work out well for my family. My father died there, and my brothers . . . well, they were men of few scruples and fell into bad ways. They ended up being sent to prison. I'm afraid the gold camps just brought out the worst in them, and they never found any gold. Well, not that they actually panned for themselves."

"Oh goodness, child. What became of you then?" Mrs. Jenkins asked.

"I left." Addie offered nothing more, and thankfully no one asked.

"But the two of you were good friends while there, as I understand it. At least that's what Mr. Hanson was telling me earlier this morning."

Addie looked at the pastor and nodded. "Yes, we were."

"Addie and I were very close," Isaac said, reaching over to squeeze her hand. "In fact, we had pledged to marry after I finished school."

She could feel the color drop from her face. Never had she expected Isaac to make such a declaration.

"Marry! But how wonderful," Mrs. Jenkins declared. "And now here you are together. Have you set a date?"

Addie pulled her hand away from Isaac. "We were only children when we made such promises." She looked at Pearl, hoping the woman might think of some way to change the subject.

"Speaking of children, Mr. Hanson, how old are your nieces?" Pearl asked without hesitation.

Isaac smiled. "They are ten and six."

"Oh, how sweet," Mrs. Jenkins said, nodding. "Such a delightful age."

"I've told them stories about Addie," he continued. "They call her Princess Addie, and I am her fair knight in shining armor. They looked forward to meeting her almost as much as I did in finding her again. I've looked for her ever since finishing college, and finding her at the expo was such a blessing."

"And what did your nieces think when they finally got to meet Addie?" Mrs. Jenkins asked.

"They adore her. They're always nagging me to have her to the house or to go and meet her somewhere. They are completely devoted."

"Well, once you're married, I'm sure they will see plenty of Addie." The pastor's wife smiled at Addie. "I do hope you'll marry soon."

"Addie is very busy right now," Pearl offered.

Anger stirred inside Addie. How dare Isaac show up here and talk about them marrying and put her in this awkward position?

"Surely one is never too busy to marry the love of their life." Mrs. Jenkins's voice took on an air of romantic charm. "They were blessed enough to find each other again. I'd say they've already had a lengthy engagement."

"That's my way of looking at it," Isaac agreed. He looked at Addie and smiled.

Addie returned his gaze with a scowl. The entire table conversation was now devoted to her marrying Isaac. How could she hope to make them understand that this would never happen? Without simply declaring herself to be a soiled woman damaged by the life imposed on her, how could Addie hope for them to understand?

Pearl seemed most sympathetic, and when a lull in the conversation came, she spoke up. "I do believe it's important to take such things slowly. Especially with so many years between childhood promises and where you are now. I would never encourage either of you to rush into anything. The years have a way of altering feelings and plans."

"It hasn't altered my feelings for Addie, unless it has made them stronger," Isaac assured.

"I hardly think a dinner table is the place for such declarations," Pearl said before Addie responded. "Perhaps you might save this for another time."

Isaac continued looking at Addie. She knew the look on her face was one of pleading mingled with rage, praying he would drop the matter and let them return to innocent topics of the fair and life in Seattle. Addie had to force herself to remain seated. She longed to run from the room and put the entire matter behind her.

Isaac finally nodded. "Yes, I suppose you are right. Forgive me for my excitement in the matter. I've only just found Addie after a long many years of searching. I'm afraid my enthusiasm often gets the best of me."

"It's not a problem to us," Mrs. Jenkins replied. "As spiritual leaders for our congregants, we have often had strange topics of discussion at our dinner table."

"Indeed, we have," the pastor countered. "And there are sure to be many more. At least a wedding is a pleasant topic."

The rest of the dinner went off without any additional

reference to Addie and Isaac marrying. Addie felt exhausted by the time they rose to make their way to the expo. She thanked the pastor and his wife for a delicious lunch and then waited outside while Pearl and Otis said their good-byes. Thankfully, Isaac lingered behind and made no attempt to speak with her.

"Well, that was most uncomfortable," Pearl said as they took their seats on the trolley. "I'm so sorry you had to endure that, Addie."

"It's over with now. I can't blame them for their reaction to Isaac's comments. He's the one I hold accountable. He should never have brought up anything about marriage."

"No, he shouldn't have."

"The boy clearly does love you, Addie," Otis said, rubbing his mustache. "I've never seen anyone more taken by a potential mate, unless of course it was me." He smiled at Pearl. "I was and remain completely devoted to this lady."

Addie smiled. "You two are wonderful together. I've never seen two people better suited. Now, let's just forget the lunch and conversation there. I want to put it aside and focus on the work at hand. The camera sales have been quite spectacular, and I want to see them continue that way."

"Oh, indeed they have." Otis shifted in his seat. "I sent off another order with a request for rush delivery. It costs extra, but we must have them. People are enjoying the cameras, and I know we'll sell out this week if not next."

Addie could hear the excitement in his voice. It pleased her that the plan had been successful. "The girls have done a good job of taking photographs and convincing folks that they too can master the camera for themselves."

"I'll soon have enough money to buy my own place downtown," Otis said. "It will be the culmination of all my dreams and plans."

Addie was glad she could be a part of that. Pearl and Otis were precious to her, and she wanted only for them to have what they needed and desired. They were good, sensible people, and their dreams were too. They weren't looking for riches and wealth, just a way to make a living that would keep them comfortable for the rest of their days.

She thought of her cottage and the life she had planned to live there. It angered her that some unknown stranger had stolen that from her. It made her even angrier that she had allowed it.

"I think I'm going to return to my cottage soon."

"Oh, but it's only been a few days," Pearl said, taking hold of Addie's arm. "Don't rush back. There could be another break-in."

"Why should there be?" Addie asked. "Whoever broke in now knows that there is nothing of value to be had. Why would they return?"

"Well, someone else who hasn't tried to rob the place might get the same idea. I'm not trying to scare you, but wouldn't it just be better to stay with us until after the expo closes?" Pearl asked.

"That's months away, and while I enjoy living with you and Otis, I want my own home." Addie glanced around the trolley, hoping no one was listening to her. "I've been thinking about what you said regarding fear and doubt. I've let both run my life for far too long. I need to take steps toward ridding myself of those chains."

"I know I encouraged you to cast aside fear and doubt, but not at the risk of putting yourself in danger."

"Now, Pearl," Otis joined in, "we must trust that Addie knows what God is calling her to do. We must all have faith that God will guide her and that she will listen. Isn't that the better way?"

Addie looked at Pearl. "I can't say that I'm past all fear and doubt—that would be a lie. But I am trying hard to overcome, and I want to trust God for my future. In order to do so, I need to return to the cottage. I know that's where I'm supposed to be."

Later that day, after the expo closed the shops, Addie made her way to the cottage, still thinking of her conversation with Pearl and Otis. With each step closer to the little house, Addie felt more and more apprehension. Was this the right thing to do? Had she just imagined that this was the direction God was leading?

She paused when she reached the bottom of the walkway. The cottage looked quite peaceful, and an abundance of flowers bloomed along the front of the little porch. It had been a place of hope and joy for her, and Addie was determined that it would be again.

Making her way up the path, she drew a deep breath and prayed for strength to cast aside her fear and doubt. She stepped onto the little porch and reached for the doorknob.

A feeling of icy fingers trailed up her spine. The hair on the back of her neck stood up, and Addie couldn't help but drop her hold. She turned abruptly, feeling as though someone was watching her. Her gaze darted from one side of the yard to the other.

There was no one there.

"Enough," she said aloud. Addie reached for the doorknob again and inserted her key in the lock. "Enough."

The latch clicked, and the door opened. Addie calmed her nerves and glanced inside before stepping forward. Everything looked just as it had when she and Mary put it in order. She let the breath she'd been holding go and stepped into the house.

14

What was the new church like, Uncle Isaac?" Mina asked as Isaac joined them in the backyard garden.

"It was quite nice. I like it very much. The pastor and his wife invited me to come to luncheon, and it was delicious."

"We had pawns for lunch," Lena said, sounding quite dejected.

"Prawns, Lena," her mother corrected.

Lena nodded. "I hate prawns."

"Now, now, Lena," her mother interjected, "there were other things to eat that you quite enjoyed."

Lena nodded. "We had carrot soup. It was good."

Isaac laughed. "We had salmon and rice with vegetables. Oh, and a berry salad that was made with early berries. It was quite refreshing."

"We were just looking at the blackberries in the garden," Mina declared. "They are growing really fast this year, and Mama said we might have some early ones next week."

"Yum," Isaac replied, rubbing his stomach.

"Did you see Mama's roses? The ones over by the carriage

house?" Mina asked. "They're so beautiful. I think you should get married by them. They smell so good."

"I'll keep that in mind," Isaac said, looking to his sister with a grin.

"When can we see Addie again?" Lena asked, tugging on Isaac's coat.

"Well, I just saw her at lunch. She's very busy, you know. But she told the pastor and his wife how much she loved meeting you girls and how dear you were."

Mina clapped her hands. "I knew she would love us because we're going to be a family."

Lena joined in the clapping. She often mimicked her older sister, but just to show her own flair, she twirled around, making her pink dress puff out and reveal the tops of her white knee socks. She was quite the character, and Isaac couldn't resist lifting her into the air and whirling around with her. Lena giggled and threw her arms wide as if to embrace the breeze.

"Well, now that your food has had time to settle," Isaac's sister began, "I believe it's time for you girls to take a nap."

"Oh, don't make us go," Mina said, leaning hard on her mother. "We are having a grand time."

"I know, but remember, your father wants to take you to the exposition tonight. There is going to be a concert with handbells."

Mina sighed and pushed off from her mother's side. "All right. I do so want to hear the bells."

Isaac put Lena back down. "You know what? I think I'd like to hear the bells, too, so maybe I'll go take a nap as well."

Mina giggled. "You don't have to take a nap, Uncle Isaac."

"I know, but that's where we're different, Mina. I actually want to take one. I'm very tired. Lunch wore me out."

"Because of Princess Addie?"

Isaac didn't mean to frown, but he did, and the girls were immediately at his side.

"Don't be sad, Uncle Isaac. Princess Addie is so good, and she will marry you soon. I know she will," Mina encouraged.

Lena nodded enthusiastically and put her arms around Isaac's leg. "She loves you."

"And we love you, too." Mina hugged him opposite her sister.

Isaac had to fight to keep his balance, but the girls' affections were like a balm on his tender heart. "Thank you. You are always so good to me." He hugged them both. "But now you must go get your nap so that we can go hear the bells."

The girls detached themselves and hurried toward the back porch steps. Isaac watched them go, almost sorry that he'd sent them away.

"They are the best of us all," he told his sister.

"Yes." She came closer to Isaac. "I'm sorry that lunch was difficult for you."

He met her gaze and extended his arm. "Care for a turn about the gardens?"

"Of course." She looped her arm around his and let him lead the way. "Do you want to talk about it?"

"I just don't understand what's happened. Addie and I were so close, and she's not unkind, but she's acting almost as if it never happened."

"But you said that you could see in her eyes that she still loves you."

"She does. I know she does, but something is keeping her from allowing herself to act upon that love. She's afraid, and I don't know why."

"You have no way of knowing everything she endured after you left Dawson City. Perhaps she gave up on ever finding you again, and now that she has, she doesn't know what to do about it."

"She can marry me. That's what she can do about it."

"Have you asked her to do that?" Elizabeth's question came as a surprise.

"She knows that's my intent. We even discussed it at lunch. The pastor's wife asked if we'd set a date."

"You did what? Oh, Isaac, please tell me you didn't put that poor girl on the spot."

Isaac hadn't considered that it might have been uncomfortable for Addie. He knew it was awkward but thought nothing more. "She seemed almost embarrassed. I can't explain it."

"Of course she was. Such conversations are private, and you put her there in the middle of her friends and pastor and demanded answers she apparently cannot give. I'm surprised she didn't get up and leave the room."

"Was it really so wrong?"

"To put her in that position?" Elizabeth asked. "Yes, imagine how you might feel if the roles were reversed."

"But I thought my enthusiasm would only prove my love hasn't changed."

"You're thinking only of yourself, Isaac. Think of her. You owe her an apology. Then, after she has time to recover from all that happened at lunch, I think the two of you need to have a long discussion on the matter. You need to air it all out. The past and the present. Otherwise, I fear there will be no future for you."

Isaac thought on that for a moment. What if there was no

future for them together? He had never allowed for another dream—another possible result. He had determined to be a college teacher of history, and that was about to happen. He had determined to marry Addie after he graduated and took a good job, and now that the opportunity was before him, shadows were cast over those plans.

"I don't want a future that she's not in," he admitted. "From the first moment I met her, I knew she was the one for me. She makes me whole."

"Then give her time, Isaac. Give her time and love, and be gentle with her." Elizabeth paused their walk and turned to face her brother. "If she had a broken leg, you wouldn't expect her to get up and run. Something in Addie is broken. Give her time to heal. Don't push her. Let her know that you'll give her all the time she needs."

He hadn't thought of it like that. "I guess I just figured seeing me again—being reunited would heal the past and the long separation between then and now. But now I see that's not the case. I know she hasn't had an easy life. People have really hurt her, and I don't want to be one more of those."

Elizabeth gave his arm a pat. "Taking extra time for something you truly want isn't always bad. You came to your position with the college only after spending time teaching elsewhere. You graduated from college only after a lot of hard work and time." She turned back and started them walking again. "And Isaac, don't forget to pray about this."

"I've never stopped." It was only his hope in God that was getting him through this matter.

"I'm so excited to come and spend the week with you, Addie," Bertha said, putting down the small bag she'd brought.

"So am I." Mary put her coat over the back of a nearby chair. "I love my roommates, but this will be so cozy. Just us three gals."

Addie smiled. "I'm thankful that you agreed. I want so much to live in my house again, but being here alone was just too daunting."

Mary was more than accommodating. "Of course it was. You're only human. After having someone ransack the place, I don't blame you for feeling overwhelmed."

"Maybe if you stay with me this week, folks will see that there's more than one person here and not think they can impose on me." Addie had given it a great deal of thought and was relieved to find Mary and Bertha happy to help her out.

Addie turned on a couple of lamps. It seemed she craved the light to make her feel safe. "I bought some roast beef sandwiches for our supper. The shop was just about to close, but I managed to get there in time."

"Oh, did you get them from Michael's on the Pay Streak?" Bertha asked, eyes wide.

"I did."

"Oh, I've wanted to try them, but they were much too expensive for me to buy. My family has needed every cent that I could bring home."

"Well, then this is your reward for being a good sister and daughter." Addie laughed and motioned to the kitchen. "Come, I have them warming in the oven."

A short time later, they sat down at the little kitchen table to eat. Besides the sandwiches, Addie had purchased some pineapple for them to have as a sort of dessert.

"My parents have been so impressed with the money I've made working for Mr. Fisher," Bertha said. "They were worried at first that most of our salary was dependent upon camera sales. They told me that if I wasn't making a decent and reliable salary by the end of two weeks, I'd have to quit and take another job. They need my help to be regular."

Addie dabbed her mouth with a napkin. "I knew the cameras would be popular. For so long now, people have wanted to have the ability to take their own photographs. It's becoming easier and easier for folks to take trips, even if they aren't rich, and having photographs allows them permanent memories."

"I've enjoyed getting to spend some time looking at the exhibits too," Mary said between bites. "I never imagined the world held so many wonders."

"I knew there were a great many wonders," Bertha declared, "but I never thought I'd have a chance to see any of them. I'm so glad they decided to have the exposition in Seattle."

"It has done wonders for the city," Addie said, slicing into some of the pineapple. "The university is benefitting tremendously. When the expo leaves, they will have gained several permanent buildings for college classes, not to mention all the beautiful landscaping."

They chatted about the city and college for nearly twenty minutes while lingering over their supper. Addie loved the relaxed feeling that came from being with friends.

"The only thing bad about working for the Fishers is that we have to work with Esther," Bertha said, suddenly changing the subject. "She has been nothing but troublesome. She's opinionated and harsh, and constantly picks on the people she knows won't stand up to her."

"Like me?" Mary murmured.

Addie could see the situation was embarrassing to the young woman. "We don't have to talk about it, but it would do you good to learn how to stand up to her."

"My father used to tell me to keep my mouth shut and let my actions defend me. I suppose that's why I'm not quick to get after her when she starts in."

"I believe our actions are a good defense, but I see no harm in putting Esther in her place when she's out of line," Addie said. "I'm not talking about a big argument, but I certainly wouldn't allow her to tell lies about you."

"And she will," Bertha said, pointing her index finger at Mary. "I've told you some of the things she's said about you and the others. She makes up all of that stuff to get attention and put herself in a position above everyone. She thinks she's better than all of us."

"But God knows the truth," Mary said, reaching for her water. "I trust God to defend me."

Addie thought on that for a moment. Trusting God to defend her from the past was something that sounded most appealing. But she didn't believe it was possible. Too many people could speak to the things that had happened to her. Too many people could point a finger and speak the truth. Surely God wouldn't defend someone from the truth.

She was still thinking about that as she crawled into bed that night. Jesus said that the truth would set her free, but the truth of her life in Dawson City seemed far more likely to bury her alive.

"But isn't it already doing that?" she whispered to herself.

15

I want you girls to sell a lot of cameras today. Remember, families are most likely to purchase them, so focus your sales pitches on the man of the family. Point out the importance of having the photographs as something tangible to keep over the years. Remind them how quickly everything changes, and those little ones grow up fast. Play on the heart-strings of the mothers," Otis suggested as the Camera Girls readied themselves to go out on the exposition grounds.

He glanced at the clock. "It's opening time. Go and make yourselves useful." He left them and went to his darkroom.

Addie took over. "Remember to be polite and pleasant. Don't be afraid to show the examples you have of photographs that come from the Brownie. People need to be able to see what they can expect. Above all, have a good time and enjoy yourselves. If you're in a good mood, it will encourage others to be as well." Most of the girls exited the building to go about their day. Only Mary and Esther remained.

"They can't expect much from Mary," Esther said. "She's a terrible salesperson. She just wanders around out there and says nothing to anyone. I've even seen her hiding herself away so that she doesn't have to work."

She seemed to be saying it just for the sake of making trouble. "Esther, I've had more than enough of your lies," Addie said. "You will apologize to Mary or risk losing your job."

Just then Otis returned from the darkroom, and Esther gave the pretense of bursting into tears. "She just threatened me," Esther declared, running to Otis as if for protection. "She said she'd hurt me if I didn't sell more cameras."

Otis looked at Addie. "What's this all about?"

Addie rolled her eyes, but it was Mary who stepped forward. "Esther is lying. Addie simply told her to stop lying about me."

It was the first time Mary had stood up for herself and someone else. Addie couldn't help but smile.

"I'll leave you to resolve all of this," Otis said to Addie.

Esther grabbed his arm. "But that's like leaving a bank robber in charge of the bank. She wants to hurt me."

"If you feel you are in danger here and want to quit your job, I can pay you what you have coming," Otis told Esther. "I wouldn't want you to be here if you felt threatened."

"I . . . well . . . I need this job. I have to stay," Esther replied, looking as though she'd just lost her last friend. "Don't fire me."

He pulled his arm away from her grip. "I wasn't suggesting that. Besides, I put Addie in charge of you girls. If you get yourself fired, it will come through her."

Shaking his head, Otis left the counter and returned to the darkroom. Esther turned back, and Addie fixed her with a hard gaze.

"You've only worked for us a few weeks. In that short

time, you've managed to make most everyone here miserable in some form or fashion. Why not try to get along, Esther? Most of these girls have formed strong friendships with each other—with me as well. You're only doing yourself harm."

"I don't want to be friends with the likes of you or Mary. You're both poor and trashy, and I have no desire to lower myself to be liked by you or to like you." Esther gathered her things and headed out in a huff.

Mary came to Addie's side. "Sometimes she really scares me. I fear she might well do something this time to make me pay for having spoken up. But at least I did it."

Addie smiled. "You did, and I'm proud of you. Esther isn't anything to worry about. I've known a lot of Esthers in my day. They like to run off at the mouth, but seldom do they have the ability to follow up on their threats."

The door opened, and Isaac Hanson stepped inside. Addie stiffened and turned away, uncertain as to what she might say. She was still so frustrated—angry really—that he had made such a scene at the pastor's.

"Addie, I need to talk to you for a minute."

She drew a deep breath to steady herself and looked at Mary. "You'd best get out there."

"Are you sure?" Mary asked, looking past Addie to where Isaac stood.

"I am. Go on now." She turned to face Isaac. "I don't have much time."

"I just wanted to apologize," he said as Mary exited the building. "I know what I did at dinner yesterday was inexcusable. Elizabeth helped me to see that. I never meant to make you uncomfortable."

Addie could see the pain in his eyes. He loved her. He

loved her just as much as he ever had . . . maybe more. And she loved him, but the past made it impossible for them to have a future.

"I accept your apology." She knew he wanted some further explanation. "Isaac, we haven't been together in a very long time. I'm not the same girl you knew back then. Please try to understand."

"I am, and I'm really sorry. I've looked for you for such a long time that my excitement at having found you keeps getting the best of me."

She gave him a slight smile. "I forgive you, but now I must get back to work."

"I understand." He started to go and then stopped. "Addie, please don't give up on us."

She didn't have the heart to tell him that the circumstances of her life had already put an end to them. Still, she couldn't bear his grief. "Please give me time, Isaac."

By noon, most of the girls had returned the cameras and taken reloaded ones out again several times, but Esther was nowhere to be seen. Addie figured she was playing a game with them, punishing them with her absence as a means of paying them back.

Addie wouldn't care, but it would affect the sales for the day, and she didn't want anything to cause problems for the Fishers.

"I'm going to take my lunch time and see if I can locate Esther," Addie told Pearl as she prepared to head out.

"Don't do that. You're entitled to your lunch same as

everyone else. Use company time to find Esther—after all, it is a company matter."

"I know, but as angry as she was this morning, this may take a while."

"If it does, it does." Pearl offered her a sympathetic smile. "Being in charge is never easy, but you've handled these girls wonderfully. Otis and I trust you completely to handle the matter."

"Frankly, I think this should be Esther's last chance. She's done nothing but stir up trouble amongst the other girls. Her sales are minimal, and she's getting to be more difficult to deal with."

"We will leave that up to you, Addie. I know you wouldn't fire someone for personal reasons."

"No, but I have been tempted," Addie admitted. "Esther is just one of those types who makes it very hard on others. I have tried to befriend her, but she wants no friend. I've tried to offer her kindness and the benefit of the doubt, but she wants none of that either. She's just very difficult."

Pearl patted her arm. "I'm sure you'll know what to do. Now, don't miss your lunch on account of this. I brought some extra sandwiches and vegetable strips if you want to share what we have."

"That's all right. I can always run over to the cottage if need be."

Addie headed out along the avenue, keeping an eye out for Esther. She hated that the girl was being so difficult. When they'd first advertised for workers and had the girls show up for interviews, Esther had been amiable enough and seemed quite smart. She hadn't revealed her true nature.

Making her way toward Arctic Circle, where there were

fountains and water cascades, Addie wondered how she might handle the situation with Esther. She didn't want to further the girl's rage and negative attitude, but since she hadn't been back at any point during the morning, it was clear she wasn't earning her keep.

Addie figured telling her flat out that she had to improve her sales or lose her job would definitely constitute a threat as far as Esther would be concerned. Still, Addie needed to put her foot down and make sure that the girl understood the risk of loafing around the expo and doing nothing.

She walked for over an hour before finally spotting Esther. She was sitting with a young man and talking. Her camera was put away, and she showed no signs whatsoever of working. Addie wasted little time.

"Miss Danbury, we need to talk."

The young man looked up and grinned. "We're kind of busy talking ourselves."

"I am sorry to interrupt your discussion," Addie said, "but Miss Danbury is my employee and currently on the clock. So, you see, I must take precedence."

The man frowned. Addie figured him to be no older than twenty, and he was clearly quite taken by Esther's flirtatious nature.

"Perhaps you and Miss Danbury could arrange to meet later, after her working hours are done. She will finish at five thirty."

"Oh, bother. Why don't you just say what you've come to say and leave me alone?" Esther snapped. "I have no desire to be further embarrassed by you."

"Then perhaps your young man will leave us to our discussion." Addie looked at him, and it seemed to have the effect of a schoolmarm on her student.

He jumped to his feet. "I'll take a walk and return here shortly."

Addie waited until he was a good way down the sidewalk before turning to Esther. "We've seen nothing of you this morning and worried that perhaps you had taken ill."

"I'm not ill. I simply didn't find anyone who wanted their picture taken. It hardly seems reasonable to come back to the shop if I have no need to."

"Checking in is for your safety as well as for us to know that you are doing your job. You clearly haven't been doing your job while sitting and chatting with that young man."

"Oh, but I was. He wanted to know what I was doing here at the expo, and I told him." She gave Addie a snide look and lifted her chin in defiance. It was an unspoken challenge to be sure.

"I'm going to give you the benefit of the doubt, Esther. Which is far more than anything you would do for me or the others. However, you're falling way behind everyone else in sales and even photography. You've been hired to do a job, and that job is not being done. If you are unable to do it, I am going to have to dismiss you and hire another girl."

"You can't do that. I need this job."

"Then do the work." Addie could see the anger in Esther's eyes. The girl was clearly unwilling to meet her halfway in this. "Esther, I didn't set out to be your enemy. I, too, was hired to do a job. Training you and supervising your work are my main duties. If you cannot do as you promised, then you must go."

"This isn't fair. You hate me because of the others. Mary has told you all sorts of stories about me, and that's the only reason you're threatening me now."

"Do you not feel you owe Mr. Fisher a fair day's work for a fair wage?"

"He pays mostly on commission, so if I choose not to sell cameras and make no commission, how is that any of your business? He's not out anything, and I'm the one who takes the loss." She got to her feet and placed her hands on her hips. "Now leave me alone."

"You have until tomorrow at quitting time to prove that you're going to do your job, Esther. If I don't see vast improvement, I will be forced to dismiss you."

Addie turned to go but stopped when Esther muttered something. "What did you say?"

Esther's eyes narrowed. "I said you're going to regret this."

"I doubt it." Addie walked away then, having no desire to listen to any more of Esther's threats or excuses.

Heading back to the photography shop, she passed the young man Esther had been talking to. He was already caught up speaking with one of the theater girls who was wearing a sparkly costume that showed off a fair amount of flesh. It would seem Esther would need to find another young man.

Esther Danbury wasn't used to anyone getting the best of her. Addie Bryant had been a thorn in her side since coming to work for Fisher Photography. Esther very nearly growled in her frustration and stormed off toward a less populated part of the fair to get her thoughts in order.

"Say there, miss, I wonder if I could have a word with you."

Esther turned and found a large, well-muscled man. His dark brown hair was neatly trimmed, as was the mustache and beard he wore. His uniform was that of a grounds worker.

"What do you want?"

"I saw you talking to that woman a minute ago."

"What of it?" Esther didn't try to hide her irritation.

"Addie Bryant, wasn't it?"

"Yes, what's that to you?"

He laughed. "It looked to me like she was giving you a bad time of it. She's good at that."

Esther let out a sigh. "How would you know?"

"She's my baby sister. We haven't seen each other in seven years, and I'd like to surprise her. That's where you can help me."

"I have no desire to do anything that helps that woman or brings her joy." Esther started to walk away.

"Me either," the man replied. "I hate her nearly as much as I've ever hated anyone."

Esther was completely drawn in by this. If Addie's own brother hated her, then her feelings were more than justified. Addie deserved whatever she got.

"Why do you hate her?" Esther asked, making her voice more alluring. She turned on the charm and edged closer to him.

The big man grinned. "It's a long story, but I see you have time to listen."

"More than ample time. Let's walk over to the park by the water," Esther suggested. "I want to know everything you can tell me about that sister of yours."

"Dr. Hanson, I must say you come highly recommended. Your references from Harvard, as well as those from your current employer, left us little doubt that you were the man we needed for the history department," the current president of the university, Thomas Kane, announced.

Isaac so seldom told anyone of his PhD that the title *doctor* seemed strange attached to his name. It was, however, one of the requisites for the job at the university.

"Thank you, sir." Isaac shifted in the hard wooden chair. He'd been summoned that morning to meet with President Kane and was anxious to see what the man wanted.

Kane picked up a letter. "And you handled all of your studies in a reduced number of years, so it's clear that your intelligence is above average." He put the letter aside. "I asked you here today to discuss a project that we consider important. We are keen to expand the history department, and in doing so, I wonder if you might be prepared to create an agenda for a class that would focus on the history of the Pacific Northwest."

Isaac smiled. That area was his favorite focus of study. "I'd be delighted. Would you like the studies to include Alaska?"

"I would." Kane got to his feet, and Isaac did likewise. "I believe it's critical for the education of our students to know about the world around them. We teach a survey course that includes the Pacific Northwest, but I believe we owe it to ourselves to dig deeper. We are going to see this university grow with the times and be the finest the West has to offer."

The pride President Kane held for the institute was apparent, and Isaac couldn't help feeling proud that he had been chosen to be a part of it.

"How soon would you like a class syllabus for the Pacific Northwest studies?"

"I'd like to have it in two weeks if that's possible. I know you are already hard at work preparing for your other classes, but I would like to instate this study as soon as possible."

"I can have it to you in that time." Isaac looked forward to putting it together.

Kane extended his hand. "Thank you, Dr. Hanson. I will look forward to reviewing it with the head of the department."

Isaac exited the building thinking of his apology to Addie. She said she needed time. Given that he was going to have to put together a syllabus in two weeks for a brand-new class, Isaac knew he'd be busy. Maybe it would be enough time to help her see that they still belonged together.

16

Addie finished her lecture and gave the audience a smile. "I'd be happy to take questions."

A young girl, probably no more than thirteen, raised her hand and Addie pointed to her. "Yes, what is your question?"

"How did you know how to build a boat once you got to Lake Bennett?"

"There were men who knew how to build boats who stayed on to help the folks heading north," Addie explained. "Sometimes you were able to hire a crew to build the boat for you, or they might even have some already built. You could rent a boat, possibly, but that was far less likely. Building your own was something you took control of and could count on.

"My brothers and father knew a little something about putting a boat together, but of course, they were far from experts. However, with the help of an expert, it took them very little time to put together a waterworthy vessel. Sometimes folks didn't want to pay for an expert's help and put together their own creations without knowing anything about boat building. They usually ended up sinking, or their vessels got dashed on the rocks."

Addie looked out over the audience. "Does someone else have another question?"

A boy raised his hand. "You said there were two trails north, the Chilkoot and the White Pass. How'd you know which one to take?"

"We didn't, really. The White Pass wasn't as steep or difficult. Horses were able to make the trip, and there were groups in Skagway who hired out and took folks north. However, it was a very muddy and narrow trail, and many of the horses died, which is why they sometimes called it Dead Horse Trail. The Chilkoot was much steeper and icy. By the time we arrived, the railroad out of Skagway and up the White Pass was already being built. It complicated things, and my father was never one for complications. I think he figured the Chilkoot was the path of least resistance. Of course, they were both quite arduous, and thousands of people died trying to get rich.

"I have time for one more question." She chose a red-headed boy.

"Did you see any bears?" This question brought laughter and jeering from his classmates.

"I did," Addie answered quickly. "I also saw wolves, and once a man brought a dead mountain lion into town. The Yukon was a very dangerous place." She noted the time and gave the audience a smile. "I must bid you farewell now, but I hope you'll all line up to the side of the stage and get your class photo taken. Teachers, you can pick these up at Fisher Photography on the Pay Streak."

The audience clapped, and Addie stepped from the stage

feeling good that she'd been able to share from her life experiences. Her time spent in Dawson City had always been more negative than positive, but the experience of telling the children about her time there did indeed seem to heal her from the bad parts. The children were eager to hear the stories—at least most of them were.

"Addie, do you have a minute?"

She stepped from the stage and allowed Isaac to help her down the stairs. "Hello, Isaac." It was getting easier to see him, but not less painful. "I'm heading back to the photography shop. You're welcome to walk with me."

He took hold of her arm and guided her through the crowd. But instead of making his way to Pay Streak, he paused at the Klondike Circle and led her to a bench where they could sit.

Addie didn't feel like arguing with Isaac about her schedule, so she took a seat and waited to hear him out. He looked quite dapper in his tan suit and blue shirt, but the expression on his face was rather serious.

"We need to talk, Addie. I would have chosen a better time, but I never know when that is exactly. I thought of coming to your cottage but didn't want to be disrespectful of your reputation."

Addie forced a smile. "That's all right. What did you want?"

"I wanted to make sure you were doing all right. I really feel bad for the way I treated you at the pastor's."

"I'm doing all right, Isaac. I've been very busy with my various jobs."

"I know you have. I have been as well. I have to create a syllabus—a sort of outline for a new class they want to give at the university."

"How nice."

"Addie, are you all right?" Mary asked, coming up to where she and Isaac sat. "Are you sick?" She reached out to touch Addie's arm. "I came to walk with you back to the photography studio and saw you come this way instead."

"I'm fine." Addie got to her feet. "Really I am. Isaac, it was nice to see you, but I have to get back to work. We'll have to talk another time."

"Addie, I hope we can talk about . . . things . . . soon." He was on his feet and took hold of her hand. "Please."

She nodded. "I owe you that much, but right now I'm too busy. Perhaps after church tomorrow." She wasn't at all sure why she'd recommended that, but now that it was out of her mouth, Addie decided not to take it back.

"All right, may I take you to lunch?"

Addie said nothing but gave a nod before turning away to join Mary. "I'm glad you showed up," she told her friend.

"Was he bothering you?"

"No, nothing like that. Isaac is a good man. He loves me quite dearly."

Mary smiled. "Are you two planning to marry?"

"We were at one time. I just don't think that will work out now. Too much has happened since we spoke our promise to one another."

An odd look crossed Mary's face. "Too much for true love?"

Addie shrugged. "I believe so."

At least he had her word to meet him tomorrow. Isaac fully intended to hold Addie to her promise. He would plan some simple picnic for their lunch, and that way he could have her to himself. Elizabeth's cook would be able to help him.

"Why do you bother with her?" a female voice asked.

Isaac turned to find one of the Camera Girls looking at him. She was very pretty, and her green eyes were quite startling.

"I'm afraid we've not been introduced."

"I'm Esther Danbury. Addie is my boss and not at all a very nice one."

Isaac laughed, bringing on a scowl from Esther. "I'm sorry," he apologized. "It's just that I've known Addie since we were children, and she's always been very nice. I've never known anyone to speak against her that way."

"Well, she's not nice to me. She threatens me all the time and promises me trouble. I've tried to please her, but it seems she has something against me." She gave a shrug. "It seems she also has something against you."

"My affairs are none of your concern." Isaac felt irritated with the young woman. Her beauty was apparently only skin-deep.

"I didn't mean to offend you, mister," Esther said, frowning. "I tend to speak my mind. I forget that not everyone appreciates that. I hope you'll pardon me for being so open."

"Of course," Isaac replied. "Now, if you'll excuse me."

He headed off toward Pay Streak. His annoyance at Esther's comments seemed to follow him through the exposition. Despite the growing crowds, Isaac had never felt more alone. He wanted to keep his spirits up. After all, Addie agreed to meet him after church. But there was something that seemed so final in her look and tone.

Father, I've tried to give this to You over and over, but it would seem each time I slip back to take it with me rather than leave it in Your hands. Isaac continued to pray as he walked through the mass of people.

You're my only hope. If You don't change Addie's heart, I fear I'll lose her. Please, Lord, don't take her from me.

Isaac made his way home and found Elizabeth instructing the housekeeper when he came in. She glanced his way, but Isaac turned to go into the music room, knowing that if she saw his expression, she'd know something was wrong.

He didn't make it far before she caught up to him. "Isaac, what is it?"

"What is what?" he asked innocently.

"Don't play games with me." She closed the pocket doors behind her and motioned to the settee. "Sit and tell me everything."

He sighed and unbuttoned his coat. He waited until she sat before joining her. "Why do you always seem to know when something is wrong?"

"Because I'm your big sister and I love you." She smiled and turned to face him. "Tell me what happened with Addie."

"How do you know it's Addie and not something else? Say, the university?"

She fixed him with a raised-brow expression. "Let's not waste time. I have guests coming this evening, in case you didn't remember, so I haven't time for games."

"I had forgotten, but even so, it's not my intention to play games. I just feel at a loss for words. I tried to speak to Addie about my feelings and apologize. We were interrupted by one of her friends, and I didn't have time to really discuss the matter. But she did agree to meet me after church tomorrow."

"That's something. What is your plan?"

"I intend to tell her that I love her and ask her to marry me when she's ready."

Elizabeth gave a nod. "And where do you plan to do this?"

"I hadn't really figured that all out. I thought maybe I'd take a picnic, and we could slip away to the park."

"Why don't you bring her here? Stuart and the girls and I will be out, but I can arrange for the cook to fix you a nice lunch."

"You don't think it would be inappropriate to invite her here without you present?"

"No, the housekeeper and cook will be here, as well as my maid and the valet. You'll have plenty of people in the house. They will make it appropriate but not interfere. I'll arrange a nice lunch for you both, so don't worry about that. You can take the smaller carriage to church and not have to walk back."

"That's kind of you, Lizzy. I appreciate your efforts on my behalf."

She smiled. "I want things to work out for you, Isaac. I've so long heard about Addie that I'd enjoy having her as part of the family." She gave him a hug. "I'll keep praying, too. Sometimes the only way to bring these things about is through prayer."

"I don't believe God would have brought us back together to forsake us now. I know she's meant to be my wife."

"Make sure to count the number of cameras we have in stock every night and record it here," Addie told Eleanor. "Then move on to the film, the cases, and on down the line."

Eleanor smiled. "That seems simple enough. I don't mind being the one to take inventory every night if need be. I used to do that back in Kansas for my father. Besides, I think it's only right I do something extra since you've allowed me to take so many of my own pictures."

"But you're already paying for those," Addie said. "I've seen some of them and am quite impressed. If only they could be in color. Those flowers sometimes look like they're going to burst right off the postcard." Addie nodded. "All right, I'm going to let you get back to your photographs. Just remember to take care of this tonight, and tomorrow Mary will do the job. You two can trade off."

Eleanor grabbed up her camera equipment and case. "Thanks for putting your trust in me. You won't be sorry."

"I'm sure you're right." Addie immediately sobered as thoughts of Isaac and their impending meeting came to mind. She began to go through the addresses for the pictures that still needed to be mailed out. The girls numbered each photograph and added that number and their name to the top of the address. They kept meticulous records of what number roll of film they were on, as well. The precision kept the photos from being mixed up and sent to the wrong family or person. But Addie's mindset wasn't good, and she tossed the postcard photos aside and sighed.

"Addie, what's the matter?" Pearl asked. "You've seemed off your feed since coming back from your lecture. Are you all right?"

She nodded. "I'm out of sorts to be sure, but I'm fine. I agreed to meet Isaac tomorrow after church."

"Well, you have the day off. It might work out well for you two to just sit down and get everything out on the table. Honestly, Addie, it's easy to see you have feelings for him."

"Of course I do. I love him."

"Then tell him. Give him a chance to work through this with you."

Just then Esther walked into the shop with her camera. She cast a glance at Addie and Pearl, then moved to where she was supposed to deposit the full camera and take a freshly loaded one.

Addie turned away from the counter to the table behind her. There were several boxes she'd been working to unload, and she focused her attention on that instead of talking to Pearl.

Pearl, however, was not going to leave the matter alone. "You know you'll both feel better once things are resolved." Her voice was barely a whisper.

Glancing over her shoulder, Addie changed the subject. "It's been nice having Bertha and Mary stay with me at the cottage, but they have to go back to their own homes, and I'll need to make a decision."

"Maybe you should arrange to rent the place out and stay with us a while longer. I wouldn't want you to live in fear."

Addie glanced to where Esther was talking to Otis. She didn't seem at all interested in Addie and Pearl's conversation. Addie relaxed a bit. "I have even thought of selling it. It's never going to be without the memory of what happened. For as much as I love that place, I just don't know if it will ever be home again."

"Well, you could either rent it out or sell it. But you needn't rush to do anything. It's not like you need the money."

"No, that's true. There's still plenty in the bank."

"And if you come back to live with us, your expenses will be minimal like before."

"Oh, Pearl, I don't know what would be best. I'm praying about it, but I just don't feel like my prayers are getting past the ceiling."

Esther made her way back across the shop and paused in front of Addie and Pearl. "I want to make sure you saw that I brought back my second camera, and it's not even noon."

Addie nodded. "Good work."

Esther's eyes narrowed as her expression grew haughty. "You're going to regret not being nicer to me, Addie Bryant." She turned and let her chin lead the way out of the shop.

"That girl is trouble," Pearl declared. "She hasn't a kind word for anyone."

"So long as she does her job and doesn't insult the customers, I suppose we can put up with her." Addie didn't want to dwell on Esther. Not when Isaac rested so heavily on her mind.

Tomorrow might well be the end of their friendship altogether, and Addie would have to decide what to do about the future. After all, Isaac intended to make this area his home. He had a job at the university and was attending Addie's church. She would have to be the one to go if they couldn't find a peaceable way to settle the situation.

But where would she go? She had no one in the world besides her friends here.

"Hey there, Hiram," Esther said, sauntering up to the big man.

202

Hiram looked up from where he'd been poking trash with a stick and putting it in his bag. "Esther, fancy seeing you here."

"I've been looking for you everywhere. I heard something I thought you might like to know."

"What's that?" He stopped what he was doing and leaned against the fence.

"Addie was just talking about selling her house. I guess someone broke into it, and that's spoiled it for her. She said it doesn't feel like home anymore."

"Well, isn't that interesting." Hiram gave her a lazy smile.

"Pearl reminded her that she didn't need to sell it right away since she had plenty of money in the bank." Esther decided to embellish a little. "In fact, she's quite wealthy."

Hiram nodded. "Always knew she'd gotten out of the Yukon with a lot of gold."

Esther's eyes widened. "Gold? She struck it rich?"

"Yeah, married a man who made a fortune from a gambling hall and brothel."

She gave a little gasp. This was a delicious turn of events. Esther was certain no one else knew about that. "Was she really married?"

"Yeah, although I don't know why the man bothered. He already had her as his mistress."

Esther tried not to look as delighted as she felt. "A mistress? Oh goodness, and here I thought she was a moral woman."

"Oh, Addie was pretty moral. It wasn't her doing that made her a mistress," Hiram admitted. "Shep and I needed the money." He laughed. "What can I say? She was available, and we sold her."

A giggle came from Esther. How it delighted her to

imagine Addie in such a position. She could hardly wait to use the information against her. Maybe that would shut her up once and for all.

"Look, we should have an arrangement," Hiram said, giving it thought. "Why don't you do this. If you want to get ahold of me, you can leave a message for me over there by the boat dock. There's a wooden sign down there, and it has a little box attached for maps of the exposition. You could leave me a note underneath the maps. I'll check it during the day around noon and when I quit for the day."

"That would be easy enough," she agreed.

"Good. That way if you hear something I need to know, you don't have to worry about finding me. I wouldn't want either of us to get in trouble and lose our jobs."

"Your sister keeps threatening to fire me anyway."

"Well, we don't want that. Be nice to her, and maybe we'll both benefit from it." Hiram gave the girl a smile. She was quite pretty, and with any luck at all, maybe he could have a bit of fun with her. "Say, what do you do with yourself after work?"

17

Addie nervously waited until the church service was over to seek out Pastor Jenkins. He had spoken of God's great forgiveness of sin and how easy it was to be cleansed of it. Addie knew that she could pray and ask God to forgive her. Isaac had once told her all about that and how by turning from sin and asking Jesus to be her Savior, she would not only be forgiven but have eternal life. At the time, it had sounded quite appealing, but also difficult. How could God forgive sin without seeking to punish first?

Of course, there were earthly consequences. People would always have to deal with the circumstances they created by sinning. Very few people could walk away unscathed, but Pastor Jenkins told them God offered complete absolution.

"You don't have to be afraid for the future," he had said just before closing the service. "God holds your destiny. If you've put your trust in Him, you have nothing to fear."

She wanted to believe that so much, but how could she?

"Pastor Jenkins, could I talk to you for a few minutes?" She knew Isaac would be looking for her. They had met up prior to the service, and he had told her he was taking her to his sister's house for lunch, and then they could have their talk. She'd asked Pearl to find him and tell him she'd be delayed a few minutes.

"I'd be pleased to talk with you, Addie. It would seem the sunny day has sent my congregants from God's house in a hurry."

She glanced around, happy to see no one was lingering to talk to the pastor. She breathed a sigh of relief.

Pastor Jenkins led the way to the front of the church. "Would you like to sit here or in my office?"

"Your office, please. Mrs. Jenkins can come too," she said as the woman approached.

"Of course. Selma, Addie would like to talk to us for a moment."

"How nice. I was hoping to find you and tell you how pretty you look in that summery gown," Mrs. Jenkins added.

Addie had worn her nicest dress, a lavender layered muslin with ivory cording and lace. "Thank you. I don't have to work today, so I thought it would be nice to dress up."

"Since you don't have to work, would you like to come to the house and have lunch? We could talk there?" Mrs. Jenkins offered.

"No, I have a luncheon date already. That's why I can't delay too long. It's just that this is rather important, and I need to talk to you before I talk to someone else."

The husband and wife exchanged a look, then gave Addie a nod. "Well, come right on with us."

Once in the pastor's tiny office, they took seats, and Addie folded her gloved fingers together to avoid twisting the material of her skirt.

"What's on your mind, Addie?"

"Your sermon today. You said that God will forgive my past sins. You said that a person has only to ask forgiveness and turn from sin. I want to believe that, but my sins are great."

The pastor smiled. "I doubt they are greater than my own, and God has forgiven those."

Addie felt her nerves getting the best of her. "Maybe I shouldn't have come." She glanced at the door.

"Whatever it is, Addie, you can talk to us. We will keep your confidence and advise you as best we can."

She drew a deep breath and let it out slowly. "When I lived in the Yukon with my father and brothers—it wasn't a good life. They were cruel. When my father died, my brothers . . . sold me to a man who owned a gambling hall and brothel."

"Oh, Addie." Mrs. Jenkins reached over and took hold of her hand. "You poor child."

"I wasn't made to work in the brothel—well, I did cook for the girls." Addie lowered her head. "But I was made to be the man's mistress. He did later marry me, but the harm was already done. I guess I just want to know if God can really forgive me."

"Oh, my sweet child." Mrs. Jenkins put an arm around Addie and hugged her close. "Addie, none of that was your fault or choice. You didn't seek to be a mistress. You were forced into it. Of course you're forgiven. It was never your sin, Addie. It was the man, or men in this case, who forced you into that life."

"I feel so ashamed. Isaac wants to marry me, but he knows nothing of my past. I can't impose that on him."

"Why not just tell him the truth? If he truly loves you, it won't matter," Pastor Jenkins said.

"I know it won't matter to him, but, Pastor, it might well matter to others. He has the job he's always wanted. What if he marries me, and someone there recognizes me? What if my brothers learn about our marriage and want to make trouble for us? I can't have Isaac risk his job for me that way. He's fought far too hard for this."

"I still say you need to just tell him the truth," Pastor Jenkins said.

Addie nodded. "I figured you'd say that. I plan to tell him, but how do I deal with him beyond that? How can I convince him that he can't marry me for his own sake?"

"I don't believe that's the truth of it, Addie. This is the twentieth century, after all. People are far more open in their understanding of the Bible and God. You did nothing wrong, but even if you had, it would be forgiven. Either you believe that, or you don't. Addie, you are forgiven, and you love Isaac. Isaac is forgiven and loves you. I'd say the two of you belong together."

This wasn't at all what Addie had figured to hear. She looked at Selma. "Do you mean to tell me that you don't think any less of me, knowing that I was a man's mistress and lived in a brothel? Does that not bother you at all?"

"Addie," Mrs. Jenkins began, "you know nothing of my sins. None of us want folks to know about the sins we've done. But in this case, you committed no sin. Your heart was with Isaac, and the wrong done to you was not your fault. My child, I weep for you and the insult heaped upon you. But even if it had been your sin, it would be no worse than my own."

"Sin is sin," Pastor Jenkins said. "God abhors it all, but Jesus washes it away. He takes it on himself, and it's no longer our burden. Do you trust Him to do that for you, Addie?"

"I know He can."

"But you wonder if He has? Or if He will? Is that it?"

Addie met his kind eyes and nodded. "I don't feel worthy of forgiveness."

"No one is worthy. We don't get forgiveness because we have earned it. It's a gift—a loving gift from a loving God. God made the way for us to be reconciled to Him. He gave us Jesus, and you must now trust that He died for your sins and the sins of others. You must see that He loves you and has brought you out of that hopelessness and sin into life everlasting."

Addie considered that for a moment. "I do believe that. It's just so hard to understand why God allowed it to happen. If He truly loves me, why would He let others hurt me?"

"That's a hard question for Christians. Why do we suffer loss? Why doesn't God prevent bad things from happening to us?" The pastor smiled. "That's where faith comes in. We have to trust, and when we do, our faith grows a little more. God loves you, Addie, and He always knows exactly where you are and what's happening to you. Remember that. You're never alone."

She left the church and found Isaac waiting with the carriage just outside the door. She could see the look of love in his eyes and knew beyond any doubt that if not for the problems it would cause him, she would happily spend the rest of her life with Isaac.

"Is everything all right?" he asked.

"Yes, I needed to speak to the pastor, but all is well." She forced a smile. Why couldn't that be the truth?

"I'm eager to show you where I live. Of course, it's not my place, and I will eventually find myself a house near the university to save time and money."

Addie nodded. "I understand." She started to allow him to help her up when she heard someone call her name.

"Addie!"

She turned and found Mr. Fisher hurrying across the church grounds. "Can you come quickly? It's Pearl. She's not feeling well, and I need your help."

Addie looked at Isaac for one long, regretful moment. "I'd better see what's wrong."

He nodded. "Let me see if I can be of any help as well."

They went with Mr. Fisher to where Pearl sat resting. "What happened?" Addie asked.

"I got dizzy and started to faint," Pearl replied. She rubbed her temples. "I'm not sure what happened. I'm sure I'll be just fine in a moment. Please don't worry."

"I'm not worried. We're going to get you home, and I'm going to take care of you," Addie said, looking to Isaac. "Sorry about this, but could you drive us to the Fishers' place? They haven't a carriage."

"Of course," Isaac replied. "I'll bring the carriage around."

Addie looked to Mr. Fisher. "I know you have to get to the expo shop. I can manage helping Pearl, and Isaac can help as well. You go on ahead."

"Oh, thank you, Addie." He wrung his hands and looked at his wife. "Do you think she's really all right?"

"I can't be sure, but I think perhaps she just overdid things. It is warm and sunny, and she's dressed rather heavily for such a day."

Pearl nodded. "I'm sure that's all it is, Otis. Go and open the shop at the expo. Addie has the day off, and she will take care of me."

"Very well. If you're sure." He hesitated a moment, then

turned and hurried away. As he passed Isaac in the approaching carriage, he gave a wave. "Thank you, Mr. Hanson."

An hour later, Pearl was settled in her bed, and Addie bid good-bye to Isaac. "I'm sorry about this, but I promise to make it up to you. We will try again soon."

Isaac smiled and reached out to touch Addie's cheek. She felt the warmth of his hand against her face, but it was the warmth of love in his eyes that made her knees feel weak.

"I'm going to hold you to that," he said. "Please let me know how she's doing."

"I'll get word to you one way or another," Addie promised. She watched him go, and Pastor Jenkins's words came back to her. *"God loves you, Addie, and He always knows exactly where you are and what's happening to you."*

Addie glanced heavenward. "Then I suppose You didn't want me talking to Isaac today." She smiled. "I didn't want to talk to him either . . . at least not about the past." She closed the door and went upstairs to where Pearl was resting comfortably.

"I'll fix you something to eat," Addie said, feeling Pearl's forehead.

"Thank you, Addie. I feel much better now. Not so dizzy, but a bite of food would perhaps settle my uneasy stomach."

Otis showed back up around six thirty. It was still plenty light outside, so Addie decided to head to her cottage. Mary had mentioned possibly staying the night, and Addie wanted to make sure she was there for her. They'd both had the day off, or it would have been simple enough to ask Otis to tell her what had happened.

Addie didn't really mind. She knew that Pearl was tired of being fussed over anyway. Pearl assured her she was feeling much better and would see Addie and the others at work the next day.

On the long trolley ride, Addie thought of how all of her plans for the day had been completely thrown aside. She had hoped to explain to Isaac and get him to see reason. His future would depend on him understanding the risks at hand.

The other thing occupying Addie's mind was where she could move. There was no one to turn to who didn't live right there in Seattle. She had wandered through the exposition exhibits more than once and knew there were a great many devoted to towns in Washington. Perhaps she should look at them again with real consideration as to a move. The sisters she'd purchased the cottage from were in Spokane now, and Spokane had its own building at the expo. She could go there and research the possibility of making a move. There was also a building exhibit for Yakima County. Perhaps that would give her insight.

The trolley brought her to the expo stop, and Addie got off and began a leisurely walk back to her cottage. A band was performing for the evening concert, and the marching music was quite lively. She smiled. Overall, the AYP had been a pleasant experience, and Addie was glad Otis and Pearl had wanted to get involved. She was equally happy that it had turned out to be such a blessing for the couple. Soon, Otis would have enough money to move his shop to a better location. He could have the place of his dreams with a large storefront and plenty of room in the back for his darkroom and developing.

There were lights on in the cottage, and Addie smiled. No doubt Mary was already there, making herself comfortable. Addie had given her a key to come and go as she pleased. It would be nice to have the girl's company. Mary was coming out of her shyness more and more, and she and Addie always had a great deal to talk about.

Addie made her way up the pathway and reached for the door. It was unlocked just as she'd figured it would be. "It's just me, Mary."

Only it wasn't Mary who responded.

"Hello, baby sister. Fancy us meeting here."

Shep stood to her right. To her left and seated in her favorite chair was Hiram. He was the one who had spoken. He was as big and mean-looking as she remembered.

Addie started to back out of the house, but just as quickly Hiram was on his feet and closed the distance between them.

"Oh no, you don't. It took much too much time to locate you, and I'm not letting you go that easy." He yanked her into the house and slammed the door closed behind her.

"Let me go!" She pulled away, but he held her fast.

"I'll let you go when I'm good and ready, Addie." He pulled her around to the chair he'd vacated and pushed her down.

She fell back against the cushion and looked up. "What are you doing here? I thought you were in prison."

"We were," he said, nodding. "Got out to help with moving Vancouver expo materials. Got early release for that and good behavior."

"Aren't you happy to see us, Addie?" Shep asked, coming to stand beside Hiram.

"No," she said, not caring that it would irritate her brothers. "I had prayed to never see either of you again."

"Well, just goes to prove there ain't no God. At least not one that listens to your prayers," Hiram replied.

Addie wasn't going to sit for this. She started to get up,

but without warning Hiram hit her hard in the face with his fist. She saw stars and thought she might pass out. She fought against it. The last thing she wanted was to be left to the mercy of these two.

"What do you want?" she asked, rubbing her sore eye.

"What do we always want? Money." Hiram smiled. "And I know you have plenty, including a certain gold-nugget neck-lace that will make me a pretty penny."

"I'm not giving you two anything. Not one cent. Now get out of my house, or I'll start screaming, and the patrol will come."

Hiram chuckled. "It would seem you've grown brave in our absence, but it won't do you any good, Addie. You can threaten all you like, but if you don't do things our way, I'm gonna kill Isaac Hanson."

She felt her color drain. "Isaac has nothing to do with this."

"Well, he means something to you, so that means he does. You'll cooperate with us, or he dies."

"And money is what you want?"

"For starters. I think Shep and I will be staying with you for a while, so you need to make sure and get some comforts for us here. Food and whiskey to start."

Addie couldn't begin to make sense of all that was hap-pening. How could they be here? How did they find her?

"God loves you, Addie, and He always knows exactly where you are and what's happening to you."

Well, Lord, if You know now what's happening . . . if You're here with me . . . I could surely use some help.

18

After a restless night, Addie finally got up and dressed. Hiram had taken her bedroom, and Shep had taken the guest room. This left Addie with the sofa in the living room. She didn't really mind, but she knew these arrangements weren't going to work for long. She needed to get back to Pearl and Otis. They would be able to protect her.

Or could they? The horrible thought of Hiram tormenting them left Addie realizing that she couldn't go to anyone without risking their lives. Hiram had already threatened to kill Isaac. The thought of Isaac lying dead was almost more than Addie could bear. She wouldn't be able to bear it if her loved ones were hurt by Hiram as a means of punishing Addie.

She hurried around the place, hoping she might get her things together and sneak out before her brothers woke up. She was nearly ready to walk out the door when Hiram opened the bedroom door and strolled out, yawning.

"Where do you think you're going?"

"I have a job. If I don't show up, they'll send someone looking for me."

"That's too bad. You and me are going to the bank today."

Addie fixed him with a blank look. She knew he expected her to turn thousands upon thousands of dollars over to him. The gold-nugget necklace in particular intrigued him. No doubt he had dreamed on that thing many a night in prison. Addie couldn't help but wonder if he would go away and never bother her again if she just gave it to him. She knew it was worth a fortune, and maybe that would be enough to make Hiram happy. Unfortunately, she didn't think her brother was the type to be contented with that alone.

"You know, I've been thinking," Hiram began, "we sold you too cheap the first time. I'm bettin' that given you've turned into a fine-looking woman, we could get even more money for you this time around."

"I'm not going to be your pawn, Hiram." She knew she couldn't fight him with brute strength, so she would have to outsmart him. The only trouble was Hiram could be quite the thinker when he put his mind to it.

"And how do you propose to stop me?"

She could see the challenge in his eyes. Hiram enjoyed intimidating people and making them feel helpless. Addie crossed her arms against her body. "You've always under-estimated me, Hiram."

For the briefest moment, there was a look in his eyes that suggested doubt. That gave Addie a sense of strength. It was good to know that she could make Hiram doubt himself. Even if just for a moment.

She took up her hat from the peg by the door. "I have to go to work now."

Hiram crossed the room and took hold of her arm and

bent it back behind her. The pain was immediate and unbearable.

"Let me go!"

"You'd best listen up, Addie. You can put on a brave front and pretend you have some sort of power to fight me, but you don't. You're going to do exactly as I say."

"If I don't go to work, they'll come looking for me. Maybe even send the police. Is that what you want?"

He loosened his hold. "You're going to get me that money. I know you have money in the bank."

"I do. I have a few hundred dollars, and after thinking about it all night, I've decided I will give it to you, but only if you agree to leave me alone."

Hiram let go of her altogether and laughed. "Why should I agree to that? You can bring in some real money if I sell you to the right person."

"I will never let you sell me again, Hiram. This you should understand."

"Well, Shep and I intend to be around for a while. We figure to stay here with you. You've got comfortable beds, and this gives us easy access to the exposition."

"I don't care what you do, Hiram, but I will not be a part of it." Addie retrieved her hat from where it had fallen. She secured it to her head and reached for the door. "I am going to my job at the photography studio. I'll meet you at the expo-gate trolley stop at noon."

To her surprise, Hiram said nothing more. He didn't even affirm that he'd be at the trolley stop. Addie didn't care. She just wanted to get away from him as quickly as possible. Once she got to the studio, Addie hoped she might figure out what else she could do. Hiram wasn't going to go away without having his way. She could threaten all she wanted, but Hiram would merely see it as a challenge.

She walked slowly. It was still a good hour before the exposition opened. Addie usually got to the shop early, but this was a little too early even for her. Despite the hour, the exposition was already coming to life. People were preparing for the day. Shops were opening and exhibits were setting up. It wouldn't be long before the noise level would increase with the sound of machinery and people.

As if on cue, the Ferris wheel started up with music and lights. Addie had thought she would like to take a ride on the contraption but so far hadn't made it. Now, given all that was happening, she probably never would.

No matter what else happened, she had to protect the people she loved. It really didn't matter if she gave Hiram her money. He had guessed she had a lot more than a few hundred dollars, even though she had denied it and would continue to do so. She needed to have that gold for her own move.

When she'd first arrived in Seattle, Addie had asked about trading the gold for cash. But it hadn't been easy to learn what to do without arousing suspicions. The last thing she had wanted to do was present herself as a young woman with a lot of gold, and so the gold and jewelry had gone into the bank box first thing. She knew it would be protected from theft, and she could take some time to think things through. And instead of needing to cash it out, Addie had gotten a job and room right away and hadn't needed to change her valuables to cash. Of course, Hiram wouldn't know about her bank box.

She reached the photography shop and found she was the

first one there. She took out her key and opened the door. Inside was as quiet as a church on Saturday morning. She put away her things and started the routine of preparing for the day. She first checked the cameras and loaded film into them if they weren't already loaded. With this done, she began setting up the display counter with cameras and accessories. Otis had been so excited by the sales that he had ordered some of the carrying cases and plenty of extra film. Addie arranged them with the pricing information Pearl had created. Next, she decided to change out some of the window photos. It had proven to be a great idea to post photos in the window to draw attention to what the camera could do. Otis had taken some of the more attractive photographs and put them in special frames to make them look all the better.

Once all of this was done, it was close to eight o'clock, and Addie knew the others would soon be flocking in to ready themselves for the day. Her plan was to work the shop in the morning, then meet Hiram and hopefully get back to the shop in time to spend the afternoon out strolling amongst the people visiting the expo. She would check on the girls and make sure they were doing their jobs and perhaps even take a few pictures.

"Addie, you're here early," Pearl said, following her husband into the shop.

Turning to face her friend, Addie smiled. Pearl, however, did not return the expression. She looked immediately upset and came to Addie's side.

"What happened? Where did you get that black eye?"

"Black eye?" Addie hadn't had a chance to look in a mirror as she dressed for the day. She touched the place where

Hiram had punched her. "I fell. I didn't even notice that my eye was black. Is it truly bad?"

"It is. I have some powder. I suppose we could put some on and make it less noticeable."

Addie nodded. "That would be good. I'd hate to scare the customers."

"How did you fall and hit just your eye?"

"Well, my arm hurts too." And it did. Hiram's manhandling left Addie sore from her shoulder to the wrist. "I guess my eye just bruised more easily. Of course, I've not looked. I could have bruises on my arm as well."

"What exactly happened?"

Addie hadn't considered that she might need a more detailed story. Thankfully, some of the Camera Girls entered the store just then. Addie went into the back so that no one else would comment. Pearl eventually joined her and brought her the powder.

"Here, let me help disguise the bruising." She very carefully powdered the area and stood back to survey her work. "It will do. Today's looking overcast so perhaps the light won't reveal too much."

"I'm sure I'll be fine. Thank you, Pearl."

Addie puttered around in the back, putting extra materials and supplies close at hand for the darkroom and then tidying up and unboxing new cameras. She tried not to think about her upcoming meeting with Hiram. She wanted nothing to do with him, and yet she knew he would continue to haunt her so long as he thought he could get something from her.

"I have to leave Seattle," she muttered.

That was really the only way to keep Isaac and the others safe. If she fled, Hiram and Shep would follow after her. Of this she was certain. Since Hiram already had in mind to sell her off again, he wouldn't just allow her to flee. She could make her first destination obvious so that Hiram would rush to follow. This would get him away from the people she loved. The second leg of her escape would be more difficult to trace but give Hiram just enough to keep moving away from her friends. By the time Addie was done, she would disappear completely and leave Hiram and Shep wondering where she had gone. And that was the question: Where would she go?

She knew no one and wasn't at all familiar with any other place. How could she make a new life if she had no idea of where that life should be made? It was obvious that disappearing in a big city would be easier than a small town. Maybe San Francisco. From there she could sell the gold and buy passage on a steamer to New York. That would take Hiram some time to figure out. From New York, she could even go abroad. Now there was an idea. Hiram and Shep would never be able to afford that.

When noon rolled around, Addie found Pearl. "I'm going to be gone for a little while. Maybe an hour or a little more. I have a couple of things that I want to tend to."

"Would you like company? I'm sure I can put Bertha in charge and get away."

"No." Addie hadn't meant to sound so adamant. She shook her head. "I'm sorry. I didn't mean to snap. I just need to have a little time to myself."

Pearl smiled. "I completely understand. Sometimes a girl just needs that. You've been more than faithful to this job and have worked long over the hours owed to us. You take all the time you need."

"Thank you." Addie pulled off an apron that she'd put on

to keep her clothes fresh. She hung up the apron and took down her straw boater. "I'll be back as soon as possible."

Several customers entered the store just then, and Pearl was busy tending to their needs. It was easy for Addie to slip out of the shop. Unfortunately, she ran into Esther on her way out.

"Well, look at you. Looks like you got bossy with the wrong person." She gave a self-satisfied smirk.

"Hello, Esther. On your way to lunch?"

The younger woman looked as though she were considering something witty to say, then shrugged and headed for the door. "It's noon, isn't it?"

Addie didn't respond. Instead, she picked up her pace and made her way to the trolley stop. She found Hiram pacing back and forth.

"I thought you'd changed your mind and I'd have to come down to that shop and belt you again."

"I'm here and so is the trolley." She drew a deep breath. The last thing she wanted was to move away from the expo, where at least there were some folks who cared about her well-being, and go downtown with her brother. Hiram would just as soon throw her in the sound as tolerate any lip or protest from Addie.

"It's a good thing you agreed to do this," Hiram said as they took seats on the trolley.

"What would you have done if I was completely broke?"

He laughed. "I knew you wouldn't be. Even in the Yukon you had a way of always having money. You're too frugal. Pa always said that of you."

"Frugal? I did just buy the cottage. Paid cash and didn't even barter the price. That doesn't sound overly frugal."

Hiram looked at her for a moment. "You've turned out to be an odd one for sure. I've seen Hanson hanging around with you. I'm surprised you two haven't run off to find a judge to marry you."

"I have no intention of marrying Isaac or anyone else."

"Didn't like it much with Moerman, eh?"

"Sam was kind to me. I just don't intend to ever marry again."

"Well, that will remain to be seen. If I find someone who offers the right price, you'll do what I say."

Addie wasn't about to argue with him on the trolley. She turned away from him and looked out the open window.

"It's a good thing you've learned to keep your mouth shut. I wouldn't hesitate to hit you just because we're on the trolley."

Still, she said nothing. He frowned as if something had gone wrong. Addie hoped that her silence would silence him. To her surprise, it did. When they reached their stop for the bank, Addie got to her feet and glanced back at him.

"Come on. This is our stop."

The sidewalks downtown were crowded with businessmen. Occasionally, there were women dressed in smart-looking walking suits, but otherwise it was clearly a man's world.

Addie entered the bank as the skies began to sprinkle rain. She sighed in relief. As upset as she was, she'd forgotten to bring her umbrella.

The bank was a beautiful creation done up in a Greek Revival style. The outdoor columns were marble, as was the bank's interior floor. The ceiling soared overhead, trimmed out in elaborate moldings, while the teller stations were highly polished brass with marble counters. Pearl had once described it as outrageous excess, but Addie thought it beautiful.

"I'm Adeline Bryant," she told the teller. She produced a bank book. "I'd like to withdraw my savings."

The man looked over her book, then glanced up at Addie and Hiram. "Are you sure you want to take it all?"

Addie looked to Hiram. "Yes, all of it," Hiram declared. "Do what the lady says."

The man nodded. "Very well." He counted out her money a couple of times. Four hundred thirty-six dollars. He wrote something down in her book.

"I've closed the account," he said.

"Thank you." Addie hadn't intended for that to happen, but that was fine. She knew that in leaving the area she'd have to re-establish a savings account elsewhere anyway.

She prayed that the man would know nothing about her bank box and when he curtly dismissed her after counting out the money, Addie breathed a sigh of relief. She turned and handed Hiram the money before they had even left the bank.

"There. Now you have it all. You heard the man. He closed out the account. There's nothing more."

Hiram frowned but took the cash. "I figured you'd have more, Addie. What about the gold you took out of the Yukon?"

"What gold?" She looked at him in disbelief. "I snuck out of town dressed as a poor boy. Where was I going to get gold? Furthermore, where was I to hide it during my escape?"

She could see Hiram was studying her as if to decide the

truth of the situation, so she hurried to continue. "I had the necklace, of course. I wore it under my clothes, but I sold it. I had to live all of these years."

"You didn't need a hundred thousand dollars."

She gave a laugh. "I had no idea it was worth that. I figured I was lucky to get what I did. Just a few thousand is all I thought it was worth."

"A few thousand? You sold that gold-nugget necklace for a few thousand?"

She didn't want to lie, so she changed the subject. "I'm no expert on gold. Besides, I just bought my little house. Cash was required for that transaction. Too bad you didn't show up sooner."

"We can sell it. After all, I figure we'll leave town."

"And go where?"

They were walking back to the trolley stop in the light sprinkling of rain. Addie was certain they'd be soaked to the skin by the time they got back to the expo.

"I have a hankering to go to California," Hiram replied. "I've heard there are all sorts of opportunities there to get rich fast."

"I hope you and Shep will leave soon."

"I told you, you're coming with us."

Addie saw the trolley in the distance. She turned to Hiram and shook her head. "I will not come with you. Never. Not under any circumstances. You might as well get that in your head right now. You have what you wanted, so take it and go to California."

"I don't believe that the necklace is gone. I don't believe that there's no gold. You must be hiding it somewhere else."

"Believe what you want, Hiram, but it doesn't change a

thing. Do you honestly think I'd be living as I have if I had money? You're a fool if you do."

He slapped her hard across the face, causing several gasps from the women standing in line behind them. Hiram turned and scowled at them. No one said a word.

For Addie, it was just one more reminder that she had to leave as soon as possible. Hiram would stop at no amount of torture to get what he wanted, and she wasn't at all sure how long she could be strong.

Sunday came, and Isaac was looking forward to seeing Addie at church. He hoped to again offer her lunch and have their much-needed conversation about the future. Instead, when he arrived at church, he found that Addie wasn't in her regular place. Pearl and Otis Fisher were there, but there was no sign of Addie. After the service, Isaac hurried to catch up with them and find out where Addie was.

"We don't know," Pearl replied. "She missed work yesterday and sent no word to us. She's missed work almost all week, in fact. We tried to find out what was wrong. We even sent Mary to the cottage a couple of times, but Addie wasn't home."

"That doesn't sound at all like her." Fear edged his heart. "When she's been at work, has she complained about any ailment or problem?"

"No, but she did show up with a black eye on Monday," Pearl replied. "She said she fell and also had a sore arm and shoulder. I fear, however, that she didn't fall. Addie's quite agile. I can't imagine her having such troubles unless she's fallen ill."

"When did you last send Mary to the cottage?"

"Thursday. Mary said there was a mess at the house, but that Addie wasn't there."

Isaac rubbed his jaw.

"What do you know about Addie's brothers?" Pearl asked.

The question took Isaac by surprise. "Why do you ask?"

"Bertha thought she saw Addie near the house with a large man. He seemed to be arguing with Addie about something."

"Her brothers are big men. I've been concerned about them showing up. Of course, what are the chances of them finding Addie after all this time?"

"Probably the same as it was for you, Isaac." Pearl frowned. "I'm really worried about her."

"I'll share something in confidence with you. Addie's brothers were in a prison outside of Vancouver for the last few years. I wrote to the man in charge of the prison to ask if they'd been released yet. I should hear something soon. When the letter comes, I'll let you know."

Pearl nodded, and a tear slipped down her cheek. "I'm so worried about her, Isaac."

"I am too. I'll go to the cottage and see if she's returned."

Addie was being held prisoner by her brothers, and try as she might, she found no hope of freedom. Twice she had tried to sneak off in the middle of the night, but that had only resulted in a sound beating and Hiram tying her up at night.

She was worn and hungry. They were starving her to get her to cooperate. Hiram and Shep had no consideration whatsoever for her needs, and Addie was beginning to fear she very well might die.

Mary had been in to check on her, but the threesome had hidden in the bathroom and waited until she left. Thankfully she was never compelled to check the bathroom.

"Someone's coming up the walk," Shep said, getting to his feet. "It's Hanson. No doubt he's looking for Addie."

"Really?" Hiram asked sarcastically. "Do you really suppose he is?" He cursed and grabbed Addie by the hair. "Get to the bathroom. Come on, Shep, let's get ourselves hidden." They followed Addie to the bathroom and closed the door.

"I do wish your friends would just leave well enough alone," Hiram said, putting his hand over Addie's mouth. "I'm getting tired of this. Can't even have lights on at night."

"We could just pack up and leave," Shep declared. "I'm getting tired of this place."

Addie prayed fervently that Isaac would just go. She feared what Hiram would do to him if Isaac somehow managed to make it inside.

Loud knocking echoed through the house followed by a muffled voice calling out to her. "Addie! Are you in there?"

The doorknob rattled as he sought to gain entrance. There was a long pause and then another knock.

Hiram tightened his hold on Addie. "Not a sound, or I'll wring your neck." As if to prove his point, Hiram wrapped his free hand around her throat.

Isaac could be heard circling the house and calling to Addie, but after a while, everything went quiet.

Addie couldn't help but feel a sense of relief. Isaac would remain safe so long as she served Hiram's purpose. That was all that mattered. Addie knew the time had come to tell

Hiram about her gold and get him to leave Seattle. Even if it meant she'd have to leave too. She couldn't risk Isaac and the others falling victim to her brothers. She just couldn't let anyone else get hurt.

"She wasn't there, Pearl," Isaac said, having returned to the photography shop. "I looked in every window. There wasn't any sign of anyone."

"Where could she have gone?"

Isaac shook his head. "I don't know, but I do intend to find out."

He left the shop and walked along the avenue trying his best to figure out what to do next. It would probably be best to go to the police. Let them know that Addie was missing. Perhaps the police could even gain entry to her cottage and search for clues inside.

Isaac couldn't fight off the sense of dread. Addie had to be in trouble. And if he couldn't find her, he couldn't help her.

But God can, a voice seemed to speak to his soul.

Isaac nodded and shoved his hands deep in his pockets. Yes, God could help her and would. She belonged to Him, and Isaac would pray and give it all over to God. Well, most of it. He was still going to speak with the police.

That evening Isaac related everything that had happened to Elizabeth after the girls had gone to bed. He didn't want to worry them about Addie's situation.

"She just disappeared. I wish I'd checked on her when she missed the first day of work, but I didn't know. I was too busy working on that syllabus. Now who knows where she is and if she's all right?"

"You can't blame yourself, Isaac. She's a grown woman who has been making her own choices for some time. I know you're worried, but what if she just decided to leave? What if your pressure to marry was just too much? I don't want to hurt you, but sometimes a person can only take so much."

"But I apologized, and I don't intend to pressure her anymore." Isaac shook his head. "No, I'm telling you, Lizzy, something has happened to her. She's in trouble. I just know it."

19

The letter from the federal penitentiary arrived two days later. Hiram and Shepard Bryant had been released after helping to transport goods and displays to the Alaska-Yukon-Pacific Exposition. They had received an early release for good behavior.

Isaac felt ill. He leaned back in his desk chair and stared at the ceiling. Fate had dropped them in Addie's lap. But Isaac didn't believe in fate. God had obviously allowed this to happen, but why?

"Hasn't she suffered enough, Lord?"

He sat listening to the silence. Elizabeth and the girls were out making calls, and Stuart was at the university for a meeting. Even the servants were quiet.

Isaac decided he couldn't sit and do nothing. He folded the letter back into its envelope and stuffed it in his pocket. He needed to let the Fishers know what he'd learned, and he needed to find Addie and get her away from her brothers.

It took forever to get a trolley to the expo. Even though they were running on time, each trolley seemed more crowded than the one before. Isaac finally managed to squeeze onto one, although there was standing room only.

When they reached the expo, he showed his pass to get in and hurried down the Pay Streak to reach the photography shop. It was surprisingly empty when he made his way inside. Pearl popped in from the back room, and when she recognized Isaac, a look of worry passed over her face.

"She's not here."

"I feared she wouldn't be." He pulled out the letter. "Her brothers were released from prison. Not only that, but their last duties were helping to transport goods to the expo and set up the exhibits from British Columbia."

Pearl's hand went to her mouth. Isaac crossed the room and put his arm around her. "I'm sorry to just blurt it out like that, but I'm still in shock myself. It's obvious they have a hand in whatever is going on with Addie."

She pulled back her hand. "What are we going to do? What if they've taken her away?"

"I don't know on either account." Isaac stepped away from Mrs. Fisher and shook his head. "I need to find Addie."

The door opened, and to their surprise, Addie herself stumbled in. She was disheveled and had a bloody face. Both gasped.

"I . . . I . . ." She started to crumple, and Isaac moved with lightning speed to catch her.

"Addie, Addie, talk to me," he murmured as he lifted her into his arms.

"Bring her in the back. Otis put up a cot for me to rest on. We can put Addie there."

Isaac nodded, and Pearl led the way. He placed the unconscious love of his life on the cot and grimaced at the abuse she'd suffered. Anger surged through him. If Hiram and Shep had been in the room, he would have attacked them.

"Do you have some water and a cloth?" he asked.

"I'll get them for you and then go for the doctor." Pearl quickly returned with a basin of water and a cloth. By now Otis had heard the commotion and had come to see what was happening.

"Is there a problem, Pearl?" he asked, coming into the room. He spied Addie on the bed, and his brows immediately went together as his eyes narrowed. "Who did this?"

"I'm fairly certain it was her brothers," Isaac said, trying to clean away the blood to see how bad her injuries were.

"Her brothers are here?" Otis asked.

"Yes, we just found out," Pearl replied. "Poor sweet child. I must go for the doctor."

"No, let me. You stay here with our Addie."

Pearl nodded and came to Addie's side. "I can do that if you like."

"No." Isaac shook his head. "I want to do this. I love her and promised I'd always care for her. Even if she doesn't want me."

Pearl sat down beside him. "Oh, Isaac, she loves you so much. You need to know that even if she won't say it."

"Then why does she reject me?"

Addie moaned, but still didn't open her eyes. Pearl reached over and unbuttoned the high-necked blouse. She gasped and pulled back.

Isaac saw immediately what had caught her attention. Addie's neck was red and rubbed raw. Someone had tried to strangle her or had restrained her by tying a rope around her neck.

"We're back, Pearl. I have the doctor," Otis called from the front of the shop.

The doctor entered the room and immediately pushed Isaac aside. He took the chair Isaac had been sitting on and placed his bag on the cot beside Addie.

"What happened to her?"

"We think her brothers attacked her," Isaac said. "But we don't know for certain. They are around and have great hatred for her, so it stands to reason."

"She's nearly dead. I must get her to the emergency hospital," the older man declared after a cursory examination. "It's at the north end."

Pearl cried and buried her face against Otis, while Isaac stood in silence. In that moment, he knew he was capable of murder. He wanted nothing more than to kill Hiram and Shep Bryant.

"I can carry her," Isaac said, tamping down his rage.

The doctor nodded. "Then let us hurry."

The expo's emergency hospital was quite a ways from the photography shop, and once there, it became apparent that they didn't have all the necessary things to help Addie.

"I have a car," the doctor announced. "We'll take her to Seattle General Hospital."

"I'll go with her," Isaac announced.

"May I also accompany her?" Pearl asked.

"Of course, but we must hurry. She's bleeding, and the pressure building in her head must be relieved." The doctor motioned to Isaac. "Bring her to my car, and let's hurry."

It was nearly nightfall before Isaac heard any report on Addie's condition. She had been sent to surgery, and he and Pearl had sat waiting for some word. At six o'clock, a doctor clad in white surgical clothes appeared.

"I'm Dr. Anderson. I operated on Miss Bryant. Are you her family?"

Isaac got to his feet. "We are."

The doctor nodded. "She's in stable condition now, but she's suffered a terrible ordeal. Her arm is broken, and there are multiple lacerations on her back from what appears to be a whipping."

Isaac gripped the back of the nearest chair. Pearl came to his side. "Will she live?" she asked in a strong, steady voice.

"She will. At least, I have every confidence that she will, now that we've relieved the pressure in her brain. You'll be happy to know that we were able to do the surgery without shaving too much of her hair. I know that's important to most ladies."

"I wouldn't care if she was bald, so long as she's going to be all right," Pearl declared.

"Can we see her?" Isaac asked.

"Not tonight. She must rest. I don't have any idea of when she'll regain consciousness, but I suggest you come back tomorrow." And with that, he was gone. Hurrying away to no doubt help someone else.

Isaac turned the chair around and sat down hard. He had been so afraid she would die. What would he have done if she had died? He'd spent so long trying to find her . . . knowing that she was the one and only woman he would ever love.

He lowered his head in weary sorrow. *Please, God, let her heal and live.*

"Isaac, we only live a few blocks away. Why don't you come stay with us tonight? It's close enough to walk."

He barely processed Pearl's words. "I can't leave her."

"You heard the doctor. No one can see her tonight. Come on home with me. I'll get you some supper. There's no sense in letting yourself get sick. Addie's going to need all of us to get through this."

He looked up at Pearl. "I want to kill her brothers. I know that's shocking, but I cannot help myself in thinking the world would be a better place without them."

"I agree and feel the same, but we both know murder isn't in us to do. We might think it is as we rage over what has been done to our dear friend, but God did not make us that way, and He certainly hasn't grown us that way."

"I feel as if I've failed her over and over. It's no wonder she doesn't want me."

"She wants you, Isaac. She's just afraid."

The next morning, Isaac and Pearl were at the hospital bright and early. They were excited to learn that Addie had regained consciousness and had even had some broth and juice. A nurse accompanied them to the private room Addie had been given. The doctor wanted to ensure she would have not only quiet and rest but also safety. Isaac told the nurse he would pay any amount of money to see Addie receive the best care possible. She looked at him oddly, then just nodded and continued leading the way to Addie's room.

When they arrived, Isaac couldn't help pushing ahead. He

went into the room without thinking of whether or not she might be sleeping. She wasn't.

Addie half sat, half reclined in the iron bed. Her head was wrapped in white bandages, and there were stitches in cuts above her eyebrow and lower jaw. Her face was terribly bruised. Isaac grimaced.

"Surely it isn't that bad," Addie managed to say from swollen lips.

"You're still beautiful, if that's what you're asking." Isaac drew nearer to the bed, noting that her arm was cast in plaster. "Oh, my sweet Addie."

"How are you feeling?" Pearl asked, coming up to the bedside.

"Terrible. My head and arm hurt. My back and neck and . . . well, everything hurts," Addie admitted.

A knock sounded behind them, and two uniformed policemen entered the room with a man in a suit following close behind.

"Miss Bryant?" the suited man asked.

"Yes," Addie murmured.

"We need to talk to you about what happened. The expo authorities are quite insistent that we get to the bottom of this situation. They are concerned that guests of the expo may be at risk."

"Well, how good of them to worry about others," Isaac said, his sarcasm thick. "Never mind that Addie nearly died. What about us being concerned for her first and foremost?"

The man looked at him. "Are you family?"

"She's soon to be my wife," Isaac replied without hesitation.

"Well, I am here to find out what happened and hopefully capture her assailant."

"Her assailants are her brothers. Isn't that right, Addie?"

Her eyes widened a bit. "Yes, how did you know?"

"It's not important. I only just found out. I wish you would have told me so I could keep you safe."

"Where are your brothers now, Miss Bryant?"

"I'm not sure. They were staying at my house. When folks came to check on me, they insisted we hide. I suppose there might have been times we were away from the cottage when folks came. Hiram kept insisting I go with him and Shep rather than wait at the house while they went for liquor or other supplies." She reached for a nearby glass of water, but Isaac got it first and helped her to take a few sips.

"What happened to cause this?"

"I wouldn't give them what they wanted."

The suited man frowned. "And what was that?"

"My gold-nugget necklace."

"You have a gold-nugget necklace?"

Addie nodded and eased her head back against the pillow. "I was given the necklace when I lived in Dawson City. I brought it with me when I left and have it hidden away. My brother Hiram wanted it so he could sell it and leave Seattle. He intended for me to go with them. I said no."

"I see." The man wrote down notes in a little leatherbound journal. "And so he beat you?"

"Beat me, bound me, put a rope around my neck, and tried to choke me. At one point he took a belt to me. Most of it was done by Hiram, but Shep kicked me several times when I was on the ground."

"Can you describe your brothers for me?"

Isaac listened as Addie gave a detailed account of Hiram and then Shep. He worried about how taxing this interrogation must be for her. Still, he wanted the police to immediately find and arrest the two ruthless men.

"Miss Bryant, do you believe they will attempt to come here to see you?"

Addie looked to Isaac. He could see the fear in her eyes. "They wouldn't dare," Isaac said before she could speak. "I'll be here to protect and guard her."

The nurse stepped in just then. "Everyone needs to leave now. Miss Bryant must rest." She ushered the police to the door.

"We'll be back if we have any further questions. But I think once the expo officials realize this is a personal matter, they'll rest from further demands of an investigation."

"Does that mean you won't seek to find her brothers?" Isaac asked.

"We will of course keep an eye out for them, but you must understand we can only do so much. This is a mere family feud, and Seattle is a big city. We hardly have time to interfere in every fight that takes place between family members. Hopefully her brothers have cooled off and will realize just how wrong they were to have taken advantage of their sister."

Isaac wanted to roar. "You mean that's it? She nearly died, and you won't even have her brothers arrested?"

"Do you intend to file charges against them?" the man asked from the door.

"Of course she does," Isaac answered for her, then looked to Addie, who nodded.

The suited man stepped forward. "You want to put your own brothers in jail?"

"That's where they belong. They won't only beat me,"

Addie said, shaking her head slightly. "They'll hurt anyone who gets in their way. You must find them—before they kill someone."

The man studied her, then nodded. "We'll do what we can."

"Now, everyone out of the room," the nurse insisted. She herded them toward the door, but Isaac didn't budge.

The look in Addie's eyes was sheer terror. He reached out and took her hand. "What's wrong?"

"I don't want everyone to go. What if Hiram comes here?"

"I won't leave you alone," Isaac promised.

"Unless you're her husband," the nurse said from the door, "you will have to go."

"I want to be her husband, but I'm apparently not good enough." His tone clearly revealed his sorrow.

Addie shook her head. "That's not true. That's never been the case. It's me. I'm not good enough. You don't know about the past."

Isaac smiled and kissed her fingers. "I know everything, Addie. I visited your brothers in prison, and they told me everything. Probably even made some stuff up. I don't care about your past. You had no say in any of it, but I want you to have a say in your future . . . and I want a say in it too."

20

Isaac wasted no time in getting help. He went to the police station first to speak to the officer in charge. Explaining the situation and the danger that the Bryant brothers could pose, Isaac finally got someone to take the matter seriously. Then he arranged for the Pinkertons to come to the house. Isaac once again gave all the details of what had happened and related the situation as best he could.

"Do you know for a fact that the necklace exists?" one of the Pinkerton men asked.

"I don't have any reason to believe it doesn't," Isaac replied. "I've personally never seen it, but I have heard from those who have. Her best friend in the Yukon told me it was a birthday present worth thousands, if not hundreds of thousands, of dollars."

The man jotted down notes, while his partner picked up the questioning. "You said that the two men in question have a criminal history."

Isaac nodded. "They were only recently let go from the prison at Vancouver." He reached into the desk drawer and pulled out the letter he'd received and handed it to the man.

"Here's proof of that. While living in the Yukon, they were constantly in trouble for everything from fighting to thievery. It was felt certain by most folks that the two had even committed murder. It wasn't unusual for men to go missing up there, and no one ever knew for sure what happened to them."

"Did the law not get involved?" the Pinkerton asked.

"There wasn't much law to begin with. The Canadians offered what they could, but the influx of thousands upon thousands of people made it impossible to keep up. Even though the Canadians recorded each person entering the country, they had very little ability to keep track of them afterward."

"But they were never arrested for murder?"

"Not that I know of," Isaac replied.

"Do you have a photograph of them?" the other man asked.

"No." The irony wasn't lost on Isaac. Here Addie's job was to photograph everyone she could, but there was nothing to show the Pinkertons regarding what the two men looked like.

"We can get a photo from the prison." The Pinkerton looked to his partner.

"For the time being," Isaac said, "I just want her guarded so that no one comes to bother her unless they have permission. I can give you a good description of what they looked like last time I saw them."

"Good. Let's go ahead with that," the man replied.

Isaac nodded. "Hiram is older and bigger. He's probably six three and two hundred fifty pounds. He has brown hair—dark. Blue eyes and may or may not be sporting a beard and mustache. He wore them in the Yukon because shaving wasn't convenient and in the colder weather it offered some protection. Shep is six foot or so and probably only around one hundred ninety pounds. He's not very smart, and I think he relies heavily on whatever Hiram tells him to do. For instance, he'd never come up with doing all this on his own. He's mainly someone to come alongside and offer muscle."

"Any distinguishing marks?"

Isaac thought for a moment. "I know Hiram had a long scar down his right forearm. Got that in a knife fight. At least that's what he boasted. Otherwise, I can't recall anything in particular."

"We'll get right over to the hospital and put men in place. It's not going to be without expense, though."

"I don't care what it costs. I want to know that she's safe. I don't want any further harm to come to her. I want her to be able to rest knowing that she won't wake up to find one of her brothers at her bedside."

"Well, we can certainly guarantee that." The man closed his notebook and looked at Isaac. "We'll see this through, Dr. Hanson."

"You have our guarantee," the other agent offered.

Isaac showed the men to the door and had just headed back to the library when Mina and Lena showed up.

"Are those men going to help you save Princess Addie?" Lena asked, hugging her arms around Isaac's waist.

"Yes, they are. Those men work for a company called the Pinkerton National Detective Agency. They are very good at offering people protection."

"So they're going to stay with Addie and keep her safe?" Mina questioned.

"That's the plan. I asked for two men to be with her at all times. That way if Addie's brothers show up to cause her harm, there will be more than one man helping to keep her safe."

"That's very smart to do," Mina replied. "If there was just one man and he had to run after one of her brothers, that would leave her alone for the other brother to do as he pleased."

Isaac nodded. "You really are much too smart for just being ten."

She smiled. "I learn a lot from you, Uncle Isaac. I wish you were my teacher."

"Well, while I'm here, I'll do what I can to help you with your learning." He hugged them both close.

"I should have known that I'd find you girls wherever I found my brother. Girls, you were very naughty to escape your nanny. She was frantically looking for you," Isaac's sister admonished her offspring.

"Don't be too hard on them, Lizzy, they are just trying to help Addie."

She gave them a sympathetic nod. "Very well, but for now you need to get back up in the nursery."

They moaned a bit at this, but after Isaac assured the girls he'd come to see them later, they finally went without further protest.

"Whenever I can't find them, I have only to look for you, brother dear."

"Like I said, don't be too hard on them. They really adore Addie and want to see her safe."

"How did they find out about her being in the hospital?" Elizabeth asked.

Isaac shrugged. "It wasn't me. I would guess they were eavesdropping and got most of their information that way. Those two are quite good at ferreting out whatever information they want."

Elizabeth took a seat on the red leather sofa in the library. She had been such a great source of comfort and encouragement to Isaac and when she motioned for him to join her, Isaac did so.

"I think the Pinkertons are a good idea, Isaac. I'm glad that you're not trying to go this alone. In fact, I've cancelled my trip. I want to be here to help in whatever way I can."

"That's so good of you, Lizzy. I recognize that I need help in this. I've always known my limitations, and this time it's overwhelming me. I hate seeing her so injured. What kind of animal does such a thing—especially to a family member? But I keep remembering the way they treated her in Dawson City. They were always so cruel to her." He ran his hands through his hair and shook his head. "I wanted so much to keep her safe."

"She's in God's hands, Isaac. You told me that yourself. You gave her over to the Lord, and now we must trust that God has her."

"But that doesn't mean we sit idly by."

"And you aren't."

Isaac met her gaze. "I feel so bad that I can't do more."

She reached out and squeezed his hand. "You are doing all that matters. You have been there for her from the start and continue at her side. Don't be so hard on yourself, Isaac."

"I just couldn't go on if anything happened to her," he replied.

"God will make a way in all of this, little brother. Do not limit Him, and furthermore, do not hinder Him."

Addie woke with a start and glanced around the dark hospital room. The door to her room had been left ajar so that just a little light shone in from the hallway. It made strange shadows on the walls and caused her to pull the covers a little higher.

Her throat hurt from where Hiram had tried to strangle her. It made her think of the necklace, and its heavy weight around her neck. Why hadn't she just given it to him?

She knew the answer. This was no great mystery. She saw the necklace as a means of procuring her own well-being—her rescue. She supposed she put more faith in that necklace than she put in God.

"I never meant that to be the case," she murmured.

The medication they'd given her made Addie far too groggy to think clearly. She closed her eyes and tried to forget everything that had happened, but it seemed impossible to put from her mind.

Hiram was insistent that she had more money and that she give it to him. His tirade started with a few slaps to her face and then gradually became combined with fisted hits to her body. Addie hadn't been treated in such a fashion since she was a child, and it was all too much. At one point, she started to fight back, hoping it would dissuade Hiram and Shep. Show them both that she was stronger now than when they'd last been together. But they were unimpressed.

"You're gonna give me what gold you have," Hiram had

told her. *"I can do this all day and night if need be. I doubt you're as capable of enduring it."*

Addie made a dash for the door but forgot that Hiram had tied a rope around her. She felt her air cut off as he grabbed for her neck and held her in place.

"I ain't got much patience left, Addie. Where's the gold?"

Addie turned to fight off her assailant and woke to a nurse trying to calm her. "It's all right, Miss Bryant. Please calm down, or the doctor will need to give you something."

Addie opened her eyes and struggled to focus. For a moment, only Hiram's image registered, but as she progressed into wakefulness, Addie saw the nurse's concerned expression.

"I'm sorry. Just a bad dream."

The nurse handed her a glass of water. "Here. Try to clear your thoughts and relax. It's nearly morning, and the doctor will be by to see how you're doing."

"I'm fine. I just want to go . . ." She shook her head and fell silent. She wanted to go, but to where? She might have said *home* at one time, but Hiram and Shep had taken that sweet cottage and turned it into a nightmare for her.

"It's all right, Miss Bryant. Just relax." The nurse's voice was soothing. "You're safe here. Your fiancé arranged for Pinkerton men to guard you night and day. No one will be able to get through to hurt you."

Addie thought of Isaac and his comment that he knew everything . . . that he'd visited her brothers in prison, and they had told him *everything*.

No doubt they even managed to embellish the story and make it ten times worse. Although Addie knew that would have been hard to do. Her life in Dawson City had been nearly as bad as she could have ever imagined it. Of course, she was grateful not to have been sold to whatever man wanted her. Poor Millie had endured that. How she had still managed to go on living and feel the hope that it might one day be over, Addie couldn't imagine.

The nurse made sure Addie was comfortable and then turned off the light. "Rest well, Miss Bryant. You are safe."

Addie wanted to believe that, but never in her life had it really been true. She had longed for that sense of security, that feeling of protection, and yet it eluded her.

"There is rest in the Lord. Peace in His presence. Allow yourself to be comforted."

She remembered the pastor speaking those words to his congregation once after a family from the church had tragically died in a fire.

Was that really the trick to all of this? Was she not allowing God to comfort her—to share His peace? Was her inability to fully trust God and let go of her own fears the reason that she never felt that full comfort, that rest?

"God, I don't know what to say," Addie admitted. "I want to rest in You and to know Your peace. I do long to be comforted, and yet I know my faith is so very weak."

She closed her eyes. "Forgive my unbelief. Please forgive me, Lord. I know I'm not nearly grateful enough for all You have already done. I know I should be happy to have found Isaac again and know that he still loves me. But I'm so afraid. Not just of Hiram and Shep either. I'm afraid of people knowing the truth about me and condemning me—casting me out of good company so that the only company I'm allowed is that of bad, disreputable folks."

Addie felt her body relax a bit. She knew God was real

and that He was known for His Word and faithfulness. Trust had never come easily to Addie, but she wanted to trust in God more than ever before.

"Forgive me, Lord. Please just help me to believe—to trust in You and know that You are with me always. Even when, or perhaps especially when, I feel all alone and without hope."

When Addie awoke some hours later, it was Pearl's face she first saw. The woman's look of concern caused Addie to smile.

"Good morning, Pearl."

"Good morning, Addie. I'm so glad to see that you are doing better. I've been so very worried about you."

"I'm sorry for that. Sorry, too, that I'm not there to do my job at the expo. How are things going?"

"Quite well, but Otis is very worried about you. He was threatening to close down the shop in order to be here with me. I convinced him that you were on the mend and were sure to come home with us after the doctor released you. I think it's the only reason he agreed to keep working."

"Poor man." Addie struggled to shift her position.

"Here, let me help," Pearl said. Together the two carefully maneuvered Addie into a more comfortable position.

The door opened, giving Addie a terrible start. She pressed back into the pillow and closed her eyes. It was silly, she supposed. It wasn't like harm or devastation couldn't see her just because she'd closed her eyes. She opened them again.

"Here's your breakfast, Miss Byrant." A young woman,

clearly a junior nurse, crossed the room. "Are you up for having it on your lap?"

Addie nodded. "That would be fine. Thank you."

"The doctor said to tell you he wants you to eat it all. He will not even consider you going home until you are able to eat a proper meal." She smiled. "I think you should like this well enough."

Addie looked down at the plate of scrambled eggs. Beside that were two pieces of toast and a bowl of hot cereal. There was also a glass of orange juice and cream for the cereal. "This looks like an awful lot of food, but I'll do what I can. You can remind the doctor I'm only just starting my recovery."

The young woman giggled and shook her head. "We never tell the doctor that he's wrong. It just isn't done." With that she hurried away to deliver other meals.

"It looks surprisingly good for institution food," Pearl said, examining the tray.

Addie sampled the eggs. "It's not so bad, I suppose. Lacks any seasoning, but it's all right."

She ate for a few minutes in silence while Pearl waited. She was such a dear friend, and Addie was touched that she'd taken time out of her day to be at the hospital.

"I'm afraid I don't feel all that well," Pearl said without warning. She got to her feet and turned to Addie as if to say something more. As if in slow motion, she moved slightly to her right, then collapsed to the floor in a dead faint.

"Help!" Addie yelled as loudly as she could. "Somebody help us."

One of the two Pinkertons looked in on the situation. He immediately noted the problem. "I'll get someone."

Addie was already trying to get out of bed, but with a broken arm, she wasn't having much luck moving the tray.

Two muscular orderlies entered the room with a nurse at their side. They got a gurney and lifted Pearl onto it. Without another word, they whisked her away. The nurse turned to follow.

"Is she all right?" Addie asked, unable to imagine what had happened or why.

The nurse paused at the door. "The doctor will see her, then decide what's to happen next," she assured.

The wait was excruciating. Addie forced herself to eat, hoping that by doing so the time might pass faster. It didn't.

Finally, Pearl herself peeked into the room. "Did I scare you?"

"Pearl! Are you all right?" Addie patted the edge of the bed. "Please come sit and tell me what happened."

Pearl crossed the room, leaving the door open. "Perhaps this way it won't feel quite so stuffy in here."

"Of course. Open the window if you like."

"No, this is fine. With a small private room like this, it just seems so terribly close."

"Is that what made you faint?"

Pearl smiled. "In part. I was hoping to share some news with you about my health. News I only learned about recently. You've been gone and then hurt, and there wasn't any time to tell you."

"Tell me what, Pearl? Are you ill?"

"Not at all. In fact, I'm in the best shape of my life. At least that's what the doctor said."

"Then what?"

"I'm with child. Otis and I are going to have a baby."

"Oh, Pearl!" Addie put her hand to her mouth in surprise.

"I kept feeling lightheaded, and Otis insisted I see the doctor. With the busyness of the expo and all that we had to do for it, I completely missed the signs that this might be the reason for my feeling unwell at times. When I put all the pieces together, it was clear that after hoping for over twelve years, we are finally expecting a baby. Imagine that, and me forty-five years old."

"Oh, that's such good news. Oh, Pearl, congratulations. Please sit down and rest. You've been through so much this morning."

"I'm fine, Addie, and I'll be even better when you are back home with us." She took hold of Addie's hand. "I just need to know that you're in a safe place."

Addie said nothing about the plans she'd had for leaving Seattle. Instead, she squeezed Pearl's fingers and smiled. There would be time for sorrow later.

21

Hiram threw down his boots and cursed. He'd been so stupid to leave Addie alone. He had thought she was unconscious from one of his beatings. He knew she was wounded. In fact, from the way she held her arm, Hiram was pretty sure he'd busted it. So how could she have escaped? Better still, where was she now?

Shep was absolutely no help at all. He did nothing but complain about the dump they were living in. The one-room apartment was barely big enough for one man, much less two. The small bed wasn't suited for sleeping double, so Hiram had told Shep they'd sleep in shifts. The important thing was that one of them be on watch at all times.

"Did you hear anything about Addie?" Shep asked, coming awake. He stretched and got up from the bed.

"Not a thing. The people at the photo shop are being quite closemouthed about her. I wasn't even able to find Esther and see what she knew." He plopped down on the single chair in the room. "This is getting harder by the minute. I'm sure she's gone to her friends, but there doesn't seem to be any sign of her with them."

"Maybe we should just move on then. If she's with her friends, they're gonna put the police onto us. There's no doubt about that."

Hiram shook his head. "I've got to try and get in touch with Esther. Maybe I'll go back to the expo around closing time and see if I can find her. She's bound to know something."

Addie was pleasantly surprised to wake up from her nap and find Isaac at her side. She tried to smile, but the cut on her lip and the swelling made it almost impossible.

"It's nice to see you awake. How are you feeling?" Isaac asked, reaching out to take hold of her hand.

"I'm doing much better. I can finally sleep without startling awake at every sound. Thank you for the Pinkerton men. I want to reimburse you when I'm out of here. I know it cannot be cheap to have men posted round the clock."

"I won't hear anything more about reimbursing me. Addie, I love you, and I want to marry you."

She said nothing for a long moment. Finally, she decided what needed to be discussed could no longer be put off. "Isaac, you said you knew everything about me. Or something to that effect."

"Yes, I think I know most every important matter that pertains to you."

"Then you must know that I'm ashamed of my past and all that was forced upon me."

Isaac's gaze turned sympathetic. "Addie, you did nothing wrong. Nothing at all."

"I was a mistress to Moerman before he married me."

"I know. Millie told me. Then, of course, when I caught up with your brothers in Vancouver, they told me all sorts of things. I don't even know what's true and what's not, but I can tell you that it doesn't matter at all. I hate that you suffered and that it torments you still. That's what I care about. Otherwise, those things are unimportant and need to be left to die in the past."

"But you deserve so much better than a damaged princess," she said, thinking of the girls.

"You are so precious to me, Addie. I know I've been pushy at times, but if you could only see yourself through my eyes, you'd know that the past doesn't matter to me. I lost my heart to you the first time I saw you in the Yukon. You're more precious to me than silver or gold."

"Oh, Isaac, you make it all sound so simple."

"It is simple as far as I see it. I know you feel the pain of all that has happened and all that was put upon you. I just want to help you heal. I know that together we can overcome everything that's happened."

"You make me believe it can be that way too."

He smiled. "Don't be afraid, Princess Addie. Let me be your brave knight and rescue you from the dragon."

"Yes, well, Hiram and Shep are indeed dragons. They're vicious and cruel and all for the want of gold."

"Your gold?"

She nodded. "I have gold and jewelry in a safety deposit box at the bank."

"Millie told me about the gold-nugget necklace. I thought it might have something to do with Hiram's demands, but I didn't realize you still had it until you told the police about it."

"He wants it, but I won't give it to him. Even if I do, it won't be the end. He already demanded I go away with him so he can sell me to the highest bidder when the time is right."

"No one wants that to happen. Addie, a lot of people love you, and we will fight to keep you safe, no matter what."

She smiled despite the pain. "I can just imagine you all donning armor. The girls too. By the way, how are Mina and Lena doing?"

"They're fine, but they're worried about you. Elizabeth even cancelled her trip to California. They all want you to get well soon. I told them that I very much hope you will marry me right here in the hospital, and then we can have a formal ceremony in the church later. What do you think?"

"Marry in the hospital?" Addie shook her head. "But why?"

"I want to be in charge of protecting you. I want to make certain everything that can be done is being done." He paused and gave her a slight smile. "And most importantly, I love you. We've been apart much too long. I want you to be my wife, Addie. I will never want another."

"But what about your job? What if someone found out that I lived in a brothel, mistress to the owner? What kind of reputation would you have then?"

"It's none of anyone's business what happened in the past. I've prayed long and hard about this, Addie, and I am convinced that God will deliver us from the past. No matter what happens, I am putting my trust in Him for our future. I know He plans one for us . . . together."

Addie relaxed a bit, but her anxiety was far from gone. "I fear it could bode so badly for you. You've been hired on at the university, and their standards are quite stringent. Even though I'm not the person I was in Dawson City, what if the truth comes out? What if someone learns about my past and presents it to the president of the university? What if he's so appalled by it that he fires you?"

"Then we move on and allow God to show us where we're to go. I'm not afraid, Addie, and I don't want you to be either. You've been through so many terrible things. I'm not going to be just one more on the list."

"You could never be terrible to me. A little overbearing, yes, but not terrible," Addie said, shaking her head.

"I know I have been out of line, but my enthusiasm got the best of me. I wanted to pick up where we left off. I just knew that you must still feel the same way about me. That you would remember our love for each other."

"Your memory was all that kept me going. I still have the tintype you gave me. You wrote 'Remember Me' on the back, and I've kept it close to my heart ever since. I suppose it might be lost to me now, but it has otherwise been with me since living in the north."

"So you admit that you still love me?"

Addie could see the hope in his eyes. "Of course I still love you. I'll never stop loving you."

"Then marry me, Addie. Don't let them win. Your brothers might think they can control you. Control us. But we need to show them that they can't. Marry me here in the hospital. I'll arrange it all."

Addie wrestled with her heart. She wanted to say yes and throw caution to the wind. If problems came down the road, then they'd face them together. Saying yes would mean that everything she ever longed for was finally within reach.

"I can see that you want to say yes." Isaac's expression lit up with joy. "I know you do."

"I do, but there's still so much that frightens me. I don't want you to be hurt in all of this. What if my brothers come after you? They've threatened to kill you before, what's to stop them from trying it?"

"I don't know. I suppose nothing, but Addie, I don't want to live like that. I refuse to live in worry and fear, watching and waiting for trouble around every turn. I believe God has ordained our union, and I won't be afraid to move forward with it. I don't want you to be either."

"I'll marry you." The words were simple, but hearing them impacted Addie quite thoroughly. She had agreed to marry Isaac. She was going to be his wife, perhaps mother to his children. She trembled at the very thought of her love for him.

Isaac understood and leaned forward to half embrace her. "You won't regret this. I promise. We're going to be happy together, Addie. We're going to have a good life, and God will oversee the rest. I'm going to go now and make arrangements. We'll get the pastor to come up here and perform the ceremony. Then later when you are well, we can have a church wedding with all the frills you like."

"I don't need frills. I just need you."

Esther sat with the other Camera Girls waiting for Mr. Fisher to speak. He and Pearl had called a meeting before allowing the girls to go about their business. They said it was critical, and that no one was to be excused from it. She couldn't help but wonder if that meant Addie Bryant too. She hadn't seen Addie in days and wondered if maybe the girl had managed to get herself fired. Maybe that was what this meeting was all about.

"Girls, I'll get right to the point of this meeting," Otis said, coming to stand at the front of the small photography shop. "Some of you know that Addie Bryant was attacked and viciously beaten. She was very close to death, but we managed to get her to the hospital, and she's now recovering. We don't know for sure who was responsible for this, but we believe it was her brothers."

Esther felt as if she'd been hit in the stomach. Her breath caught in her throat. Was Addie's near-death experience due to what she told Hiram?

Otis continued. "I have descriptions of each of them so that you might be on the lookout for them. I don't want any of the rest of you harmed, so I want you to team up in pairs to cover the expo together. I realize that this could have the effect of reducing your salary, so I plan to go over your sales and make sure that you keep an average wage."

Esther pushed her guilty conscience deep down. It wasn't her fault. Addie brought this all on herself. After all, it was a family matter. She couldn't be to blame for that.

The girls murmured amongst themselves. Esther knew that several of the girls were already planning whom they'd work with. No doubt Bertha and Mary would go out together. Most of the girls had made good friends in the job, but Esther had put off having much to do with anyone. She was superior in every way to these young women. Most of the Camera Girls came from poor backgrounds and families who had absolutely no social standing. Esther's family wasn't that way. At least not really. They did struggle for money, but that was because of her father's medical bills.

"I want each of you to keep an eye out for these men. They are considered very dangerous," Otis said, handing out pieces of paper.

Esther glanced down and saw that they were very accurate descriptions of Hiram and Shep.

"Don't try to do anything to encounter these men on your own. If you see them, then find the nearest policeman and let them know. I don't want any of my girls hurt."

"Oh, it's just terrible," one of the girls declared. "Poor Addie. She never hurt anyone and to think of her nearly dying."

Esther swallowed the lump in her throat. She didn't like the way guilt was resurfacing. She didn't know that Hiram would actually try to kill Addie. She knew he disliked her, as Esther did, but that degree of physical harm was never even a thought.

Finally, they were dismissed. Esther found herself without a partner, however, so Pearl suggested she just stay in and help with the shop.

"I wouldn't want you out there risking your life, and neither would Addie."

"She wouldn't care about me," Esther muttered.

"Nonsense. She'd care very much. I know you don't seem to get along very well with the other girls. I figure it's probably a rivalry thing. You want to make more money than the other girls, and they no doubt feel the same. But I know Addie doesn't feel any malice toward you."

"Maybe she should." Esther felt more and more compelled to make her confession. After all, what would happen if Hiram decided to do to her the same as he'd done to Addie?

"Esther, I've watched you work, and I know that you're

most unhappy. Otis tells me that your father has been ill, and that you're working to help pay his medical expenses."

"Yes." She put up her defenses. "What of it?"

Pearl shrugged. "It's just that I know it must be hard for you. It's never easy to see our loved ones suffer. You're a good daughter to care so much for your family."

It had been a long time since anyone had offered Esther praise. She did her best to remain unmoved and said nothing.

Pearl smiled. "I'm sure they must appreciate you very much. I know if I had a daughter offering up her time and money in such a manner, I would cherish her. Addie's the closest thing to a daughter that I've ever had. She's been so good to us, and I pray fervently that no additional harm comes to her. But with her brothers loose out there, I fear the worst."

Esther nodded, looking to the ground. The battle going on within her was almost too much to contend with. How could she continue to keep her secrets when what she knew might save Addie's life? Hiram Bryant meant nothing to her. He might even mean to harm her to make sure she didn't tell anyone about him. That filled Esther with sudden fear.

"I have to tell you something," she blurted out. "Something about Addie's brothers."

Pearl fixed her with an odd look. "What do you know about her brothers?"

"I've met them. Well, mainly Hiram."

"When did this happen?"

Esther immediately felt defensive. "I don't know. It was just a while back."

Pearl came to stand directly in front of her. She took hold of Esther's hands. "Esther, please, you must tell everything you know. These men aren't to be trusted."

She bit her lower lip. "Addie was reprimanding me for something and was quite harsh. When she left, this man showed up and told me he was Addie's brother. That was that. He wanted me to help him to get in touch with her . . . alone."

"Well, you see where that got her."

"I didn't know he would hurt her. I didn't know that there would be any trouble," she lied. She had always known that Hiram meant some harm for Addie, and Esther had thought it an adequate recompense for all that she'd done to cause problems.

"Where are Addie's brothers now?"

"I don't know. I only ever knew that if I needed to tell Hiram something, I could leave him a note. He said he would check from time to time and get in touch with me."

"We need to let Isaac know about this. He'll know how we should handle this." She fell silent and looked at Esther with a look of pity and reproach. "I wish you would have let us know when he first approached you. Knowing that her brother was in town—here—would have helped to keep her safe."

Esther shook off anger at the look on the woman's face. She wasn't going to allow the others to make her feel guilty. She'd done nothing wrong.

"Well, it's not like they can do anything to her while she's in the hospital," Esther said, pulling away from Pearl. "I'm sure the police will find Addie's brothers before she can be hurt again."

An hour later, Isaac and two uniformed policemen stood in the photo shop, listening to Esther relate her story. It was quickly decided that Esther would leave a note for Hiram in the regular place and hope that she could entice him to meet with her one more time.

Esther carefully penned the request, suggesting that Hiram could meet her near the Swedish building and Ferris wheel at exactly four o'clock the next afternoon. Esther had told them that they needed to give him plenty of time to get the message. She figured at least a day.

"Hopefully he'll respond quickly, and we'll have our man," one of the policemen declared. "I'm anxious to see him caught."

Isaac shook his head. "For a department that considered this nothing more than a domestic squabble unworthy of their attention, I'm surprised to find you saying so."

"I don't happen to agree with my department. I think this is a critical issue, and we must encourage change. My own mother and sisters have been victims of such treatment."

Nodding, Isaac offered an apology. "I am sorry to misjudge you. It's just this whole thing has caused me nothing but grief. Addie won't be able to rest properly until her brothers are caught and put away."

"I'm finished," Esther said, holding up the folded letter.

"Good. Now take it as you would have before and put it where Hiram will find it," Isaac said. "If we are unable to catch up to them before tomorrow, you'll have to go to the appointed place and wait for Hiram. We'll have men nearby to keep you from harm."

Esther hadn't realized she'd need to be a part of the capture. "Do I have to be there?"

"I know it's a frightening proposition," Isaac said, sounding quite sympathetic, "but we must make it look as legitimate as possible. Hiram is a smart man. He won't be easily caught, I fear."

Esther nodded. "So do I."

22

Hiram maneuvered through the crowd of expo attendees. He hoped no one would recognize him. The last thing he wanted to do was have some sort of run-in with Addie's friends. Then again, he was desperate to know where she was and how he could get her back in his custody. He'd been a fool to leave her alone at the cottage. That was a mistake he wouldn't make again.

He checked the box where he'd directed Esther to leave him messages and, to his happy surprise, found one waiting. He hurried to pocket it and then moved away from the crowded areas to find a place to read the note.

He finally found a secluded path. Young couples often strolled here to be hidden from view, but luckily no one else was around. He sat down on a rock and pulled out the letter.

"Must see you," he read aloud. He read on in silence noting that Esther wanted to see him at four o'clock by the Ferris wheel. He had no idea what time it was. They'd returned to the expo around noon. He'd given Shep the task of picking up their final pay and giving notice that they'd quit their jobs. That way, he figured if their boss knew what was going on and had the police watching for them, they'd only get Shep. Shep had been too stupid to worry about the matter. The thought of getting paid was all that he had on his mind.

They were supposed to meet up by the new ferry launch as soon as they each concluded their business, so Hiram tucked the note back in his pocket and made his way down to where the ferry would dock for passengers.

As a man passed by, Hiram asked him the time. "Three thirty," the man responded and continued up the graveled path.

"Thanks." Hiram glanced around for Shep, starting to feel a sense of irritation. That's how it always was when something was about to go down. He didn't feel afraid, just frustrated—annoyed really. He supposed it was due to the control of the situation being stripped from him.

Where was Shep? Why hadn't he gotten back already? Had he got caught?

Hiram really hadn't given a lot of thought as to how he'd handle matters if his younger brother did get apprehended. For Hiram, life had always been an every man for himself operation. Shep knew the dangers, even if he wasn't very bright. If Shep got himself arrested, Hiram would leave him be. After all, the main goal was to find Addie and get that necklace. Not to risk getting himself thrown in jail.

Just the thought of Addie caused his irritation to grow.

Once again Hiram kicked himself mentally for having left her alone. He had thought her far too injured to flee. He was almost certain he'd broken her arm, if not her ankle. The beatings he'd given her were fierce, and at one point, he'd even worried that he had killed her. When he and Shep had left, Hiram knew he could hardly drag or carry Addie out of the cottage without a neighbor noticing.

Had it not been for needing Shep to carry stuff for their move, he might have left him there to watch over their sister. But it was too late now. Somehow Addie had managed to get loose. But where was she, and how could he get her back without an all out war?

Shep arrived a few minutes later. He handed Hiram the money he'd collected and gazed out across the water. "Looks like the ferry's comin'."

"It is, but we're not going to take it. I had a message from Esther. She says it's urgent I meet her at four o'clock."

"What time is it now?"

"Getting close to four. I figure we'll make our way over to the Ferris wheel, where she wanted to meet. We can stay out of sight while we wait for her to show up."

"Do you suppose she'll tell you where Addie is?"

"Could be that's why she called the meeting," Hiram replied. "She's got to know that we're wondering where Addie is."

"What if Addie never made it to her friends?" Shep asked. "What if someone else found her and took her?"

"Took her where?"

Shep shrugged. "The doctor or the hospital. She was hurt pretty bad."

Hiram hated it when Shep made sense. He had been so fixated on Addie going to her friends that Hiram hadn't really considered any other possibility. What if someone else had found her and taken her for care?

"Come on," Hiram said, nudging Shep. "Let's make our way to the Ferris wheel and see what Esther knows. There's no sense standing here speculating."

The expo was more crowded than normal. It was Saturday,

after all, and that was the day when most families were able to attend. A marching band was performing at the bandstand, which only served to raise the noise level to unbearable levels. Hiram longed for peace and quiet but knew it could never be had here at the fair.

They reached the appointed place, and Hiram pulled Shep behind a ticket booth to hide them from the passing crowd. It wasn't long before Hiram saw Esther walking along, looking around as if she didn't have a care in the world. She was certainly a beauty. Pity he couldn't take a little time out to better explore the possibilities with her. But the facts being what they were, Hiram was already risking a lot just to meet up with her.

As she drew near, Hiram stepped out from behind the ticket booth and waved to her. She saw him immediately and crossed the road to get to him.

"I wasn't sure you'd be here," she said, glancing over her shoulder.

"I'm here. What do you have to tell me?"

"Uh . . . well, the police have the cottage under constant surveillance."

"I already figured that. We were on our way to leavin' when Addie snuck off. I suppose she's with her beloved Mr. Hanson."

"No, she's still in the hospital," Esther replied, again glancing back over her shoulder.

"What's wrong? You seem mighty nervous."

"I'm not. Not really. I don't want the Fishers to catch me not working. They can be real sticklers." She cleared her throat and started to look at Hiram, then glanced away.

Hiram felt icy fingers on his neck. Something wasn't

right. This wasn't the brazen flirt he'd known Esther to be. He started searching the street even as he reached for his knife.

"Keep an eye out, Shep. I think we've been had."

Esther started to move away, but Hiram caught her and pulled her close. "You set me up, didn't you?"

"I didn't have a choice. Once they found out about our connection, they demanded I contact you."

Hiram cursed and pulled Esther with him. "Come on, Shep. Cut behind the machine house."

Esther tried to wrench away from Hiram's hold, but he managed to tighten his grip.

An officer stepped out from behind a large sign. "Stop where you are. You're under arrest Hiram Bryant, Shepard Bryant."

"I'll kill you for this," he whispered against Esther's ear. He maneuvered her in front of him and put the knife to her throat. "Back off or I'll kill her."

He couldn't be sure how many officers were involved in this attempt to capture him, but he figured they wouldn't press their advance so long as he had Esther at the point of death.

"You're surrounded, Bryant. You can't escape. Let the lady go." At that, several other policemen emerged from various hiding places. They formed a kind of horseshoe position around Hiram and Shep. The only way out was to the right.

"Fat chance of that." Having cleaned these grounds, Hiram was well aware of places he could slip away. He lowered his voice. "Shep, remember that house that had the heavy growth of shrubs?"

"The one we said would make a great place to hide?"

"Exactly. That's where we'll head. Once we clear the po-lice, you go to the left, and I'll take right."

Shep nodded. "I'll see you there."

"I won't go with you," Esther protested. "I won't."

Hiram pressed the knife into her neck. "You'll do as I say. Now move."

She stumbled as he pushed her forward. By now the of-ficers were commanding people to move back. Making a clearing would not be to their advantage so Hiram gave Shep the order. "Go!"

Shep took off in a flash, and Hiram did likewise, dragging the unwilling Esther. After a few yards of trying to manage her, he finally let go, sending her onto her backside. He had no idea if the police would stop to see to her or just follow after him. It didn't really matter. Hiram had to get away. He wasn't going to prison for any reason, but especially not for beating his sister.

Isaac looked at the officer and shook his head. "What do you mean they got away? How could they? You said you had plenty of men to help."

"He took the young lady hostage."

"Esther?" Addie asked. "Is she all right?"

The man nodded. "She is. He made a small cut on her neck, but otherwise she's fine."

"I can't believe you had them and then let them go."

"They could hardly let Hiram kill Esther," Addie said, patting Isaac's arm as he stood beside her bed.

"I realize that, but now they know we're looking for them."

"They already knew that, Isaac." Addie shook her head. "Hiram knows we won't just let him get away without a fight."

"So what do we do now?" Isaac asked the uniformed man.

"That's where I come in." A tall man in a three-piece suit strolled into the room as if he owned it. "I'm Joseph Carnegie. No relation to the man who builds the libraries. I'm a detective with the police department. I've been talking to your Pinkertons and think we've come up with an idea."

"For what?" Isaac asked.

"For capturing Miss Bryant's brothers."

Isaac glanced at Addie and then returned his gaze to Carnegie. "Go on."

"We're going to arrange for a front-page story about Miss Bryant being hospitalized. We're going to make it quite clear that although she had guards in the beginning, we no longer see her position as endangered."

"In other words, you want to set Addie up as bait to catch her brothers."

"Yes." The man was matter-of-fact. "Do you have a better idea?"

Isaac considered the situation. "I just don't want Addie in harm's way. She's already gone through far too much. If something goes wrong . . ."

"It won't," the man assured. "We're going to put police officers in the uniform of orderlies. They will be positioned in every possible place to afford Miss Bryant the best protection. We'll even put one here in the room—perhaps two."

"It still sounds too risky."

"You know very well, Dr. Hanson, that Miss Bryant's brothers are after the necklace and any other gold she might have. They aren't going to kill her before she has given them that."

"Maybe not, but if they manage to get in here and take her, they'll beat her again." The color had drained from Addie's face, and Isaac felt bad for discussing the matter in front of her. "Why don't we go somewhere else to talk about this."

Addie grasped his hand. "No, please. I want to know what's happening. I want to put an end to this here and now. I can be the bait."

"I don't like the idea." Isaac squeezed her hand.

"But in a few days, I'll be leaving the hospital."

"As my wife," Isaac replied. "You know that everything is arranged for us to marry."

"I do, but if we can capture my brothers here at the hospital, then they won't be able to follow me to wherever I go to live. We cannot put your family in danger. I would never forgive myself if something happened to those beautiful girls."

"I hadn't considered that." Isaac had arranged with his sister and her husband for Addie to move in as his wife until they could find a place of their own. However, he had figured on the Bryant brothers already being safely put away in jail.

"This is probably the only way to tempt them out of hiding," the detective said. "We'll all but give them a key to the hospital and draw them a map to where she is. I honestly think they'll find themselves too tempted to leave it alone. Especially once we stress that Miss Bryant is soon to be married. Perhaps we can even say that she plans to leave the area. The more desperate they feel, the more mistakes they'll make. I assure you that we will capture them this time."

Addie nodded. "We must do it this way, Isaac. We must."

"Very well. When?"

"I'll see to it that the article is in the paper tomorrow. Do you have a photograph of yourself, Miss Bryant? For the newspaper?"

"Mr. Fisher does. You could get one from him."

He nodded and left without another word. He definitely came across as a man of no nonsense. Isaac had to admit the man seemed more than capable of getting the job done. But then, so had the others.

He looked to Addie. "Are you sure about this?"

"I am. This has to end. I had hoped the police could catch them with Esther but after hearing about her peril, I can't abide putting anyone else through that."

Isaac let go his hold and took a seat on the bed beside Addie. "I agree it has to end. I don't want you to live your life in fear."

She smiled. "Strangely enough I feel at peace. I have some fear at the thought of how this will play out but not of what might happen to me. I think I finally see the power of God's influence over my heart and mind. I've been so afraid most of my life. So sure that God didn't really care because He hadn't kept me from harm. But through all of this, I feel His presence more than any other time. I know He's with us, Isaac. Before now, I couldn't have said that."

"I'm glad you know that He's here. I suppose I should be glad that the circumstances have brought you to a deeper faith, but if it were up to me, you would never have had to suffer."

"And I would probably never have come to see the truth. You once told me that the affairs of our days were in place to bring God glory. The good, the bad, the sorrowful, and the joyful. All to His glory."

Isaac nodded. "Yes, all to His glory."

She touched her hand to his cheek. "So then this is as well. To His glory."

23

"Well, would you look at this," Hiram said, holding up the newspaper.

He and Shep had barely headed out for breakfast when the newspaper boy on the street started calling attention to the story about a local heiress. Hiram normally wouldn't have wasted the money for a paper, but he saw the photograph of his sister.

"What's it say? Did she die?" Shep asked.

Hiram waited until after the waitress poured them coffee and left. "It says she's an heiress with a vast amount of money, including a gold-nugget necklace worth over one hundred thousand dollars." He pointed his finger at the middle of Shep's chest. "Didn't I tell you?"

"You did." Shep put several spoonfuls of sugar in his coffee.

"It says she's in the Seattle General Hospital, and that the police and Pinkertons have decided she's safe enough to pull the extra guards from her room. She's supposed to leave the hospital altogether tomorrow." He read on further to see if anything else might be helpful. It wasn't.

He glanced up and smiled. "Now we know right where she'll be, and with a little bit of luck, we can get her out of that place."

"But then where are we gonna go? Can't stay here, not since she's had her picture in the paper and all."

Hiram nodded. "I'm already thinking about that. I have no idea where she has her necklace and gold, but we need to get that straightaway. After that we can get out of the area. I think maybe we should head down to Sacramento or San Francisco. Those towns are good sized and should be useful to us. That area of the country also knows about dealing with gold."

The waitress returned with their breakfast. "You fellas want anything else?" She fixed Hiram with a smile.

"No, nothing," he said, hoping his gruff tone would keep her from coming back.

She frowned and put their ticket on the table. "Pay up front."

Hiram didn't bother to reply. Instead, he focused on the food and considered how to go about his plans. He wasn't going to get caught again. If this was some sort of setup, and it was always possible that it was, Hiram was going to be two steps ahead of the law.

The day passed without any new developments or difficulties, much to Addie's relief. She knew what had been done with the newspaper and what was planned; however, she had serious doubts about whether or not they could accomplish what they intended.

Since their childhood, Addie had always known what a conniver Hiram was. He was smart and mean, and the combination gave him a natural edge. Poor Shep was just a follower. Without Hiram to boss him around, Shep would most likely stay out of trouble. But not Hiram. There was something in him that just demanded he break the law and take matters into his own hands.

"We won't be that far away in case something does happen," Pearl told Addie as they finished up their visit. "Otis even suggested we come and stay with you somehow, but I know they won't allow it."

"No, and you must keep out of harm's way. You have the baby to consider," Addie said, smiling with delight. "I'm going to love spoiling this child."

"And I will let you, so long as we get out of this." Pearl sounded more than a little worried.

"Try not to fret, Pearl. I know we're in God's hands, and that things will come together in His perfect way. I can see now how often we go through things that we'd rather not— things not of our doing or choosing. But God has a plan in how those situations will change our hearts and grow us in Him. I'm just glad you never gave up on me."

"How could I? You've been as dear as a daughter or sister to me," Pearl replied.

"Are you ready to go?" Otis asked from the open doorway.

"I am." Pearl leaned down and kissed Addie's cheek. "Tomorrow all of this should be behind us, and you will marry Isaac. I'm so excited for that to happen."

Addie met her loving gaze. "I am too. I'm also glad that you agreed to stand with me, for I have no dearer friend."

They shared a quick embrace, then Pearl headed for the door. "We'll be back early in the morning."

"It might be best to call first and see what's happened. I wouldn't want you to get in the middle of it."

Pearl nodded and took her husband's arm. "Until tomorrow then."

Addie waved to them and settled back into her bed. Her arm still hurt something fierce, but the other places where she'd been hit were starting to calm and heal. She couldn't imagine wanting to hurt someone the way Hiram must have wanted to hurt her. For all her anger toward him, Addie couldn't bring herself to desire his pain.

"God, I know You could still change his heart. He could come to an understanding of who You are and seek forgiveness." She murmured the prayer even knowing that such things were not likely to happen.

"Want some company?" Isaac asked from the open door.

"I'd love some, but visiting hours are over."

He strolled into the room with a boyish grin. "I know, but I have been given special privileges." He came to the bedside and kissed her forehead.

She took hold of his hand, reluctant to let go. "I'm glad you came back. I'm not nearly as brave as I pretend to be."

"You never have to pretend with me, Addie. I want to know the truth—always."

Addie knew he meant every word, but it still amazed her that he was so determined to love her. "I do wish things could have been different, Isaac. We had such hopes and dreams. Things were going to be perfect."

"That was just childish boasting," Isaac replied. "Deep inside, we knew there would be difficulties. No one lives without sorrows and hardships. Even the very rich have their burdens to bear."

"I suppose. But I really believed we could have things fall into place without nearly so much trouble. Perhaps they would have if not for my brothers."

"Perhaps, but even so, I'd say things are falling into order now despite them."

"I do want to say that I'm so proud of you," Addie began. "You set out to get your education and become a college professor, and now you'll be that. I know you had to work hard."

"It was surprisingly pleasurable, except that you weren't there." He kissed her fingers and pressed her hand to his cheek.

"No, I was mostly here, and the life I had was good, thanks to Pearl and Otis. They were so dear to take me in. I would have been all alone to face who knows what kind of fate without them."

"For that, they have my deepest gratitude. I hope we shall always be good friends."

"I think they would like that very much." Addie suppressed a yawn.

"You need to get some sleep. The doctor said that rest was the most beneficial thing to aid in healing. You sleep, and I'll stand . . . or, rather, sit guard." He kissed her hand again and moved to the nearby chair. "I'll be right here beside you."

"Isaac, thank you." Addie searched his face, satisfied that his feelings were all that he had declared them to be. "Thank you for not giving up on me, even after I'd given up. My hope was so depleted, and my relationship with God wasn't at all what I needed it to be. You are an amazing man of God to

279

have kept such faith over the years. I shall always remember that and thank God for it."

"I love you, Addie. I will always love only you."

"And I love you, Isaac. More than I ever thought I could love anyone."

She closed her eyes, secure in the warmth of that love and so much more. God had brought her to this place and time, not without difficulty, but perhaps with just enough that Addie could see how precious this love was. Not only Isaac's love but also God's.

Addie awoke with a start. She heard a commotion outside. The room was dark, and she had no way of knowing if Isaac was there except to call for him.

"Isaac!"

"Hush, I'm here. But from the sounds of it, I think your brothers are too."

A shot rang out. Shaking, Addie curled into a ball on the bed, wishing there were somewhere else to go. The police had listed her as being in a room down the hall. They emptied everyone else out of the area, and Addie wished they'd moved her far away from the scene as well, but they thought she needed to stay just in case her brothers managed to get help from one of the hospital staff. They kept her in the same hallway, but told as few people as possible which specific room. Hopefully there wouldn't be anyone to help Hiram and Shep.

The shouting and noise increased. Addie pushed her face deeper into the pillow and prayed.

She felt Isaac's hand on her shoulder and reached out to take hold.

"Don't be afraid, Addie. I won't let anything happen to you."

Another shot sounded—this one closer than the other. Addie edged toward Isaac and prayed again. *Please, God, deliver us from this evil. Please don't let the innocent be hurt.*

Everything went silent, and for several minutes, Addie wondered what had happened. When the lights came on in the hall and then her room, she ducked her head against Isaac.

"It's all over." Detective Carnegie strolled into the room as if nothing of importance had just happened. "Your brothers were both shot, Miss Bryant. We will need you to identify their bodies."

"Bodies?" Addie sat up in bed. "They're . . . dead?"

"Yes." He frowned. "I may also lose a good man. They stabbed him, and he's been taken to surgery."

"I'll identify the bodies," Isaac said. "I know them both, and I don't want Addie having to be a part of something so gruesome."

Carnegie nodded. "Then come with me, and let's get this done. I'd like to wrap things up here so that the hospital can go back to their normal routine, and I can get some sleep."

Addie loosened her grip on Isaac, although she didn't want him to go. She knew that things would be all right now, but still knew she'd feel better when they were reunited.

About twenty minutes later, Isaac returned to her and gave a nod. "It was them."

She waited for some sort of emotion other than relief. When none came, Addie wondered if she was just as cold-blooded as her brothers.

"I don't feel anything for them. No remorse. No sorrow. I'm just so relieved they're not able to hurt me. Does that make me an awful person?"

"No. No, it doesn't, Addie. You owe them nothing. They robbed you of so much, and you owe them nothing." He hugged her close and kissed the top of her head.

It was nearly dawn when Isaac arrived home. He did his best to keep quiet, even though he knew the cook and some of the other servants were already up and preparing for the day.

He was more exhausted than he'd ever been, and all he wanted was to go to sleep, but Mina and Lena had other ideas.

"Uncle Isaac, did you save Princess Addie?" Mina came out of the shadows and fell into step beside him.

"Did you get the bad guys away from her?" Lena asked.

"Well, I must say this is a surprise," he said, putting his arms around them. "Does your mother know you're awake?"

Mina shook her head. "We couldn't sleep. We heard you talking to Mama earlier, and we were worried for you and Princess Addie."

"Don't you know it's not nice to eavesdrop, Miss Mina?" He gave her a stern look but couldn't maintain it for long. He finally smiled. "Addie is fine."

"And were the bad guys caught?" Lena asked.

"They were."

"Will they go to jail for a long time?" Mina asked.

Isaac hated having to tell them about the violence that surrounded the situation. He knelt down. "Look, girls, it was a very bad situation, and Addie's two brothers were determined."

"Are they dead?" Mina pressed.

Isaac looked at her and nodded. "They are. They cannot hurt Addie ever again."

Mina squared her shoulders. "I'm glad." Lena nodded in agreement with her sister's statement.

"Will they go to hell because they did bad things?" Lena asked innocently.

"It's not the bad things that send a person to hell, Lena. It's not having Jesus as your Savior that separates you from God. Jesus said that He is the way, the truth, and the life, and no one can come to God except through Him."

Mina nodded. "We had that for our memory verse."

"Hell must be a terribly awful place," Lena said, looking worried.

"It is," Isaac agreed, "but we haven't any reason to fear it. We have asked Jesus into our hearts. We have put our trust in Him. We belong to Him."

The girls nodded, and Isaac stood. "I think it's time we got to bed. I'm quite worn out, and yet I'm supposed to marry Princess Addie in a few hours."

"You will still have a wedding here at the house, won't you, so Lena and I can see?"

"Well, maybe we can figure out a way to have you at the hospital. I'll see what I can do."

"Oh yes, please," Mina said while Lena clapped for joy.

He put his arm around them and headed to the stairs. It had been a long and fretful night, but through it all, Isaac had known God's presence and felt such peace as he'd never known.

He ushered the girls to the nursery, then headed down the hall to where his room was situated. After stripping off his clothes and donning his nightshirt, Isaac crawled into bed and sighed. With a prayer of thanks on his lips, he drifted off to sleep, knowing that in a few short hours he would acquire a wife. The love of his life.

24

Addie had just had her head bandages removed when a surprise visitor appeared at her door. Esther Danbury stood looking both apologetic and fearful.

"It's not visiting hours," the nurse said, collecting the discarded bandages.

"Please let her stay. She won't be here long." Addie motioned to Esther. "Come in. What brings you here?"

Esther was dressed simply in a brown-and-orange calico print. Her hair was done in a single braid down her back. She looked for all the world like she might burst into tears.

"Are you . . . sure?"

"Goodness, Esther, do come in and sit by the bed so that we can talk." Addie motioned to the chair.

Esther came forward and took hold of the back of the metal chair. "I had to come."

"I'm glad you did."

"You look . . . I mean, the beating . . . uh . . ."

"Yes, well, I am on the mend. They plan to let me go home soon. So you see, it's not so bad."

Esther slowly moved around the side of the chair to sit.

Her gaze never left Addie's face. "I had to come and tell you how sorry I am for my part in this."

Addie nodded. "Why don't you start at the beginning and tell me what happened?"

"Your brother Hiram came to me after you had been particularly hard on me one day. At least I felt it was hard, and that you were purposefully seeking me out to give me a bad time of it. He said he wanted help in seeing you."

She continued to explain all that she and Hiram had talked about and how the situation had played out with their messages and meetings.

"I never thought he'd hurt you like this," Esther said, shaking her head. "I've never known anyone like that."

"No, I would imagine not. Hiram had a lot of meanness to him, but I think there was also a fair amount of plain evil."

Esther nodded. "He just had a way of convincing me it was right to help him. I never ever thought he'd try to kill you."

"He didn't really try to kill me. If he'd wanted me dead, that's where I'd be. No, he wanted my gold and a way to live out his life without care. Hiram always felt the world owed him something."

"I heard he was dead. Your other brother too."

Addie nodded. "Yes, I'd like to think their souls are at rest, but unless they got right with God before taking their last breath . . . well, it's in God's hands. Sadly, however, I know that neither one had ever held any respect for God."

"Addie, will you forgive me?" Esther blurted out all at once. "I've done so many bad things in my life, and I've treated you horribly. I'm really very sorry, and I promise I'm a changed woman."

Addie smiled. "Of course I forgive you. You had only to

ask. Perhaps I should say not even that because I forgave you when it happened."

A sob broke from Esther. "Thank you. I was so afraid that you wouldn't be able to forgive me or that you'd die, and I'd never have the ability to ask for forgiveness."

"Now you have asked, and I have given. Seek God's forgiveness as well, and it can be finally laid to rest."

"I have sought Him. I begged Him to forgive me and make me a better person. I don't want to be all hateful and bitter. I know the girls don't like me because I've been mean to them as well."

"So ask their forgiveness too. I think you'll be surprised at how generous they can be."

Esther wiped her tears. "Thank you. You have no idea how much I needed your understanding and forgiveness. Nothing felt right. I couldn't sleep or eat or even begin to focus on doing my job."

"Then have peace of mind. It is done."

Esther nodded. "It is done."

Addie was more than a little anxious about her hospital wedding. The newspapers had caught wind of it and wanted to cover the event as a sort of closure to the front-page story they'd done on her. She couldn't help but worry that further exposure could bring out other people from her past—people who could stir up trouble and point to her questionable history.

"Don't let the devil spoil your day," Pearl stressed as she helped Addie dress for the occasion.

"It's just hard not to worry. I suppose it's a habit I need to break."

"Indeed. Worry is saying that God can't possibly manage the matter. You're the same as calling God a liar because He promised to see to your every need."

"I certainly don't mean to do that. It's not my heart." Addie considered her friend's words. "I'm glad that God already knows my heart, but even so, I will try to fight against worry."

"Take those thoughts captive, as the Bible says." Pearl frowned as she tried to figure out how to accommodate Addie's broken arm. "I think we're going to have to open the seams of the sleeve."

"Oh no! This was your wedding dress, and I don't want you to do anything to harm the gown." Addie had been so touched and surprised when Pearl showed up with the gown. Her only real regret about marrying in the hospital was that she'd have no real wedding dress. Pearl's gift had made everything perfect, but no one had considered the cast on Addie's arm.

"It's not the end of the world, Addie. It won't hurt a thing. Let me see if I can borrow a pair of scissors and get this open. The wedding is in less than an hour, and we still need to do up your hair." Pearl left for a few minutes, then reappeared with a small pair of scissors in hand. "Ask and you shall receive."

Addie was half in and half out of the gown, but Pearl wasn't daunted. She took the sleeve and started cutting the seam at the wrist.

"Now we should be able to get your arm in there." She helped Addie to maneuver the casted limb and within moments had the dress in place.

"Oh, it's just perfect," Addie said, more excited than she could ever imagine a dress making her feel. "I feel just like a princess." *Princess Addie, indeed.*

"I knew it would be a good fit. It's a little large at the waist, but I could take it in if you think it needs to be."

"No, this is just fine, Pearl. You've been such a dear to me. I can't thank God enough for the way you've been at my side all these years. I know I would have ended up in dire straits had you and Otis not taken me in."

"God always provides, dear Addie. He always provides."

Pearl finished doing up the buttons on the back of the gown. "Now for the hair."

"I'm sure it's a terrible mess after being under bandages all these days."

"We shall manage," Pearl said, beginning to brush the long, dark brown mane. "I remember when I first met you, I thought you were a boy with your hair cut so short."

Addie smiled. "I was so glad you were willing to hire me on. And that you were so forgiving when I told you the truth—that I was a girl. It seemed to take forever for my hair to grow back out." Addie shook her head. "What a mess of a person I was back then."

"But just look what God has done with that mess." Pearl chuckled.

Addie laughed. "It's true. He took a very broken and hopeless girl and changed her completely."

A knock on the hospital door startled them both. Mary peeked in and smiled. "Mind if I come in?"

"Mary, I'm so glad you could come." Addie nodded toward the Brownie camera around her neck. "I see you came to work."

"I will get you some very special pictures of the day," Mary promised. "You'll be able to make an album and show them one day to your children."

"I appreciate this so much. How wonderful to have this to remind me of our day. Although I have a feeling every detail of this day will stay with me always."

Pearl continued to twist and pin Addie's hair, while Mary set her things aside. She pulled a framed picture from her knapsack and brought it to Addie. "Besides taking the photographs, I have another wedding present for you." She handed the picture to Addie.

To Addie's surprise, the photograph was one of her and Isaac. They were standing face to face, looking quite absorbed in each other. Addie remembered the moment. It was shortly after Isaac had revealed himself to her.

"You were both just standing there so still, I couldn't help myself," Mary declared. "I don't really know why I was driven to take the photograph, but now I'm so glad I did."

"As am I," Addie murmured. She held the frame up for Pearl to see. "Isn't this something?"

"I've seen it. When Mary had it developed, Otis and I both saw it and remarked on what a handsome couple you made. Little did we know."

Addie nodded and lowered the photo. "Mary, I can't thank you enough. This is so special to me. I shall always cherish it."

"Oh, look, it's nearly time for the others to arrive," Pearl said. She put a final hairpin in and stepped back to survey her work. "What do you think, Mary?"

"It's perfect. She couldn't be more beautiful." Mary held up the camera. "Let me take a picture."

Pearl finished picking up the room while Mary took a couple of pictures. Addie could hardly remember that just the night before her brothers had been killed. She was determined to put all of that from her. This day was dedicated to God and to Isaac. She wanted nothing else to influence her thoughts.

It wasn't long before Pastor and Mrs. Jenkins showed up. They were over the moon with excitement for Addie's big day.

"I have to say this is my first hospital wedding," he told her. "When Isaac asked me to do this, I had never before considered performing such a ceremony."

"But he quickly forgot about the oddity and said yes because it's you," Selma said, coming to give Addie a kiss on the cheek. "Just look at you! As pretty as a bride should be. Why, you fairly glow, and your bruises are fading nicely."

Addie nodded. "I feel so happy. I cannot imagine being happier."

"You can never tell what God has in mind," Selma replied. "Pearl, did you arrange her hair?"

"I did."

Selma nodded. "It's quite lovely."

"She brought this wedding gown too. It was hers," Addie said.

"I see you had to open the sleeve for the cast, but it doesn't detract at all."

"Where's your soon-to-be husband?" the pastor asked.

"I suppose he'll be along any moment," Addie said.

Two minutes later, Isaac strolled into the room as if he didn't have a care in the world. He was dressed impeccably in a navy blue suit, white shirt, and blue striped tie. Behind him were his sister and brother-in-law, and, to Addie's utmost delight, his two nieces. Each of the girls was dressed in matching pink gowns with white collars and big bows that tied at the waist.

"Mina and Lena—what a surprise," she said, smiling. "And aren't you two pretty."

Isaac stopped short, causing Elizabeth to run into him. "What in the world?" she said as her husband helped to right her.

Addie shifted her focus from the children to Isaac. His sister laughed and gave Addie a grin.

"He's clearly been captivated by the bride," Elizabeth said. "Although we've never met, let me compliment you, Addie. You look quite beautiful."

"Thank you," Addie replied, never taking her gaze off Isaac.

It was clear he approved. He just stared at her without saying a word, making Pastor Jenkins roar with laughter. "You've dumbfounded him, Addie. He's purely stunned by just how pretty you are."

Isaac stepped forward and held out his hand to Addie. She grasped it and drew him closer to kiss his hand.

"You are the most beautiful woman I've ever seen, Addie."

"She's a real princess," Mina said, holding out a bouquet of roses. "Mama let us pick these for you."

Addie had no desire to let go of Isaac's hand, but she didn't want to be rude to the child. She took the offered flowers and lifted them to her face. The rich, sweet aroma was heavenly. "They're so lovely and smell so good."

Mina gave a twirl. "I knew they'd be just right."

"Just right," Lena parroted.

"And so they are. Thank you so much for thinking of me."

"Sorry for being late," Otis said, huffing and puffing as he came to join them. "I thought I might not get here at all. The trolley was terribly overcrowded."

"Well, it doesn't matter because you're here now," Pearl said. She dusted some lint from his suit coat and straightened his tie. "I believe we're ready now."

"Then let us join together in prayer," Pastor Jenkins said, bowing his head.

The ceremony was short but covered all the important matters of pledging their lives together and promising to love each other. The press was allowed in after that and immediately began asking questions and taking a few photographs.

"How do you feel about having a hospital wedding, Mrs. Hanson?" the reporter asked.

"It's definitely not the kind of wedding I dreamed about, but you know what? It's perfect in every way."

"How did you and Dr. Hanson meet?" the man pressed on.

"We met during the Yukon gold rush. We both climbed the Chilkoot Trail and made our way to Dawson City, where we came face to face."

"It was love at first sight for me," Isaac declared.

Addie nodded. "It really was. We both knew there was just something very special about the other one. We learned soon enough that together we made each other whole."

"It was a true gift from the Lord," Isaac added. "I left the Yukon after just a year there, but I told Addie I'd be back for her and we would be married. It just took a few years more than I planned on."

The reporter nodded and jotted down notes. "What about your brothers, Mrs. Hanson?"

Addie's last desire was to speak about them. Just the thought of all that had happened was more than she could bear. Thankfully, Isaac stepped in and dismissed them. "Perhaps in time she will talk about it, but you can get any details you need about what happened here last night from the police," Isaac reminded.

By the time everyone left and Pearl had helped Addie back into her hospital gown, Addie was completely worn out. She wanted nothing more than to fall asleep with the wonderful memory of all that had taken place. She had nearly fallen asleep when Isaac returned and came to her bedside. He bent down and kissed her carefully on her still swollen lips. She opened her eyes and met his gaze.

"Mrs. Hanson."

"Dr. Hanson." She smiled and giggled a bit in her half-awake state. "I remember when we used to talk about you getting your college education and becoming a doctor of history." She could hardly keep her eyes open. "I'm so happy, Isaac. I pray you won't regret this."

"I could never regret you, Addie. No matter what happens, having you in my life is more important than any of the other things I hoped to obtain." He kissed her again, and Addie sighed.

"You rest now," he whispered. "The doctor said you could probably go home tomorrow, so you'll need your strength. Once we have you at the house, you won't have to worry about a thing. We'll even hire a nurse if necessary. You'll be able to recuperate for as long as you need without concerning yourself with the details. Elizabeth and Stuart said we could live with them as long as we need to."

"That's very kind of them, Isaac, but I have money. Actually, I have a lot of money—a few bags of gold and jewelry and, of course, the gold-nugget necklace. I think we should cash it all in and buy our own place."

"What about the cottage?"

"Too many bad memories. I want to sell it as well, or at least rent it out."

"It's entirely up to you, my love. It belongs to you."

"No, it's ours. That's why I want it all to benefit our lives together. That necklace means nothing to me. I only kept it as a kind of insurance against the future. I don't need that now that I have you. I'm so happy to have found you again." Addie smiled and touched Isaac's face with her hand. "I always had your tintype to remember you by, and now—"

"Now you don't have to worry about it because you'll always have me with you." He kissed her fingers and straightened up. "I love you, dearest friend and wife."

"I love you, Isaac. More than I could ever have imagined."

Tracie Peterson is the award-winning author of over one hundred novels, both historical and contemporary. She is often referred to as the "Queen of Historical Christian Fiction," and her avid research resonates in her stories, as seen in her bestselling HEIRS OF MONTANA and ALASKAN QUEST series. Tracie considers her writing a ministry for God to share the Gospel and biblical application. She and her family make their home in Montana. Visit her website at traciepeterson.com or on Facebook at facebook.com/AuthorTraciePeterson.

Sign Up for Tracie's Newsletter

Keep up to date with Tracie's news on book releases and events by signing up for her email list at traciepeterson.com.

More from Tracie Peterson

When an accident leaves Cassandra Barton incapacitated, she spends her time compiling a book of stories about the men working on the Santa Fe Railway. But worry grows as revolutionaries set out to destroy the railroad. As the danger intensifies, Cassie and her longtime friend Brandon must rely on their faith to overcome the obstacles that stand in the way.

Under the Starry Skies • LOVE ON THE SANTA FE

More from Tracie Peterson

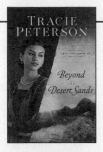

After living an opulent life with her aunt, the last thing Isabella Garcia wants is to celebrate Christmas in a small mining town with her parents. But she's surprised to see how much the town—and an old rival—has changed and how fragile her father's health has become. Faced with many changes, can she sort through her future and decide who she wants to be?

Beyond the Desert Sands
LOVE ON THE SANTA FE

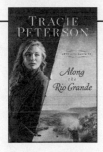

When bankruptcy forces widow Susanna Jenkins to follow her family to New Mexico, what they see as a failure she sees as a fresh start. Owen Turner is immediately attracted to Susanna, but he's afraid of opening up his heart again, especially as painful memories are stirred up. But if Owen can't face the past, he'll miss out on his greatest chance at love.

Along the Rio Grande
LOVE ON THE SANTA FE

On the surface, Whitney Powell is happy working with her sled dogs, but her life is full of complications that push her to the edge. When sickness spreads in outlying villages, Dr. Peter Cameron turns to Whitney and her dogs for help navigating the deep snow, and together they discover that sometimes it's only in weakness you can find strength.

Ever Constant with Kimberley Woodhouse
THE TREASURES OF NOME #3

BETHANYHOUSE